THE GOOD GIRL'S GUIDE TO BEING BAD

COOKIE O'GORMAN

The Good Girl's Guide to Being Bad
Text copyright © 2019 Airianna Tauanuu writing as Cookie O'Gorman

ISBN: 978-0-9978174-3-0

All rights reserved. This book is a work of fiction and any resemblance to any person, living or dead, any place, events or occurrences, is purely coincidental. The characters and story lines are created from the author's imagination or are used fictitiously.

No part of this book may be reproduced, transmitted, downloaded, distributed, stored in or introduced into any information storage and retrieval system, in any form or by any means, whether electronic or mechanical, without express permission of the author, except by a reviewer who may quote brief passages for review purposes.

Cover Design © Stephanie Mooney. All rights reserved.

To Aunt Colleen, Aunt Pat and Mom
I love you

&

To the good girls, the list makers, the dancers and dreamers
This one's for you

CHAPTER 1

I'd made it to senior year with my V-card still intact, which was easier to do than they made it seem in the movies. Heck, I'd gone all four years of high school without getting so much as a kiss. (I still refused to count that time with Billy Cunningham. Him attacking me, open-mouthed like a zombie, slobbering on my neck while I scrambled away, did not a kiss make. Gross.) Honestly, unlike some of my classmates, I'd never thought it was that big a deal.

Still…

…it was on my "Carpe Diem List"—the kissing, not the sexing…was that even a word? Gah, I was so out of the loop—but now it looked like even a kiss might be off limits.

I closed my eyes, shook my head.

The official documentation of my eternal virginal status was burning a hole in my hand.

Complete and utter devastation.

This wasn't happening. Career Aptitude Tests could be wrong, right? *Right?* The problem was I'd hoped this test would give me some direction, tell me what to do with my life. Everyone else in our graduating class seemed to know what they wanted to do, but I had so many interests in so many different things that… yeah, I'd *needed* this. The CAT was supposed to be my guide. My gaze snapped open and stuck on the one sentence that would change my life forever.

Based on the test results, Sadie Elizabeth Day is ideally suited for a career in…

"Religious or Clerical work?" My best friend barked a laugh. "You've got to be kidding me."

I frowned. "I wish. What'd you get?"

"Arts and Entertainment," he said. "Duh. But Sadie…it says you're meant to be a *nun!*"

"*Kyle*," I hissed, glancing around the crowded hall. Everyone had likely already heard. I mean, this was the kinda thing that made headlines in high school, and Mrs. Jeffries had (to my horror) announced the results aloud. But still. "Holy smokes, could you say it any louder? I'm thinking they might not have heard you in the freshman building."

"Sorry, sorry." His eyebrows rose. "But I thought that rumor was a joke. A *nun*? Seriously? Sadie, there's no way."

And there was my best friend. "Aww, thanks I--"

"Black and white are *so* not your colors."

And there was his inner smart aleck.

"Plus, good luck fitting all that amazing hair under a habit."

Kyle reached up and pushed a long blond strand behind my ear.

"You're hilarious," I said, fighting down a blush, hoping he didn't notice.

The strand of hair stayed for about a second before springing back out. Kyle was right, of course. My hair had always been unruly. Curling even after multiple passes of the straightener, frizzing at the smallest sign of humidity, slipping out of any rubber band. It was the wildest thing about me.

But man…a nun???

"There has to be a mistake," he said suddenly. "You'd make a terrible nun. You can't even sing."

"What does that have to with anything?"

Kyle tsked like I'd asked the dumbest question ever. "All nuns can sing. Just look at Julie Andrews, Whoopi Goldberg, Sally Field--"

"Hey, genius," I cut in, "those are all *fictional* nuns."

"Au contraire," Kyle said, holding up a hand. "Let's not forget *The Sound of Music* was based on a true story. I sincerely doubt the Captain would've fallen for Fraulein Maria, played by the incomparable Julie Andrews, if she hadn't been able to carry a tune. And you, my dear sweet bestie, are *no* Julie Andrews."

I shook my head. "Why are we friends again?"

"Hey, it's not my fault you're 100% tone deaf." Kyle sniffed, running a hand through his perfectly styled hair. "As to why we're friends…well. You've always had excellent taste."

"In desserts, yes. In best friends, well…I'm not so sure."

He gasped, head thrown back. "You wound me."

Despite myself, I laughed.

If I hadn't fallen in love with Kyle Bishop Jr. in my formative years, everything might've been different. But what fifth-grade girl in her right mind could resist when he was oh-so-fine? And nice…and clean-cut…and polite…and everything I'd been Stockholm-ed into thinking was "prince charming" by good ol' Walt Disney?

Kyle, my first boyfriend, had been all that and more. We'd watched movies together while he braided my hair, played dress up with Kyle being pirate to my assassin-disguised-as-damsel-in-distress—Kyle could work wonders with a mascara wand. We held hands, passed notes, shared lunches. And it was perfect. I'd thought it was love. I'd thought we'd be together forever, married with kids, happily ever after.

Until he came out to me in the eighth grade.

The funny thing was it hadn't changed anything—nothing important, anyway. Knowing that he'd never love me back hadn't made even a dent in my affection for Kyle.

I guess that should've been my first clue.

Being in love with your best friend? Not so bad.

Being in love with your *gay* best friend? Even after you find out he's gay? Yeah, there was no getting past that one.

Besides, far as I knew, high school guys didn't go for girls who A) had crazy hair and too many curves, B) literally would pick a cardigan and pearls (they were just so classic!) over anything remotely on trend and C) always had their nose stuck in a book.

Ah crap, maybe I was destined to be a nun.

"Hey, Sister Sadie, wait up!"

"Jerk alert," Kyle muttered as Zayne Humphreys and crew stepped up to us, his usual smug grin in place. Besides being born with a name that immediately put him on the douche list, Zayne was the typical jock/jerk combo. His sport of choice: lacrosse. His favorite targets: me and my best friend. The three of us had gone to school together since middle school. Kyle and he had despised each other nearly as long.

"Did you want something?" I asked.

"Yeah," he said, "I have some things I need to confess."

I sighed. This had been happening since we got the CAT results in homeroom.

"Ah come on, Sister Sadie." His lacrosse buddies snickered at the nickname. "Since you're all tight with the big guy upstairs, could you put in a good word for me? I've been a bad boy, and I'd appreciate the help. Unlike you, I party every weekend, get drunk, hook up—there's been a lot of hooking up."

The laughter got even louder as I blushed. But seriously, who said things like that?

"Isn't it like your job to pray for us sinners and all that?"

"Newsflash," Kyle said, "she's not actually a nun."

"Not yet." Zayne shifted to face him, that stupid grin still in place. "But she will be, right? I'm just getting my confessions in early."

"I think you're beyond my help," I said.

"Oh and why's that?"

"Douchebaggery isn't a sin. It's an incurable disease." I shook my head sadly. "Sorry, I can't help you there."

Zayne wasn't smiling anymore, and his co-captain Billy Cunningham (yes, *that* Billy) took a step toward me. "Is there a cure for being a bitch?" Billy said. "'Cause you could use some of that."

"Hey," Kyle said, frowning. "That was out of line."

Billy shrugged him off. "She started it."

Kyle's turn to shrug. "Actually, your boy here started it, and Sadie's my best friend. I won't stand by and listen to you idiots badmouth her."

See, this was why I fell for the guy in the first place.

"Back off, faggot."

"Hey!" I snapped. "Don't talk to him like that."

Billy scoffed. "Who's going to stop me? You or your faggot friend?"

I was about to speak up, tell Billy to shut the heck up, when a long arm came to rest heavily around Billy's shoulders, making him grimace. A moment later, a new voice joined the conversation. A voice I loathed to the tips of my toes.

"Now, now," it said, low and soft. "There's no need for name calling."

Luckily, today he wasn't focused on tormenting me.

"Speaking of which…are nuns supposed to use words like 'douchebaggery'?"

Or maybe he was.

"I'm thinking that would be a black mark on your record, Sister."

Rolling my eyes, I looked up and came face to face with my long-time nemesis. Colton Bishop was the spitting image of Kyle—they were identical twins, same ocean blue eyes paired with ink black hair, same long, lean frame—except where my bestie was all preppy Prince Charming, his twin would definitely be the villain of any story. Unlike Zayne, Colton was a true bad boy. Everything from his rep for getting into fights to his playboy persona to his I-don't-give-darn attitude put me off. He grinned at my look of disdain and cocked a pierced eyebrow. I would've killed to be able to pull off that look.

Instead, I said, "For the hundredth time: I am not a freaking nun."

Blue eyes looked me over, taking in my beat-up sneakers and well-worn jeans, my gray cardigan, pearls and my crazy hair. His eyes were twinkling by the time they met mine.

"If you're going to dress like that, you might as well be."

"Colt," Kyle said, shaking his head. "You may be my brother, and I love you dearly. But I'm going to laugh the day she decides to punch you in the face."

"She wouldn't," he smirked. Seeing his attention was elsewhere, Billy tried to wriggle away, but Colton tightened his grip. "She's too *good* for that."

"I wouldn't count on it."

"Plus, she loves this face." I felt my cheeks getting hot as he sent a knowing nod his brother's way. "Isn't that right, Sadie?"

Through gritted teeth, I said, "I have no idea what you're talking about."

"Every girl loves it," he said with a wink. "You just won't admit it."

Kyle shook his head again. "Seriously, man. Twenty bucks says she does it before graduation."

"Twenty? I'll take that bet."

"Knew you would." They shook on it, and I shook my head.

"It's just too easy. Sadie would never do something so violent."

"One of these days," Kyle said, smiling as my glare intensified, "she's going to do it, Colt. Just punch you in the face."

Colton pretended to think for a second. "Do nuns actually punch people in the face?"

I threw my hands up and started walking in the opposite direction.

"But Sister Sadie, I wasn't done confessing!" Zayne called to my back just as Colton said, "Now, Billy boy, are you going to apologize to my brother, or are we going to have a problem?"

Ignoring them both, I reached my locker—but couldn't get in because Jeff Chan and his girlfriend Addison Corbin were going at it again. Every day I saw them making out. Every day I was almost late for History because of it. And every day I thought: geez, don't their lips ever get tired?

I cleared my throat. Loudly.

The two separated long enough for Addison to shoot me a glare and for Jeff to say, "Sorry, Sister," before they moved down a locker. Two seconds later, their lips were once again suctioned together.

"Don't call me that," I muttered, quickly exchanging my books.

Sniffling brought my attention to the girl across the hall.

Could've been worse, I thought. I could've run out of homeroom crying like Serena Douglas. She'd turned white as a sheet when her results said she was destined to be a TV producer. For someone else, that would've been a great result—I, for example, would have been over-the-moon ecstatic. TV producer, life set on a course to Hollywood? *Yes please, sign me up!* But for Serena, who it was widely known had been training to join the Peace

Corps and whose parents had taken her on missions overseas the past three summers, it was a dagger to the heart.

"Hey, Serena," I said. We weren't exactly friends, but we'd been in the same homeroom since sixth grade. Plus, I could kind of relate to how she was feeling. "You okay?"

"I've had better days," she said, wiping the tears away. "How you holding up?"

"Not too bad all things considered. Wondering if my hair will actually fit under a habit, trying to see if I remember all the lyrics to 'Climb Every Mountain'. You know the usual.'"

A surprised laugh escaped her. "You're funny, Sadie. Thanks."

"I try." I shrugged.

"And hey, I guess as long as you wind up meeting your Captain von Trapp it might not be so bad," Serena said.

I nodded as she waved and walked away, her eyes looking less glassy than they had moments before. At least one of us was feeling better. The sting of my test results was still sharp, but unlike Serena, I chose to wallow in silence. Silence was good. Silence was relaxing. It was exactly what I needed—

"For real, Sadie, where do you get these clothes?"

Dear God, why? What had I done to deserve this?

"Are they specifically designed to put guys off or is that an unintentional side effect?"

Spinning around, I looked up into Colton's eyes and forced a smile. "Is your voice specifically designed to make girls want to vomit or is that a side effect?"

Colton, the jerk, laughed. "Touché."

"Where's Kyle?" I asked before he could say more.

"Still back there with the jock squad." And sure enough, looking over his shoulder, I could see my bestie still talking to Zayne Humphreys of all people. He'd left me to deal with his brother solo. Great.

"Did you make Billy apologize?"

"Yeah," he said, face suddenly serious. "Nobody talks like that about Kyle. Not while I'm around."

"Good," I said. We couldn't agree on anything else, but we agreed on this: Both of us wanted to protect Kyle. It was one of Colton's only good qualities in my opinion. "I guess you're not all bad."

"And I guess you're still in love with my brother."

Eyes narrowed, I shook my head. "Seriously, do you say things like that to make me want to run away from you? Because it's working."

Instead of backing down, he leaned in. "Usually girls run toward me," he said, voice low, "not away, but you never did. Why is that?"

The question caught me off guard. Plus, for some stupid reason, his closeness made my heart beat faster. Ugh. My back was pressed against my locker, cool against my heated skin, my heart pounding as he stood close, close enough to smell his surprisingly pleasing aftershave. But this was Colton freaking Bishop for goodness sake.

"Could you back off?" I said, trying to put a little distance between us.

"No."

"No?"

Colton shook his head, those blue eyes looking amused. "Maybe I'm just too much for a good girl like you."

You definitely are, I thought. But I'd die before admitting it.

"Maybe that's why you went for Kyle." His lips tipped up at the corners. "A less hot, much safer choice."

"Hate to break it to you," I said, lying through my teeth, "but you're not that hot. And I'm not in love with him."

"Not in love with who?"

Kyle joined us, and Colton eased away while I had a mini-panic attack. It wasn't that I thought Kyle had overheard us. I just wouldn't put it past Colton to out me to his twin, my bestie, and yes, the only guy I had ever loved.

"Who's Sadie not in love with?" Kyle repeated, looking back and forth between the two of us.

"No one," I said, begging Colton with my eyes. Kyle had no idea as far as I knew, *none*, and this would ruin our friendship. "I'm not in love with anyone."

Colton stared me down a second longer then finally said, "You think you are. One day somebody's going to prove you wrong."

What the heck was that supposed to mean?

"You guys are acting really weird," Kyle said as I gaped at his twin. "And hey, thanks for the backup, Colt. Billy's an asshole."

"No problem," Colton said. The two clasped hands and did one of those one-armed guy hugs.

Before I could really take in what was said, my phone went off. It was an email. It was *the* email I'd been waiting on for a month. But as I read, face paling the farther I went, it was so not the response I'd hoped for.

"What's up, Sadie?"

It was Kyle's voice, but I couldn't speak. I felt like the rug had just been snatched from underneath me.

"Ah, it can't be that bad," Colton said. Taking the phone from my numb fingers, he began reading out loud, "'Dear Miss Day, We have received and viewed your video submission to be featured on *Dancer's Edge* media. Though we appreciate your efforts, there is something missing, an edge if you will, to be included on our channel. Your videos are too nice, your choreography somewhat dull, and your point of view lacks real life experience. For these reasons, we unfortunately will be unable to accept your work at this time…' Shit."

That last part wasn't in the letter, but if I cursed, I'd agree with him.

"Don't let it get to you, Sadie," Kyle said.

"What a bunch of pretentious assholes," Colton said.

"You can always try again."

I shook my head, not in disagreement, but like someone coming out of a dream. Or returning from battle.

"Come on," Kyle said. "This is like what, your third rejection?"

"Seventh," I said.

Kyle winced.

"This is the seventh time they've rejected me, but it's no big deal." Rolling my shoulders back, I lifted my chin, tried to believe my own words. "Rejection is a normal part of life. There's no way I'm giving up, but…it's always the same. Too nice, lacks experience, no edge."

"You've gotta admit they have a point," Colton said. I looked up, and even if he was the bane of my existence, his look of pity spoke volumes. "Come on, Sadie, you're like Miss Nice Girl."

"Shut up, Colt." Kyle shot him a glare. "She doesn't need that right now."

Colton cocked an eyebrow. "What she needs is the truth. I would've thought being her best friend you'd be honest enough to give her that."

Turning, I asked Kyle, "You agree with him?"

"Not really," Kyle muttered.

"Not really?"

"Well…you *are* nice, Sadie," he said. "If what they want is an edgy, mean girl type, that's not really you."

"I'm not that nice," I said finally coming to my own defense.

"I'm kinda edgy."

I mean, sure I was an honor roll student who stayed out of trouble--much to my parents' delight. And yeah, the dances I'd sent in to *Dancer's Edge* were mostly happy, fun pieces and not the dark and/or sexy stuff they usually featured. And okay, yes, I preferred weekends spent in my room binge watching TV, playing video games, or reading instead of partying. Besides my gay best friend, books were my first love. So sue me. That didn't mean I wasn't edgy…did it?

A second later, Colton, who was born without a filter, answered that one as only he could.

"You're about the least edgy person I know." I started to argue, but Colton held up a finger. "You wear the clothes of a prissy librarian." Another finger. "You don't hook up." A third. "Shit, you don't even swear." A fourth. "You don't drink." A fifth. "I haven't seen you at a party… well ever."

I tried to think of a cutting retort, something to really knock him down a peg.

"You…you're…such a *jerk*," I said in my most menacing voice. It wasn't good enough. That was clear by the answering grin on Colton's face. I was just starting to realize, that when you didn't swear, your options in the insult department were severely limited.

"Face it, Sadie," Colton said. "You're a classic good girl. If those idiots want edgy, you ain't it."

It was so close to what Kyle had said I had to grit my teeth. While I silently fumed, setting his brother on fire with my eyes—seriously, would a good girl do that? Ha!—Kyle tried to change the subject.

"So Sadie," Kyle said, "you coming over to study tonight? And by the way, who the hell puts a Physics test on a Monday? So wrong."

"No, I can't tonight," I said, still staring straight at Colton. "As a matter of fact, I have a party to go to."

Colton laughed. "Oh really? You can't be talking about Eric Greene's kegger."

"It's a different party." Lifting my chin, in my coolest, ice-queen voice I said, "The guest list is pretty exclusive. I guess you didn't make the cut."

And with that, I made my grand exit, Colton's laughter and words echoing in my ears.

CHAPTER 2

The stereo was blasting Elvis Presley, the room was packed with people...and I was the youngest person in attendance by at least 50 years.

I hadn't lied.

This probably wasn't Colton's idea of a party. Actually, strike that, it *definitely* wasn't Colton's idea of a party. 1) There wasn't a keg in sight. 2) All the women were completely covered up, most of them wearing slippers. 3) It was 7:00 pm, and the party would end at 8:30 pm (bedtime for most of the residents). 4) The only fight that usually went down in this crowd was over who won at Bingo. But who the heck cared what Colton thought, anyway? Certainly not me.

"Sadie, would you be a dear and get me a slice of cake? I think Edith's already on her fourth piece—the wretch—and I'd like at least a taste of *my* birthday cake."

"Sure," I said and got up to cut my oldest friend a slice.

Birthdays were a big thing here at Shady Grove Assisted Living. On the main table—where Edith was, in fact, sitting, licking the icing off her fork—was a pound cake with a replica of The King (courtesy of yours truly), and it was going fast. Streamers hung from the ceiling, balloons blanketing the floors, and a banner on the wall read: HAPPY 79TH BIRTHDAY MISS BETTY. The residents were migrating around the room, catching up and sharing gossip. As usual, the TV in the corner was turned to the Game

Show Network, volume loud enough to compete with the music. The place still smelled like a weird mix of Lysol and baby wipes, but everyone looked happy enough.

When I came back and handed her the plate, Betty smiled. Her teeth were all crowns, she'd once told me, but they gleamed better than the real things ever could.

"Thank you, dear."

"Welcome," I said. As she closed her eyes to savor that first bite, I gave myself a mental pat on the back. I knew I'd found the perfect cake. It was blueberry pound cake, Betty's favorite, infused with real blueberries and vanilla frosting, a blueberry glaze drizzled over top.

"This is divine," she breathed. "Just divine."

"I had to go all out," I said. "It's not every day you turn 79."

Betty shot me a look. "You getting fresh with me?"

"No way." I held up my hands.

"Better not be," she said, pointing with her fork. "I have it on good authority I don't look a day over 60. It's my mama's classic bone structure." She gestured to her face. "We Lockhart women always look at least ten years younger than we actually are."

I eyed her perfectly rounded cheeks, smooth skin enhanced by foundation, eyes brightened by too-much-for-daytime mascara and perfectly applied eye shadow. Her lips were ruby red. Betty never left her room without her face on.

"You do look rather fabulous," I agreed.

She smiled again at that. "As do you…but you could use some lip gloss."

I rolled my eyes at that. It was an old argument, but Betty wasn't done.

"And mascara! What's the point in having those amazing blue eyes if you don't showcase them? You've got to use what the Good Lord gave you, Sadie. And he certainly gave us more than most."

She took a breath then jumped right to it. "Did you know that Old John tried to kiss Edith? That old bat wouldn't even know what to do with a man like him."

"Oh, and you do, do you?"

She sniffed. "I'll pretend like you didn't say that, dear. But *of course*, I would know what to do. Men are easy as apple pie for a woman like me. But *really*? Edith Duhurst? The man obviously has no sense of decorum."

"Apparently not," I agreed.

"And that Trask is no better. Just the other day he swatted me on the backside." Betty widened her eyes in feigned indignation. "I mean, I can't really blame him for wanting to do it. But where have all the gentlemen gone?"

"That's a good question, Betty," I said, trying to keep the laughter out of my voice. "So what did you do?"

"Well, you know, I felt bad for the man, so I let it go. But if he tries to get frisky again, you bet your sweet self I'll set him straight." She took a quick breath. "And then, you won't believe what Verna said to me the other day…"

I listened as she gave me a rundown of all the Shady Grove gossip, the two of us moving to the rec room next door for board games and Bingo. A lot happened behind these assisted living walls. My parents hosted Senior Night at their ballroom studio on Saturdays—which was how I'd met Betty four years ago; she was the main reason I spent so much time at Shady Grove. We had instantly bonded. Betty and I both loved movies (she'd been a celebrity makeup artist in her younger years—though she preferred the term "Hollywood starlet"), and we shared our favorites. Her first pick for me was *Bye, Bye Birdie*. Mine was *Little Miss Sunshine*. She loved to talk, and when she spoke, I loved to listen. Betty was more vivacious at 79 than I'd ever been. But we worked. In a weird, *Harold and Maude* (another of Betty's picks) kind of way, we worked.

Though I guess I'd be the dude in that scenario.

I sighed.

Apparently, it was enough to derail Betty's train of thought because she stopped right in the middle of what she was saying and looked at me. "So…tell me more about these jerks who turned you down."

I tried not to wince, still feeling the sting of rejection.

"Why haven't they liked your dance videos?" Betty went on. "Are they blind or just stupid?"

I shrugged. "A little of both?"

"What exactly did they say?"

I gave her the whole spiel: too nice, dull, no edge, no life experience, blah blah blah.

When I was done, her lips were pursed, eyes narrowed, looking me over in a way that made it hard not to squirm.

"What?" I asked.

"Well…I don't think you're dull."

"Why thank you, Betty."

"I watch your dances every week and greatly enjoy them. And you're not too nice," she continued. "You've got spunk. I saw you take on Blanche that day for the last cup of chocolate pudding."

"She's diabetic!" I said. "I was trying to help."

"Still, Blanche is very serious about her pudding. And you sass me all the time." Betty nodded as if she'd come to some conclusion. "There's hope for you yet."

I was about to argue the sass comment, possibly proving the truth of that statement, but she kept going.

"So, what are you going to do about it?"

I was taken aback. "I hadn't really thought about it."

"Well, let's think," Betty said. "You can't just let these *Dancer's Edge* people have the final word."

"What can I do?" I sighed. "If they don't think I'm good enough, that's it. I'm done. Might as well join the convent tomorrow."

"What's this about a convent?"

Cora Davies, Betty's partner in crime, walked slowly up to us, and I rose to help her into a chair. Cora had passed 79 several years back. Five-foot-nothing, silver hair crazier than my own, and wrinkles from a lifetime of laughs, though she had slowed down physically, Cora's spirit was still as lively as ever.

"Did you see Deidre just now?" she said. "I think she's found a way to cheat at Bingo. The woman never loses, I tell you. Never!"

"Maybe, she's just lucky," I offered.

She waved me off. "Now, what's this about a convent?"

Betty pursed her lips. "Sadie got some terrible news today."

"Oh no…another rejection?" Cora asked, looking to me. She knew all about my goal to be included on *Dancer's Edge*, the world's biggest online dance community. Yet another person to see me fail. Lovely. "They turn you down again?"

"Yes," I said, "and a Career Aptitude Test advised me to become a nun."

"Bah." Cora pursed her lips. "There's nothing wrong with being a nun but only if you *want* to be a nun. I'm guessing you haven't heard the Call?"

I shook my head.

"She hasn't," Betty confirmed. "And correct me if I'm wrong, Sadie, but I don't remember 'Join a convent' being on your Carpe Diem List."

"You're right. It's not." Unintentionally, my hand went to the pocket where I kept my list. They'd done an activity at Shady Grove back in July called "Carpe Diem" where the senior citizens wrote down all the amazing things they'd accomplished in life and all they still hoped to do. It inspired me to do a list of my own with the adventures I'd *hoped* to have before graduating. Right now, it felt as heavy as a lead ball, none of the items checked off yet.

"Plus, I'm not even Catholic."

"That's alright, dear. Nobody's perfect." Cora patted my hand. "Sadie, what you need is a man."

"A man?" I repeated.

The little old lady nodded, eyes sparkling. "A man who will sweep you right off your feet. Preferably a handsome devil, someone to show you the ways of the world."

"Don't you dare settle for someone plain," Betty said. "You need someone who won't be intimidated by your beauty."

"Betty. Cora."

"Yes, dear?" they said in unison.

"I do not need a man," I said. "It's the twenty-first century. Who needs men when you have birthday cake?"

I'd thought it was funny, but the joke sailed right over their heads.

"A man might help you get over that crush you have on Kyle," Betty said.

"Who says I have a crush?"

The two women just shook their heads, and I felt my cheeks warm. I'd never actually told them I loved Kyle. But I talked about him all the time, couldn't help it. They were my girls after all. It hadn't taken long for Betty and Cora, who seemed to know *everything* and were possibly the biggest gossips ever, to catch on even if I never spoke my feelings.

"Anyone who hears you talk about Kyle would know you have a crush," this from Cora. "And from what you say, he sounds wonderful. But…"

"But you need someone who can love you, too," Betty said gently.

Gentle or not, that one still hurt.

"I think men are overrated," I said, trying to lighten the mood. When you were unlucky enough to be afflicted with unrequited love that you knew, for a fact, would never be requited, sarcasm was the only defense available.

"Your problem is you've never had one before." Betty looked wistful for a moment, running the pearls of her necklace along her fingers. "Men can be lovely distractions."

"They most certainly can," Cora said then shot me a lascivious wink.

I couldn't help it. The laugh bubbled up and out of my mouth before I could stop it.

"Back to business." Betty cleared her throat while I pulled myself together. "We were discussing Sadie's love life."

Cora smiled. "Does our Sadie have any prospects?"

I sobered immediately. "Right now, my only options seem to be the Father, the Son, and the Holy Spirit."

"But you haven't even lived yet!" Cora declared.

"That's what I was saying," Betty said, meeting my eyes. "Sadie, you need to be a little wild, live your life. Show those stupid people at *Dancer's Edge* that you have what it takes. Life is too short to live quietly."

"Amen," Cora said. "If there's one thing I've learned in my ninety-two years, it's that there are no guarantees. You've got to make your own opportunities. I could die tomorrow and have no regrets. How many people can say that?"

Not many, I thought.

"Alright, alright," I said, "I hear you."

"Do you really?" Betty asked as she and Cora gave me the squinty eye.

"I do." When they continued to stare, I added, "I'll try and live louder…even if I have no idea what that means."

They looked satisfied with that. Thank goodness.

"Are you girls ready for story time?" I asked mostly to change the subject. Besides just hanging with Betty and Cora, this was actually one of my favorite parts of volunteering. "I can't wait to see what book you picked out."

There was a twinkle in Betty's eyes that I didn't trust for one second. "Oh, I'm very excited. Since I'm the birthday girl, I got to choose our reading material for the evening."

"And?"

Cora chuckled. "She picked another naughty one."

I closed my eyes. Not again.

"Oh come on," Betty said, "it's not nearly as bad as you think."

"What's the title?" I asked.

"*Falling Hard for the Highlander*. It's about a savage Scottish Highland warrior and how he seduces and falls for an innocent yet feisty English lass. Doesn't that sound delicious?"

"And it's exactly as bad as you think it is," Cora added as she handed me the book.

I'd have to check, but I was pretty sure nuns didn't read books with half-naked highlanders on the cover.

"Story time, everyone," Betty announced, and for the first time today the Game Show Network was placed on mute. The residents crowded around me, and it wasn't just the women. The men loved these stories, too. I enjoyed reading to them—some were unable to read by themselves, their eyesight long gone. But these books they liked…

There was sure to be plenty of bodice ripping.

And racy scenes.

And overall naughtiness.

No big, I thought, shaking it off and popping open the cover. I'd done this before. I was edgy. I was cool. I could read naughty romance aloud to a bunch of senior citizens. Like Betty said, life was too short to live quietly. I wouldn't even so much as blush.

Take that, *Dancer's Edge*.

CHAPTER 3

Okay, so that whole no-blushing thing?

Yeah, it didn't really work out.

I got home right at 9:00 pm and ran straight into my mother who was preparing to leave. Her red dress was skintight, strappy heels sky high. The small sparkly clutch was what Betty would call "perfect for nighttime." I was used to seeing her like this. She had on her show makeup which meant she was probably going out dancing. Again. It was the best way to drum up business for the studio.

"Hey Mom, how was your day?" I asked.

"Oh, you know how it is. One new couple signed up for classes this month. The Latin styles are always a favorite," she said, swishing her hips. "But your cheeks make me think your day was far more interesting than mine."

"Huh?"

"What's that blush about, Sadie?"

"Well, you know how it is," I said, echoing her. "Went to a party, hung out with the girls, read raunchy romance to little old ladies with a thing for men in kilts. Those guys at Shady Grove know how to have a good time."

She laughed. "Did Betty have a good birthday?"

I thought back to my last sighting of Betty and Cora: They'd been giggling, fanning themselves as they talked about the undeniably sexy Laird Blackwood.

"Betty had a great birthday," I said, "though I think her taste in books is somewhat inappropriate."

"Take it from me, Sadie. Even older women need a bit of stimulation now and then."

"Gross, Mom."

"Gross but true. Hey, is Betty coming tomorrow for Senior Night?"

"I don't know why she wouldn't."

"I really wanted to wish her happy birthday in person. She's a great dancer and an even better woman."

"She definitely is. And here, take this." Taking the shawl hanging from the coat rack, I dropped it over her bare shoulders, fluffing her blonde hair that was so like mine. The wild curls were somehow softer and fit Mom so much better. "It's supposed to be cold tonight."

"Why do I sometimes feel like you're the parent, and I'm the kid?" she asked.

I shrugged. "Maybe it's because I was born eighty."

"So not true."

"It's Friday night, Mom." I sighed, shook my head. "I'm home before ten, and my plans involve a pint of Ben & Jerry's, curling up with the remote control and studying Physics. Sometimes, I wish I was more like you."

"I don't. If you were like seventeen-year-old me, I'd probably have had a heart attack by now."

I couldn't help but think back to my CAT results, how dull and boring everyone seemed to think I was. "A test I took said I should become a nun."

"What a bunch of bullshit," she scoffed. "You're just a good kid, Sadie. There's nothing wrong with that—actually, everything is *right* with that."

"I love you, too, Mom."

"I love you more. And if you ever do decide to become a wild teenager, just give me some warning, okay?"

With a smacking kiss, she waved and walked out the door, leaving me with a perfect pair of red lips on my forehead.

Alright, I thought, looking at myself in the hallway mirror. Friday night, nowhere to go, I might as well spend some quality time with two of my favorite guys. After a day like today, I was looking forward to a little ice cream therapy.

Ben and Jerry were calling my name.

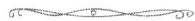

A while later, I'd watched the first season and was just starting the second of *Sherlock*, my Physics book unopened on my nightstand. I had tried. Really I had…okaaay, I'd given it about ten minutes before chucking the book aside. But seriously, on this crappy day, Physics would've been like adding insult to injury. The pint of Ben and Jerry's was long gone. I'd inhaled the Chunky Monkey like oxygen. John and Sherlock had just faced down Moriarty in the notorious pool scene when my phone buzzed a text.

"This had better be good," I muttered.

When I saw who'd sent the message, I nearly pressed ignore—but then my mind registered what it said.

Colton Freakin' Bishop: K drunk, not sober enough to drive. Need ride ASAP.

I didn't have time to respond before another text came through.

Colton Freakin' Bishop: 707 Nottingham Rd.

I typed out a quick response, trying to calm my nerves. This was only the second time Kyle had gotten drunk, the first being after his beloved dog Skittles died last year. So why had he gotten drunk this time?

Me: Of course, I'll be right there.

Colton Freakin' Bishop: sorry 2 interrupt your big "party"

Oh yeah, he sounded real sorry, I thought.

Me: No you're not.

Colton Freakin' Bishop: No. I'm not.

No way was I telling him Betty's party ended—I checked the time and groaned—over four hours ago. Huffing out a frustrated breath, I turned the TV off, pulled my clothes back on, and fired off another text.

Me: On my way.

His response came through a second later.

Colton Freakin' Bishop: Thanks, Sister Sadie. Knew I could count on you.

Me: Call me that again, and I will skinnnnn you!

I was feeling pretty great about that one. Thank you, Mr. Moriarty, for the inspiration. Colton was usually quick to respond, but this time it took at least a full minute. Smiling, I waited as the dots popped up indicating a text. The smile dropped a second later.

Colton Freakin' Bishop: Nice one, S. Very creepy. But Daddy's had enough now, and we both know I'm more bad guy than you'll ever be.

I couldn't believe he got that reference—but then I remembered I'd loaned Kyle my *Sherlock* DVDs last month.

Colton Freakin' Bishop: Catch you…later.

Gritting my teeth, I grabbed my purse, hating that he'd one-upped me. And with a perfectly placed Sherlockian quote at that! The urge to throw my phone across the room was almost as great as my urge to punch Colton in the face. There was absolutely no way I was meant to be a nun because the urge only grew stronger on the 15-minute drive to the party. The scene I found upon arrival was a sorry sight indeed.

Kyle wasn't just drunk.

He was a hot mess.

He and Colton and some girls I didn't recognize were sitting on the porch as I drove up. Actually, one girl was leaning against Kyle with a dreamy expression while he looked seriously uncomfortable. The other was sitting in Colton's lap, but whatever. That was normal, par for the course. Different party, different girl, Colton's long list of conquests continued. The music was so loud it filtered out to the street. A few red Solo cups were scattered on the lawn. As I parked and got out, Kyle launched himself at me, nearly knocking me off my feet.

"Sister Sadie," he laughed, planting a sloppy kiss on my cheek, and I stiffened. "Sadie, Sadie, Sadie. Where have you beeeeeen?"

Colton dragged him back and threw me a grin. "Glad you came. Kyle, here, has had a little too much fun tonight."

"Fun?" I repeated. "He smells like the Budweiser frog threw up all over him."

While Colton snickered, Kyle started laughing hysterically, slapping his thigh and swaying like a drunken bobble head.

"Holy smokes," I muttered, catching his arm. "Let's get you out of here."

Colton helped me get Kyle into the passenger seat then slid into the back. It wasn't until I looked in the rearview mirror and saw the two brunettes squeezed in on either side of Colton that I realized we had other passengers. Was this seriously happening?

"Did you need something?" I asked the one who'd been leaning on Kyle. She looked halfway asleep, but the other girl was busy running her hands all over Colton's chest. Sleepy Girl and her sidekick Miss Bad Taste in Boys. Lovely.

Sleepy Girl blinked as if noticing me for the first time. "Oh,

Colton said you wouldn't mind taking us home. 342 Galveston Way, please."

"Oh he did, did he?" Rolling my eyes, I shifted to face Colton. "You're kidding me, right? I'm not a freaking taxi service."

"Come on, Sadie," he said. "I figured you'd be into this kind of thing, being the do-gooder type. As you can see, Hannah--"

"It's Anna," Sleepy Girl said.

"Yeah, that's what I meant," he grinned. "Anna and her hot friend, Liz, aren't in any shape to drive."

I looked the girls over and, beneath the smudged mascara and eye shadow, saw the same glassy-eyed look that I'd seen on my best friend. Crap. Was I the only sober one in this car?

"I may have had one too many," Liz giggle-hiccupped, laying her head on Colton's arm.

And there was my answer.

"'ppreciate the ride," Anna said sleepily while Liz continuously stroked Colton's chest.

My nemesis grinned, eyebrow cocked. "It's the Christian thing to do."

If the girls had been jerks, I might have said no. If Colton and Liz were...getting busy in the backseat, I would have thrown them both out. But seeing as both girls were nearly asleep already and one couldn't keep her head up, and seeing as I was a push over, I gave in.

"Fine, whatever," I mumbled. "It's on the way anyway...but if you two start making out, I will kick all three of your butts to the curb."

"Hmm," Liz murmured, "thank you, Sister."

Colton cough-laughed, but I pretended not to hear. Even as he and Liz did what I knew they'd been going to do, and she started kissing up and down his throat, making me want to gag, I didn't react. Even as she giggled, I kept my eyes forward. In fact, I did a pretty great job of pretending I was alone in the car for the next few minutes—until Kyle started rambling.

"Nobody knows me," he said to himself. "Not my parents, not my friends. Not even my brother. No one in the whole wide world really knows who I am…except you, Sadie."

"What?" I said.

"It's like I don't even exist."

"Kyle, you're wasted," Colton said from the backseat. "You're my twin. Of course, I know you."

"No, you don't," Kyle said sadly. "You think you do, but you don't. You wouldn't love me anymore if you did."

Colton snorted. "Man, you are completely wasted. Ten bucks says you puke before we make it back home—or maybe in the car."

I shot Kyle a look. "Don't you dare."

"Deal, and don't be thinking I'm too drunk to remember, Colt," Kyle said, spirits seeming to lift as they shook on it—though, they sank again in the next breath. "Why can't anyone know me?"

My best friend looked to me, and the miserable look in his eyes made my heart clench. I knew he hadn't told anyone else. It had always made me feel kind of special, that I was the only one he'd felt comfortable enough to tell his deepest secret. But right then, I really wished he would've come out, owned all of who he is—though I couldn't even begin to understand how hard that must be. I had to believe that his family would still love and accept him like I had.

"Why can't anyone know who I am and just…love me?"

Taking a deep breath, I turned back to the road. "I love you, Kyle. You know that."

"I do," he said, and I saw him nodding out of the corner of my eye. "But not in *that* way."

In exactly that way, I thought with a pang in my chest. In the most tragic way imaginable.

"I really shouldn't have kissed Anna tonight," he breathed, head drooping to the side.

"Excuse me, *what*?"

He didn't answer.

"Kyle?" I said.

A minute later I drove into Anna's driveway and looked over to find him asleep. He'd dropped that bomb and then escaped to dreamland. Unfortunately, I wasn't that lucky.

Throwing the car into park, my mind was reeling. I didn't notice Colton leading the girls out of the backseat, walking them to the front door. All I could hear were Kyle's last words. He'd kissed someone else? He'd kissed a complete stranger? Wait a minute. He'd kissed...*a girl*? I really didn't know how to feel about that, so I settled somewhere between shocked and hollow.

My God, I thought.

Kyle, my best friend who couldn't possibly ever love me back because he was gay, had kissed a girl…

…and it wasn't me.

My eyes pricked with tears, but I wouldn't let them fall. I especially wouldn't let them fall in the presence of the person who had just gotten back into the car. Colton leaned forward, putting his head between the seats, and looked over at his brother.

"I figured we owed them both a ride considering Kyle was all over Anna at the party."

"Yeah," I said, hearing the bitterness in my tone, "and you being all over Liz had absolutely nothing to do with it."

I swallowed my feelings, locked them inside, but as Colton turned, his eyes seemed to look right through me. His clear gaze proved that he was not nearly as drunk as I'd first thought.

"You're wishing it was you aren't you," he said.

I scoffed. "If you think for one second I'd want your mouth on me—"

"Not that, you idiot. You're wishing Kyle had kissed you instead of Anna."

"Shhh," I hissed. My eyes shot to the side. Luckily, Kyle was absolutely dead to the world. "I was not."

"That's good," he said. "It didn't mean anything, and Kyle felt awful afterward. That's why he got shit-faced drunk and nearly puked on her."

"Oh," I said, looking away. "Like I said, I wasn't wishing that."

"Sure you weren't."

Pulling back onto the road, I began driving the familiar path to the Bishops' house. It was about three blocks from where I lived, and I knew the way like the back of my hand, could find their little two story in my sleep I'd been there so often. This, of course, meant there was absolutely nothing to distract me from my thoughts of Kyle…and Anna…and Kyle kissing Anna…and Anna kissing him back…and—

A low chuckle brought my focus from the endless kissing cycle to the backseat.

"What?" I said, capturing Colton's eyes in the mirror.

"I was just thinking about what you said." Another chuckle escaped.

I knew I shouldn't ask, but… "What did I say?"

His blue eyes were swimming with mirth. "In case you didn't notice, Liz was the one all over me, not the other way around."

"Oh from what I saw, it seemed pretty mutual."

"I can't help it if girls want me," he said, stretching his arms out. "Being this damn fine is both a gift and a curse. Great looks come with great responsibility."

I laughed. "Do you even hear yourself? Because you

seriously sound like such a dork, right now—and a little like Spiderman."

"And as for my mouth being on you..."

The words were like a shock to my system.

"You should be so lucky, Sadie Day."

When we reached their house, I pulled into the driveway, shut off the engine and turned to face the boy who had always known just what to say to get under my skin. His pierced eyebrow was cocked like I'd known it would be. He wore his usual grin. Colton's whole face was a mixture of smug and arrogant, and as usual, it pushed all my buttons.

"Get over yourself, Colton. Like I'd want what every other girl has already had."

Slowly leaning forward, not taking his eyes off mine, Colton rested his arms between the seats. He lifted a hand to toy with the ends of my hair.

"One kiss from me would ruin you for life."

I hated how that one sentence affected me. I didn't know why, but his words, the way he was looking at me sent a shiver down my spine. Revulsion, I thought. I was just freaked that he was touching me—well, my hair. Pushing the offending hand away, I scoffed.

"Yeah, right."

"It's a fact." Colton's chuckle feathered against my face. "I corrupt good girls like you, Sister Sadie. You really need to let loose." He plucked at the top button of my cardigan, and again, I slapped his hand away. "Stop being so buttoned-up all the time. Stop being so good."

"I'm not that good," I said, nose scrunched.

As he laughed and jumped out of the car, I met him on the other side to help with Kyle. It took several stumbling tries, but we eventually dragged him out, me taking one arm, Colton grabbing the other. Kyle wasn't helping at all. He was truly lights-out to the world, and it took some maneuvering to get him up the stairs of their porch and to the door.

"Listen Sadie," Colton began, "I'm only saying this because you're my brother's best friend. It's not like I enjoy pissing you off."

I pursed my lips, waited.

"Okay, okay." The grin was back like he couldn't help himself. "I do kinda like pissing you off. But seriously, Sadie, you need to wake up."

"Hello, I'm standing right here," I said. "I am awake."

Colton shook his head. "No. You're not."

"Colton, it's late. Your brother's arm is heavy, and I don't have time for this."

"You really go to a party tonight?"

"Yes," I said, eyes narrowed, "I really went to a party tonight."

With senior citizens and a Bingo tournament.

"Why?"

Kyle let out another groan and shifted his head onto my shoulder. Without meaning to do it, my hand rose to pat down his hair. Usually styled to perfection, right then, like everything else about him, it was a mess.

"Poor Kyle," I said.

"At least he had fun tonight." Colton shook his head as I frowned. "At least he knows how to have fun. Sadie, it's senior year, and you're sleeping your way right through it."

"I said it once, and I'll say it again because apparently you don't listen," I gritted my teeth. "I'm not asleep."

"Just because your eyes are open doesn't mean you're awake."

I blinked. "You sound like a fortune cookie."

"Whatever, smartass."

"No, keep going," I said. "I like fortune cookies. Please Buddha, tell me more."

"I was trying to help."

Kyle let out another groan.

"I don't need your help," I said. "And I have tons of fun. Tons."

Colton leaned forward. "You wouldn't know fun if it was staring you in the face."

I was about to deliver a stunning smackdown—no really, it would have been epic—but right then, Kyle lost the bet he'd made in the car with his brother. He lurched and threw up all the "fun" he'd had onto one of my favorite cardigans. I had less sympathy for him after that.

A perfect end to the worst day of my life, I thought.

Later after I had finally washed the puke out of my cardigan—it took a good thirty minutes and half a bottle of liquid detergent—I went to my computer and pulled up the *Dancer's Edge* website. They uploaded a new video at the beginning of each month, and it was almost always contemporary, hip hop or some other commercially accepted dance form. This week's dance was an amazing hip hop solo to a soulful/sexy song, and you could just feel the guy's energy coming through the screen.

After watching it (twice), I opened a new tab and pulled up my channel. There was no doubt about it. My videos, though shot impeccably, were definitely more tame…and yes, a little too nice. *Maybe instead of jive, I should try a Latin style next time?* I thought. Ballroom had never been featured, and it was my goal to be the first, to show them—and the world—just what ballroom could do. But to be honest…"sexy" wasn't my strong suit. I wasn't even sure if I could pull off "edgy." In fact, I was almost 99% sure I couldn't.

Sighing, I got into bed. I was more than ready for sleep, snuggling deep under the covers, looking forward to forgetting about today. But for some reason, even as I lay there, Colton's voice kept me up, buzzing around in my head.

Just because your eyes are open doesn't mean you're awake.

Good God, I thought. When Colton Freakin' Bishop, bad boy extraordinaire, started sounding like a poet, there was something very wrong. A change had to be made, I decided. If I wasn't so "nice," maybe I would've already been accepted by *Dancer's Edge* and checked off a few of the items on my "Carpe Diem List." If I had gone to that party tonight, maybe I would've been the one Kyle kissed instead of the one he got sick on. If I was more like Anna or Liz, maybe I wouldn't be about to end my senior year un-kissed, un-touched and…undeniably pathetic.

I didn't want to graduate high school with any regrets, was tired of living quietly.

I was so sick of being the good girl.

I just didn't know what to do about it.

CHAPTER 4

"Okay, here's what I think you should do."

Betty wasted no time finding me first thing as she and the rest of the Shady Grove residents walked (and wheeled) into Senior Night at Corner Street Ballroom, my parents' studio. Her face was even more vibrant than usual, mostly due to the spectacular evening gown she was wearing. Emerald green really was her color. The "Birthday Girl" sash and tiara were nice touches.

"I thought about you all last night," she continued. "About the nun thing. About that rejection and how those silly people think you're too sweet, too nice, unexciting, basically lifeless—"

"Geez, Betty, okay. I get it," I mumbled.

"Sorry, dear, I got carried away. Anyway, even watching a movie didn't help. It was like I couldn't sleep until I finally thought up a solution."

"And did you?"

"Yes, and Cora was wrong," she said. "Sadie, you don't need a man."

"Okaaay?" I still had no idea where she was going with this.

Betty tilted her head. "What you need...is a makeover."

"A makeover?" I repeated.

"Yes." As she nodded, the rhinestones in her tiara twinkled like stars, catching the light. "A *life makeover*. They think you're too dull? They say you lack experience? Well then, go out and get some experience. All you have to do is prove them wrong. It's not that hard when you think about it."

What she was saying made a lot of sense, but—

"Betty, that all sounds great," I said. "But how do I get life experience?"

"Hmm," she said. "I thought about that one, too. Sadie, first I need to ask you: Are you open to change?"

My mind went back to yesterday, and I didn't have to think long. I nodded.

"Well then, that brings me to step two of my solution. For your life makeover, you'll need a coach, a guide, someone to help you on your quest to break out of your shell. Man or woman, it doesn't matter. It just has to be someone who can show you how to walk on the wild side. Someone who knows how to be…well, a little bad."

I just stared.

"Don't look at me like that, dear," she sniffed. "I was a bit of a hell-raiser in my day, and you see how well I turned out."

"No, it's just…you've thought a lot about this," I said.

"Of course, I have. You're one of my favorite people."

My heart warmed. "Are you offering to be my coach?"

She laughed. "Good Lord, no! You need someone who can get out and show you the world. Trust me, dear, a life makeover is the answer to all your problems. It sounds fabulous, doesn't it?"

"A life makeover," I said, feeling a weight lift from my shoulders. "I like it. How'd you come up with that anyway?"

"Well, like I said, I couldn't sleep. So, I was watching *Pretty Woman*, and—"

"Betty," I said flatly. "Please tell me, you did not just solve my life problems based on a movie about a heart-of-gold hooker and her millionaire playboy."

Betty crossed her arms. "So what if I did? You love the idea."

I couldn't even argue because I did love it.

"Now, we just have to find your playboy." Betty clapped her hands then nudged my side. "I mean, your coach."

The lights dimmed at that moment. The idea was...brilliant. It was the perfect solution to my good girl dilemma. *One day I'm a nun, the next a prostitute. Made perfect sense*, I thought. My mind was still going over the life makeover idea as we made our way to the two seats Cora had saved us. Unfortunately, as we drew closer, I realized the seat next to mine was occupied. The woman I secretly referred to as the Home Wrecker was scowling as my mom welcomed everyone.

"Sadie," Amanda said in her usual fake tone. "How nice to see you."

"Hmm," I said noncommittally, "why are you here? Did Dad bring you?"

"Of course, he did. I'm his girlfriend."

"For now," I mumbled under my breath.

Her smile turned sharp. "What was that?"

"Oh nothing," I said. "I just haven't seen you here before. So, you like dance?"

"Uh no," she scoffed, straightening in her chair. "Your dad promised to take me out for a nice, expensive Italian dinner after this. *Little Sicily*, very high end, only the best people get in. He said enrollment has been down, so I'm here to support him."

Riiight. And the Snobs-R-Us dinner had nothing to do with it.

"Hope your mom doesn't mind me coming. I wouldn't want to trespass on her turf."

The words were perfectly delivered. The Home Wrecker was smiling an innocent smile, eyes wide. But if you looked a little closer, there was a glint of satisfaction there, a maliciousness she couldn't quite hide.

Yes, Amanda was pretty (on the surface). But she was a shameless gold digger who was twelve years younger than my dad. She wouldn't last. Dad wasn't a bad father, but he was a life-long serial cheater. There had been several other Home Wreckers in the past. I knew she'd be gone once she figured out Dad didn't have the deep pockets she was used to, but right now, she was trespassing on Mom's turf. I was looking forward to her rude awakening.

"No worries," I said, smiling. "I assume he told you about the opening number."

Before she could respond with more than a blank stare, Mom's voice rose above the chatter.

"Hi everyone! Corner Street Ballroom would like to wish the happiest of happy birthdays to our good friend Miss Betty," Mom said, blowing a kiss at Betty as everyone cheered. "I know how you like it hot and spicy, Betty. This dance is dedicated to you."

Music filled the room, smooth and sultry, as my mom and dad assumed their starting positions. Rhumba. Perfect.

The Home Wrecker sat straighter. "What are they doing?"

"They do this once a month," Betty said, speaking across me. "Just wait, their chemistry is amazing. It's the highlight of the night."

Amanda's answering frown was the highlight of my night.

As Mom and Dad moved across the floor, every eye was on them. I'd grown up with parents who had gone into marriage for the long haul, had promised to love and to cherish each other forever. But forever came and went when my dad decided that he was in love/lust with my mother's best friend, Camille (Home Wrecker #1), and when Mom decided life would be better without him to worry about. They'd divorced when I was ten, but still co-directed the dance studio.

The love of ballroom had kept them together—if not in marriage then at least in friendship. Although they hardly ever danced together anymore, one Saturday out of the month, they still performed for the students. There was something between them when they danced. Dad's flavor-of-the-month girlfriend always looked nervous when they danced.

Amanda looked pale, mouth pursed, as they moved across the floor.

Good, I thought. *Let her suffer a little.*

I wasn't delusional.

I didn't carry any false hopes that my parents would get back together, and we'd be one big happy family. Yeah, right. But seeing that look on the current Home Wrecker's face as sparks flew between my mom and dad?

Loving. Every. Second.

As Dad pulled Mom to him, lifting her leg, dipping her back for the final pose, the applause was instant. I whooped and hollered with the rest of them. Beside me, Amanda sat stiff as a board, noticeably silent, but whatever. Even she should've appreciated that performance. Rhumba had always been one of my favorites. They'd just set that floor on fire.

After they bowed, Mom said, "Thank you, thank you all so much. Now if you'll just pair up and join us out on the dance floor, we'll get this party started!"

The residents took to the floor, some girl-boy pairs, others girl-girl or boy-boy. All were welcome here. The dance studio was a safe space. There were always more women than men who signed up to take class, but it didn't really matter. Everyone just wanted to learn and have a good time.

Walter came over and said, "Cora, my love, would you care to dance?"

Her response: "Of course, you old fart. Let's go cut a rug."

As he helped her to her feet, Walter threw me a wink. He was actually 84, eight years younger than Cora. They'd been married over 60 years and were still the cutest thing under the sun. Old John came by to scoop Betty up; Amanda had gone off to talk to my father; and my mom was walking around giving pointers on proper technique. Looking up and down the row of chairs…yep, I was the only one without a partner.

Story of my life.

It was a good thing I loved to people watch, or I'd be feeling pretty lonely right now.

My eyes traveled back to the dance floor and stopped once again on Walter and Cora. They were slow dancing together, swaying really. Her head rested on his shoulder, their hands clasped and resting over his heart. There were at least ten other pairs out there. The couples circled the room like colorful spinning tops as they practiced.

Walter's eyes never left his wife.

I sighed.

"So, this is what you do on Saturday? Sit alone, looking sad, watching old people dance?"

With a gasp, I turned and found Colton—Colton Bishop, of all people!—sitting next to me, arms crossed, leaning back like he owned the place. The sight was so unexpected—him, here, at Corner Street Ballroom. It took me a moment to realize he was real and not a hallucination.

Colton shook his head. "This is pathetic even for you, Sadie."

"Where did you come from?" I asked.

"Mom found out about Kyle and the party. Of course, my brother was never a good liar. When she asked why he looked so sick this morning, he sang like a hung-over canary." He didn't look at me but lifted his chin at something in the crowd. "Mom thought this would be a good punishment."

Looking out, I spotted Kyle immediately. He'd been dancing behind a pillar with Edith, who looked like she was leading and enjoying herself immensely. She was moving to a beat only she could hear, pulling him around the floor. Now that they were getting closer, I could hear her counting: "One-two-three. One-two-three. C'mon keep up!"

I smiled as Kyle caught my eye. It looked like he was mouthing the words, "Help me."

"Dancing's too fun to be considered a good punishment," I said.

"Oh yeah?" Colton said. "You sure look like you're having a good time over here by yourself."

At that, I rolled my eyes. "Whatever. But Kyle's the one who got drunk. Why did she make you come?"

"Simple," Colton shrugged. "Because even if I'm not the one who's drunk, I'm the bad influence. I'm the one who told him about the party. I was the one who let Kyle drink. Ergo, I share in the punishment."

"Well, that's unfair," I frowned. "And did you just use the word 'ergo' in a sentence? I'm impressed."

"Now, Sadie, try and keep your panties on." He said all this with a straight face. "Like I said, I'm a bad influence. You wouldn't want to encourage me."

"But a big vocabulary is such a turn on," I said breathily.

His head whipped to face me, and I laughed—right until I caught sight of the metal on his lip.

"New piercing?" I asked.

"Nah, I got it done a while ago," he mumbled. "And were you serious about the vocabulary thing?"

"No," I laughed. The way the light played off that tiny piece of silver drew my attention straight to his mouth. It was inexplicable, and I had to force my eyes away. "Though it doesn't hurt.

Hey, tell the truth. Does that metal have anything to do with why you were sent here? I've never seen it before."

"Got it done last summer. My mom may have found out about it this morning and had a mini breakdown," he said. "Your turn. Why'd you sigh a second ago?"

"Because I was overwhelmed by your magnetic presence," I deadpanned.

"Come on, for real. What were you thinking?"

I dropped the act, looked at him a second, then shook my head. "You wouldn't understand."

"Try me," he said.

"Fine." I sighed again, this time in defeat. "You see that couple out there?"

He looked to where I was pointing.

"I was thinking, sixty years of marriage…and he still looks at her like that."

Colton nodded. "Ah, girly thoughts."

Yes, I thought, completely girly, and he didn't even know the half of it. What I'd really been thinking was: I wish someone would look at me like that.

Checking to make sure he wasn't looking, I angled my body slightly away from Colton and pulled out my list, only unfolding it the smallest amount, keeping it mostly hidden inside my hands. "Carpe Diem" was written in big bold letters and underlined at the top. Right there, just under the title, was the first and most important item on my list.

1) Fall in love with someone who will love me back.

It was also the most impossible thing. Considering I'd fallen for my gay best friend all those years ago, I knew love wasn't in the cards for me. I'd had to bury my emotions for Kyle for our relationship to survive. It was a sad fact of life, but not everyone got their happily-ever-after. Some of us just had to settle for mostly-happy-but-missing-something. But still…a girl could dream.

I sighed, looking down the rest of my list. There were no check marks, nothing crossed off as complete, no gold stars to indicate I'd accomplished any of the tasks I'd hope to when writing it. Betty was right. I really did need a life makeover.

"What's that you're reading?"

"Nothing." I jerked my hands closed before Colton could see, hastily refolding and tucking the sheet of paper back into my pocket.

Colton raised an eyebrow (the pierced one, of course).

"It's none of your business," I said.

"Whatever you say. It's not like I care anyway."

Moments later, just as I started to relax, he smoothly grabbed the end of the paper sticking out of my pocket and jogged a few steps away. The sound that came out of my throat was a combination of banshee in distress and wounded animal. For his part, Colton looked very pleased with himself.

"What are you trying to hide, Sadie?" He flipped the little square back and forth between his fingers as I stumbled toward him, arms outstretched.

"Hand it over," I said.

Not hearing or not caring about the desperation in my voice, he began to inch the paper open. I tried to snatch the list back—but he held it out of reach.

"Colton, I mean it!"

His grin broadened as I jumped and missed, but seriously, I couldn't reach my list without scaling his much taller body like a tree. It was a sign of how desperate I was that I even considered it. I must've looked silly, but I didn't care. He literally held the most personal, most humiliating document I'd ever written in his hands. No way was I letting him read that. No. Way.

"Geez, Sadie, what's the big—oomph!"

Taking advantage of his outstretched position and his assumption that I was some goody-two-shoes, I hooked my leg behind his and gave a quick push. Colton was so surprised he dropped the list immediately and went to the ground like a stone.

"Damn girl," he said, wheezed really. "Where the hell did you learn that?"

"I know several ninjas, one of whom is a girl who could totally kick your butt." I sniffed. I'd taken a few self-defense classes from a girl named Snow. She was my age, one of the coolest chicks I knew, and phenomenal at martial arts. Like Bruce Lee phenomenal. Basically, I'd learned from the best. "Ninjas, Colton. I hang with ninjas. I'd keep that in mind the next time you try and mess with me."

"Noted." Colton got to his feet, but I must not have hurt him too bad because that grin was still in place. The idiot. "Sister Sadie, prissy librarian by day, ninja warrior princess by night. Who knew?"

"I could've seriously injured you, you know," I said. "I don't think you understand the kind of mortal peril you just put yourself in."

Colton shook his head. "Yeah, okay…what was in there anyway? Was it a love letter or something? You look like the kind of girl who'd be into that sort of thing."

"What the heck are you talking about?"

He groaned. "Just tell me it wasn't to my brother? That would be so messed up."

"Colton, I repeat. What the heck are you talking about?" I said.

"The paper, Sadie, the one that made you go all ninja on me," he said, and my eyes widened. "It happened like a minute ago right before you knocked me on my ass? I just figured it had to be something really embarrassing for you to get so worked up."

Frantically searching, I scanned the area surrounding us and came up with exactly nada. The song had changed as we'd been arguing. The couples were at it again, twirling around, filling up the dance floor, but the floor here was completely clear. *Where had my list gone?* Colton distracted me so thoroughly I hadn't even remembered it. But now that I did my heart was going a mile a minute, a cold sweat breaking out on my forehead.

"Hello there, young man," Betty said, sidling up to us and eyeing Colton from forehead to foot. That twinkle in her eye was back, her timing impeccable. I felt like she'd just saved me from either screaming in dismay or bursting out into tears. "I'm Betty, and you are?"

"Colton," he said with a nod.

"Well, it's very nice to meet you, Colton. Dance with me, would you?" Betty said. "It's my birthday, so you'd best not refuse."

"I'm sorry, ma'am, but I don't dance."

"Don't you 'ma'am' me," Betty tsked, tugging on his arm. "I've never been a 'ma'am' in my whole life, and I'm not starting now, understand? It's Betty, just Betty. Now Colton, my friend Sadie looks like she could use a moment"—he looked to me then back at Betty in confusion—"and we have some things we need to discuss."

"We do?" he said, but I barely heard him.

I could've kissed Betty for taking charge and leading him away—I'd have to thank her later—but right then, I was too distraught. Getting on my knees, I searched everywhere, behind and around chairs, in every corner, anywhere it could possibly be. When I came up empty-handed a third time, I went into the back office and curled up on the couch. No one would find me here besides Mom and Dad, and they were out there teaching.

I could finally cry in peace.

Maybe it got caught on the bottom of someone's shoe, I mused, thinking of where my list could be at this very moment. *And then maybe that person got on a plane, traveled to Ireland and finally rolled down that hill like I'd been dreaming about for all these years.* A tear fell before I could stop it…and then another…and another. *Maybe it fell through the floorboards never to be heard from again.* For some reason, that thought was almost as depressing as the next. *Maybe it just got up and walked away on its own to fulfill all the un-fulfilled dreams I'd written down.*

The worst possibility, the very worst, was that maybe my "Carpe Diem List" was now in the hands of someone even more heartless than Colton Bishop. Someone who, thinking it was funny, would expose all my dashed hopes to the world. My stomach roiled, and I felt the tears fall faster this time.

At least I hadn't written my name, I thought, grasping for a silver lining, something positive about this awful situation. If someone did find the list, I could only hope whoever found it wouldn't know it belonged to me.

CHAPTER 5

"Sadie, we should talk."

I was at my locker, humming a Billie Eilish song while switching out my books for second period, feeling much better than I had Saturday. There'd been no unwelcome surprises over the weekend. I'd watched my social media accounts like a hawk but (thankfully) found no sign of my list online. No copies were on the walls when I got to school today which was a relief. To be honest, I was feeling pretty darn chipper.

But life loved to make you feel secure right when the sky was about to fall. I should've known better than to relax my guard.

"What's wrong?" I asked, frowning as I turned to face Kyle. "Your voice sounds off."

"Nothing," he said. But my best friend's brow was furrowed, eyes refusing to meet mine, and…

"Kyle, are you sweating?" I said in surprise. On someone else, it wouldn't have been odd, but Kyle was one of those people who hardly ever sweat. There were two possible explanations: Either he ran a 5k to get here, or he was seriously stressed about something.

"Sadie, we—" He stopped, took a breath. Finally meeting my eyes, he said, "I know it might be uncomfortable, but I think we need to talk about this."

"Talk about…" I trailed off, going pale as Kyle raised a hand. Between his fingers, he held a small folded piece of paper that

I instantly recognized by the lopsided daisy on one side. I had gazed at that daisy for long minutes after I'd drawn it, wondering what I should do with my life. I'd totally freaked after losing the dang thing, and now, here the paper was in my BFF's grasp. *My Carpe Diem List.* I had to clear my throat before responding. "Where'd you…I mean, that could be anyone's. How do you know it's mine?"

Kyle scoffed. "Seriously Sadie, I'd know your handwriting anywhere. I was your pen pal in fifth grade, remember? Every period is a smiley-face which is something only you do, my too-cute friend."

"I just think they make the page look happier," I muttered.

"Wow, Sadie! Just wow," he said, eyes bright. "So, you actually wrote this. When did you write it? How could you not tell me about your list?"

Looking left then right, taking his arm, I led him past the lockers to an empty corner. It wasn't more private, not really, but there was some cover from the crowded hallway. This topic was way too personal to broach out in the open.

"I wrote it this summer, " I said, keeping my voice down. "And I'm absolutely mortified that you read it. I never planned to share that list with anyone—well besides Betty, who swore to me on her makeup kit she'd never tell a soul. Now, can I please have my list back?"

"But why wouldn't you share it with me?" he frowned, keeping a firm grip on the paper. "I share everything with you."

I gave him a look. "Everything?"

"Yes, of course," he said. "You know my deepest secret, Sadie."

"I do, and you know I'd never tell a soul," I said—but he wasn't getting off that easy. Something was going on that he wasn't telling me. I knew it; he knew it. Which reminded me…

"Okay Kyle, since we share *everything*, you want to tell me why you kissed Anna last Friday?"

His lips flattened into a thin line. "I was drunk."

"Yeah for the second time in your life," I said.

Kyle stayed silent.

"Don't forget I know you, too, best friend. I guess the real question is: Why'd you get drunk in the first place? You can talk to me if you want. No judgements."

It took him a moment, but with a deep breath, he fessed up. "It's nothing really. I just kind of…like someone."

Whatever I'd been expecting, it wasn't that.

"You do?" I said, eyes widening as a thought hit me. "Who? Anna?"

Kyle rolled his eyes, his voice thick with sarcasm. "Yeah Sadie, I woke up one morning and found myself straight. Come on, of course, it's not Anna."

"Sorry," I mumbled. "I just thought since you kissed her that maybe it was possible."

"I kissed her because she kissed *him*," he explained.

"Wait," I said and held up a hand. "You're saying you kissed Anna because she kissed the guy you like?"

Kyle nodded excitedly. "Yeah, it was kind of like I kissed him through her. Like one degree of separation or something. You get it?"

"That…makes an odd sort of sense. It's kind of romantic actually," I said. But it was also pretty messed up. "Makes me feel kinda bad for Anna, though."

"Exactly. I knew you'd understand, Sadie. I felt so bad about kissing her, for using Anna that way, you know? I drank to try and forget, but I won't do that again."

"Well?" I said after a beat. "Are you going to tell me who the lucky guy is?"

"Not yet," Kyle said. "Maybe if things progress, but...yeah you're right. I guess we don't share everything."

"I get it," I said, disappointed he didn't want to tell me—especially since I'd almost had to sacrifice one of my favorite cardigans to his drinking shenanigans—but at least he knew I'd listen if he ever wanted to talk. "See there, I respect your privacy, and I understand you don't want to share all of your humiliating moments with me. Hence, why I feel so betrayed about my list."

"But your list is awesome!" he said, shaking the paper again. "There's nothing humiliating in here."

I groaned. "I still can't believe you read it."

Kyle was just trying to protect my feelings. I knew what I'd written, what he'd read—the one thing I didn't know was how it came to be in his possession in the first place.

"How did you find it anyway?" I asked. After searching the studio from top to bottom, I'd gone home empty-handed.

Kyle shrugged. "Found it after I left your parents' studio. I was cleaning my shoes, and there it was on the bottom of one of my wingtips."

Aha! It *had* gotten stuck to someone's shoe. Just my luck it was the one 17-year-old boy who always shines his shoes before bed and would recognize my handwriting anywhere. *Must stop it with all the smiley-faces*, I thought.

"When I first read it, not going to lie, I was surprised." Kyle's grin made me nervous. "It was...interesting."

My cheeks flamed as I pictured the list in my mind. Yes, there were a few...questionable items. But in my defense, I'd never thought anyone would read it!

"Honestly, I was impressed."

I blinked. "Really?"

Kyle nodded. "Yeah, I mean, it takes a lot of guts to write something like that down. How'd you come up with this anyway? I've heard of a Bucket List but never a "Carpe Diem" list. Nice twist."

"It was an activity they did at the assisted living center," I said. "Carpe Diem is a lot less morbid than kicking the bucket, and *The Dead Poets' Society* was the movie for July. They loved it."

"Who doesn't?" Kyle said. "Williams at his best, inciting those private school boys to seize the day, the drama was so on point."

"I know, right? *O' Captain, my captain*. Totally classic." Sobering, I looked down. "The sad part is I haven't actually done any of the things on my list. Not yet, anyway."

Kyle placed a hand under my chin, lifting until I met his eyes. "Kinda hard to go to Ireland when you're still in high school," he said gently.

"Yeah, but most of them don't require leaving the country."

"So, why haven't you done any of the others?"

"I don't know." I frowned. "Because I'm too much of a 'nice girl,' I guess. Plus, I'm scared."

Kyle smiled. "I could help you."

"Kyle, you know I love you," I said, "but I'd be way too embarrassed to do half the things on my list if I knew you were watching. I care too much about how you see me."

"Okay, I get that," he said. "But then what? You need someone whose opinion you don't care about?"

"Yeah," I laughed, my mind turning over what he'd just said. "That would be awesome actually. Someone I wouldn't mind making an absolute fool of myself in front of. They'd have to be brave enough to do all the things on my list. Someone less like me. Someone edgy, someone who doesn't care what other people think, someone fearless and—"

A shadow fell over the two of us at that moment, and someone (a very unwelcome someone) cleared his throat.

"Okay, what's this I hear about a list?" Colton said. His voice, that bored yet blunt drawl, always sent my hackles up. This time was no different, but his statement had me turning to glare at his twin.

"Kyle!" I said. I couldn't believe it. "You told *him*? How could you?"

Kyle took a step back hands out. "Hey, I didn't say anything."

"Good," I muttered, "because I may have had to kill you if you did."

"Geez, Sadie, I would never share your list with my brother. It's private."

"Ah, so there is a list," Colton cut in, and I hated the smug look on his face. "Sadie, if you needed my help all you had to do was ask. You didn't have to bring the old lady into it."

"What are you talking about?" I said.

"If the dancing wasn't bad enough, she kept talking about some makeover and a list and how I had to help you complete it," Colton said. "Man, that lady could talk. She wouldn't let me leave. Asked for my birth sign, relationship status, if I'd ever been suspended, how many piercings and tats I had."

I was interested in the answer to that last one. I'd always had an unhealthy and inexplicable obsession with his piercings, but that was beside the point.

"Who wouldn't let you leave?" I asked.

"That Betty woman." He shivered, a real honest to goodness shiver. "She's scary."

Any other time, I would've laughed because he looked seriously freaked—it was rare to see Colton Bishop looking anything but cocky, confident and collected. But just then, I felt like lying on the floor, curling up in the fetal position. *Et tu, Betty?* But of course, Betty would do this, I thought. She must've taken one look at Colton and decided he would be a perfect life makeover coach to introduce me to the wilder side of things. Even I had to admit, he had all the qualities on the surface. Too bad I knew better.

"What exactly did she say?" I asked, fearing the answer.

"That I should be your coach," Colton said flatly. "That there was some list you couldn't complete without me, and it was her dying wish that I help you."

"Wow," I said, eyes wide.

Betty had brought out the big guns with the whole "dying wish" thing. I knew for a fact she was in excellent health, but Colton obviously didn't.

"So, wait a minute," Kyle said to me. He looked confused, and I couldn't really blame him. It was a lot to take in. "Betty's your friend, right? The one from Shady Grove?"

I nodded. "She thinks I need a life makeover and a coach to show me how to be more adventurous, break out of my nice girl image." Colton was grinning again, but I ignored him. "To be honest, I kind of agree. Not with her choice of coach"—I shot a scathing look at Colton—"but about the makeover part."

"Okay, I think I'm following," Kyle said then turned to his brother. "Colt, she wants you to help Sadie with this?"

"Yeah," Colton said, cocking that dang eyebrow again. "She said I looked like trouble, the good kind, and that Sadie could use some of that."

I had to admit. That did sound like Betty.

"And you actually agreed to help?" Kyle said, sounding shocked.

"Hey, it was the old lady's dying wish." Colton frowned. "What was I supposed to do? Tell her no? I'm not that big of a dirtbag."

Okay, it was time to put an end to this ridiculous discussion.

"Colton," I said, "Betty was just joking about the death wish thing. She's in perfect health…in fact, she'll probably outlive us all, so you're off the hook. Despite what she told you, I won't be needing your services."

Colton gave me a slow look up and down, then with a shake of his head, he said, "I think you need my services. You're just too proud to admit it, Sister Sadie."

"Don't call me that," I said.

"What? I think the name fits with your whole uptight persona."

"Well, I've never really cared what you think, Colton. So, we're in perfect agreement."

"Oh, you care," he said.

"No, I don't," I said back.

"Then show me your list."

"What?" I scoffed, Kyle completely forgotten as Colton took a step closer to me.

"Show me your list," Colton said again, his hand extended. "If you really don't care what I think, then whip it out."

"You did not just say 'whip it out.' Seriously…ew."

"Ah, so the good girl has her mind in the gutter. Nice to know."

Kyle laughed. "If you saw her list, you'd know how much of a dirty mind she has."

"Shut up, Kyle," I said, fighting down a blush.

"Come on," Colton said. "Now, I'm curious. Betty never said what was on this list, but I told her I'd help you complete it, so I will."

God bless Betty down to her princess pink toenails, I thought. She hadn't betrayed me after all.

"I don't see why that's necessary," I said.

Colton pointed at my face. "Well, look at that. You do care what I think. Thanks, Sister Sadie, I love being right."

It was a challenge, plain and simple. The cocked eyebrow, the look in those ocean blue eyes, the tone of derision in his voice. My anger got the better of me, and I couldn't let him win.

"Fine," I said, snatching the list from Kyle's hand. Before I could think about it, I opened the note and thrust it at Colton. "Here, go ahead and read it. I'm sure it'll give you a good laugh."

Out of the three of us, I wasn't sure who was more shocked—but Colton recovered first.

"Well, alright then," he said with a grin.

As he began reading, the grin slowly fell away, replaced first by a small frown, a narrowing of his eyes followed by a clenching of his jaw. It took him a long time to get to the end. Finally, with a swallow, he re-folded the list and handed it back to me.

"Kyle's right," he said, voice gruff, avoiding my eyes. "You do have a naughty streak. Who knew? But I can't help with this. You should find someone else."

Surprised, I took the list and shoved it into my pocket. "Glad we finally agree on something."

"What?" Kyle said. "But you just said you'd help her complete it."

"I'm not the right guy," Colton said.

Kyle was looking at Colton funny like he was an alien from another planet. "You can't be serious. After all that, you bail on her? Just like that?"

"Kyle, drop it," Colton said.

"It's okay," I added. "I never wanted Colton's help anyway. That was Betty's crazy idea."

Kyle crossed his arms over his chest. "I don't see what's so crazy about it."

"What?" Colton and I said in unison.

"I'm serious," Kyle said and gestured between the two of us. "Sadie, this is the perfect solution. Don't you see? You want to do all the things on your list, but you're afraid of embarrassing yourself. And here's my brother, Colt, who's already been convinced to help you by that little old lady."

Colton shook his head. "Hoodwinked. I was hoodwinked by a wolf in grandma's clothing."

"Wow, nice vocab usage," I said sarcastically.

"You know you love it," Colton shot back.

Even as we bickered, Kyle was nodding at the two of us with a gleam in his eye. "This is going to be a perfect pairing. I can feel it in my gut."

My jaw nearly hit the floor. Couldn't he see what an awful idea this was? First Betty, now Kyle…was there no end to this madness?

"I'm not doing it, Kyle," Colton said, for once the voice of reason, and I sighed in relief. Thank goodness, he wasn't going along with this outrageous scheme. "I don't care what I said to that crazy woman. Like Sadie said, Betty's not dying, so the agreement is null and void."

"Oh, you're going to help her," Kyle said back, and I didn't like the look in his eyes one bit.

"And why would I do that?"

Kyle cocked his head. "Because I've got a hundred bucks that says you won't."

Colton scoffed. "You're seriously going to bet me? Get real."

"Two hundred," Kyle sighed. "You drive a hard bargain, brother, but I'm pretty sure you won't be able to do it anyway. Sadie's list is a tough one, so I've got nothing to lose."

"You really think some reverse psychology BS is going to work on me?" Colton said.

Kyle nodded. "Either that or your need to win will kick in. Your ego is legendary, Colt, and I don't think you could take losing to me. Am I wrong on that?"

Colton's jaw was working overtime as he stared his twin down.

"Hey," I said. " It's my freaking list. Don't I get a say in this?"

"No," they said together.

After a beat, Colton shook his head. "It's not a fair bet. There's that part about falling in love and Ireland—"

"Everything but that and Ireland," Kyle cut him off. "You have to help her do everything on the list but those two. Doesn't matter anyway. That still leaves 20 other items. I'll still win."

Colton began to grin. "How long?"

Kyle said, "I'm feeling pretty confident, so…let's say two weeks?"

"A month," Colton retorted.

"Okay, deal."

"Deal."

I felt like I was watching a car crash in slow motion as the two reached out to shake on it. Their grins were identical, the shake a pact, and as both pairs of those ocean eyes came to rest on me, I thought I might faint.

"I'll need a copy of your list by fourth period," Colton said.

"Dream on," I said back, but he leaned in so that we were almost chest to chest.

"Sadie, let me explain something to you," Colton said. "I've never lost a bet. Ever. I'm not about to start now, so from this moment forward, you'll do as I say when I say it."

"But—"

"Shhh," he said, cutting me off with a finger to my lips. I was so surprised by that touch, that one unfamiliar point of contact, I froze instantly, though if eyes could kill, he'd be dust. "One month. You're mine for a month or until we get that list of yours finished. Get used to it."

The warning bell rang, and he was gone before I could recover.

Kyle stepped in front of me next, put his hands on my shoulders. I should've shrugged him off; I would've, but my mind was still on Colton, the words he'd just said, and for some reason, my lips felt unreasonably warm where his finger had pressed against them.

"I know you're mad," Kyle said, "but I did that for you. Now, you'll get your list done…or at least some of it. I don't like to lose either, Sadie, so if you could maybe abandon ship before the last item, I'd appreciate it."

"Kyle," I said finally, "I can't believe…I mean, why would you do that? Enlisting the help of your twin, the bane of my existence? I'm not sure I'll ever be able to forgive you for this."

"Yeah, you will. You're angry now, but just remember I'm your best friend. We've made Rice Krispie treats, discovered the love of lip gloss and Benedict Cumberbatch together. Plus, just think how you'll feel after you've Carpe'd the hell out of that Diem list."

I didn't know whether to laugh or cry. As Kyle started walking away, I was still frozen to the spot, mind completely blown by all that had just transpired. Did Colton freaking Bishop just agree to be my coach? To guide me through the items of my list…and did he actually think I'd just do whatever he said for an entire month? Ha!

"One more thing, Sadie," Kyle said.

I looked up, noticing he'd turned back around. He frowned at me before completing his thought, and when he did…man, it was a doozy.

"I love Colt and everything. He's the best brother I could've ever asked for, but…just don't be one of those girls who buys into his crap. Okay? Promise me you won't fall for my brother?"

I nodded too shocked to speak.

He was gone as the second bell rang, leaving me standing alone in the middle of the hall, late for third period study hall and totally off kilter.

Don't fall for his brother? Colton Bishop?

That was one promise I was sure I'd have no trouble keeping.

CHAPTER 6

I still couldn't believe Kyle and Colton had seen my list.

And what was I thinking, showing it to Colton like that, practically daring him to read it? I mean, yeah, I'd been feeling a mixture of anger, stubbornness and frustration at the time, a trifecta of emotion that only seemed to hit me when Colton Bishop was around. But gah! What the heck had possessed me to do something so stupid?

I had no answer to that one—but I did know that Kyle was wrong. I didn't have guts. It had taken absolutely no bravery on my part to write any of my list because I'd thought it was for my eyes alone. That tiny fact, the thought that no one else would see it, had left me free to write whatever I'd wanted. My dreams no matter how silly, my goals no matter how embarrassing.

And I did.

My heart was poured onto this one little piece of paper. It included my deepest desires. Now Colton wanted me to make a copy, so he could read it again? Yeah, I'd been stupid the one time, but that was so not happening.

My eyes shifted to the list spread flat on the small table in front of me. I'd been reading and re-reading it all throughout study hall, sitting in my favorite chair, hidden between the stacks in the back of the library. No one would find me here. It was my secret spot.

CARPE DIEM LIST
1) Fall in love with someone who will love me back.
2) Roll down a hill in Ireland.
3) Be featured on Dancer's Edge—or get a million views LOL whichever comes first!
4) Talk dirty (work on better insults).
5) Stay up and watch the sun rise.
6) See the inside of a police car.
7) Get a tattoo (daisy, dragon, lyrics/book quote?)
8) Get something pierced (ears, nose, belly button?)
9) Sneak out of the house.
10) Learn to drive a stick shift.
11) Go dancing at a club.
12) Crash a party.
13) Buy lingerie.
14) Have an explosive first kiss (preferably in the library)

That one was probably the most embarrassing.

But nope, I thought, wincing as I continued to read. The four after that were equally as embarrassing but for different reasons. The one about a first kiss revealed that I'd never been kissed—and that I wanted my first one to be in the library. Lovely. But the ones following it had to do with kissing as well. Kissing in the rain, in the car, in public, in my bedroom. What can I say? I was obsessed with kissing.

And now Kyle and Colton, two of perhaps the most beautiful boys in history, knew it.

My eyes closed on a sigh. "Could I just go die now, please?"

A *click* sounded from somewhere behind me, and I spun around in my chair to see Colton standing there, looking down at his phone.

"What did you just do?" I asked.

"Took a picture," he said without looking up. "And to answer your other question, no you can't die yet, Sadie. I've got a bet to win."

I just stared.

"I figured you might not want to make a copy of your naughty list, so I decided to make it for you. You're welcome."

Standing up, I held out my hand for his phone. "Hand it over, Colton."

"Hell no." With one last look, he slid the phone into his pocket then met my glare. Colton's look was cool and assessing. "How am I supposed to come up with a game plan if I don't know what's on the list?"

"Hmm, let me think," I said, pretending to mull it over. "You're *not*. I already told you I don't need your help, and besides, I don't think Kyle was serious about the bet anyway."

"Yeah, he was," Colton said. "We'd never joke about a bet—especially not one for 200 bucks. He's had his eye on a new Gucci belt, and I've been saving up for some high-quality tinted windows. There's no way I'm losing this."

"And why would you need tinted windows?"

"So, I can hook up with girls in my car without nosey-ass people seeing in." My disgust must've been showing because he shook his head. "Don't look at me like that. I thought you'd appreciate the need for privacy what with all the 'kissing' mentioned on your naughty list."

"Gah! Will you stop calling it that?"

"What? Your naughty list?" he said innocently. "I don't know what you're so ashamed about. It's natural for repressed good girls like you to want to take a walk on the wild side."

"I'm not ashamed or repressed," I growled. "You're just being an annoying a-hole. Like always."

"Damn, that was one of the weakest insults I've ever heard. Isn't number four on the list something about talking dirty?

We'll definitely have to work on that."

I groaned and threw up my hands in frustration. "How are you even here right now? This is my spot, my special place. No one else even comes into this part of the library anymore."

Colton shrugged. "Kyle told me about it."

And I'd told Kyle about it last year when he'd needed a quiet place to study for finals.

This day just kept getting better and better.

"Holy smokes," I breathed. "Colton, can't you just forget that you ever saw my list in the first place?"

"I don't think so," Colton said, one side of his lips quirked up. "But I am willing to help you do all the things you wrote down. Out of the goodness of my heart, of course."

My brow furrowed. "And for 200 dollars," I said.

Colton held his hands out. "Where's the harm in that? I get something out of it and so do you. If you stick with me, we could have half your list completed by the end of the week."

"Really?" I said in surprise.

"Oh yeah," he said. "It'll be so easy, Sadie. We could even start now if you want."

"And how would we do that?"

Colton smirked, the light catching on the metal in his lip. "I seem to remember something about an explosive first kiss in the library."

My eyes widened as I caught his meaning, and I felt my entire face go scarlet. "Oh my gosh, that wasn't about you! I can't even believe you would suggest such a thing."

"Why not?" he said. "I didn't see a specific name on your list."

"You're you, and I'm me. I think that's explanation enough, don't you?" I said back, though as he stepped closer, I couldn't seem to take my eyes off his lip ring.

When he stopped in front of me, my back was pressed up against the bookshelf, heart stuttering.

"I'm a guy," Colton said, placing a hand on the shelf near my shoulder. "You're a girl. And it's only a kiss. It's not like this would change anything between us. You'd still be Sadie Day, my brother's annoying, too-good-for-everybody, uptight best friend."

My eyes narrowed. "And you'd still be Colton Bishop, the cocky jerk who thinks he's God's gift to women and doesn't give a crap about anyone or anything."

"See?" His gaze shifted to my lips then back up to my eyes. "We completely understand each other. That'll be important in the days ahead."

My thoughts were all jumbled up, my brain turned to mush by his nearness. The hypnotizing lip ring wasn't helping matters. Did I really want my first kiss to be with someone who was only helping me for his own benefit? If I was being honest, despite the circumstances and our hate-hate relationship, I was curious. I'd heard so many tales of Colton's prowess that I couldn't help myself. He had a reputation as being an excellent kisser. Girls had been saying that and writing it on bathroom stall walls since sixth grade. And I wanted my first kiss to be a great one, didn't I? But maybe all of those girls had been lying. The Colton I knew wasn't a very giving person. He was reckless with a side of cocky and a dislike for me that didn't bode well for a memorable first kiss.

As if he could sense my wavering thoughts, Colton said, his voice low, "I'll make it good for you, Sadie. I promise."

I swallowed. *Well...when he put it that way...*

"Don't you want to get started on your list?"

"Okay," I said quickly before I could talk myself out of it.

He froze right in front of me, and from the look on his face,

Colton couldn't believe what I'd just said. I had a tough time believing it as well. As he continued to stand there motionless, I had a horrible thought. Maybe this was a joke, Colton's latest way to embarrass me. Dangle the offer to give me a phenomenal first kiss, then rip it away with a cruel laugh just when I agreed. I wouldn't put it past him.

But the laughter never came.

In fact, as Colton eased closer, the look in his eyes was as serious as a heart attack. One hand moved to my waist while the other that had been resting by my shoulder went to tangle in my curls. I won't lie. I gasped at the contact. No guy had ever touched me like this. Well besides Kyle who had loved to play with my hair when we were kids—but it was nothing like this. Colton's hands were sure, his fingers strong yet gentle. I was pretty sure my knuckles were white from how hard I was gripping the shelf behind me, heart beating like a drum in my chest.

And he hadn't even kissed me yet.

"Sadie?" Colton said.

"Y-yes?" I said back.

"You're not going to go all weird on me after this, right?"

My eyes snapped to his. "What?"

He licked his lips, gaze shifting down to watch as I licked my own in reflex. His voice was a bit lower when he said, "Don't get any crazy ideas. I'm not in love with you or anything, so there's not going to be a happily ever after for us. Just know it's all for the bet."

"I do know that," I said, eyes spitting fire. "And you've got to be the most arrogant, egotistical maniac if you think one kiss would be enough to erase all the crap you put me through over the years. Nobody's that good a kisser, Colton."

Colton shrugged. "We'll see."

"If you ever actually do it," I retorted. "Or are you scared you've talked yourself up so much that you won't be able to deliver?"

He chuckled lightly. "Oh, I always deliver."

"Then what are you waiting for?"

"Just waiting to see if you're going to back out."

As I blushed but stood firm, Colton's eyes met mine one last time.

"This doesn't change anything," he said.

And then Colton Bishop was kissing me. His mouth was surprisingly soft as it met mine, my eyes closing on contact. More surprising? Colton, who I'd always thought of as selfish, was gentle and patient with me as I learned to move with him, to match his rhythm. And oh God, did the boy know how to kiss. His lips guided mine, caressing first my top then bottom lip. It felt so good that I repeated the action on him, earning a hum of approval from Colton. The coolness of his lip ring wouldn't let me forget who I was kissing, and my obsession came back full force. When I finally worked up the courage, I followed my instinct and pulled the ring into my mouth, giving it a short tug.

That was when I realized just how much he'd been holding back.

With something like a growl, Colton slanted his mouth over mine, and the kiss went from a slow burn into a wildfire. Unlike my inexperienced self, there was no hesitation in him. Colton kissed me like he owned my mouth. His tongue met mine in a dance I'd never done before but seemed to pick up instantly, his hand tightening in my hair whenever I did something he liked. My hands were everywhere at once. I had no idea where to put them, so as we kissed, they made a trek up his arms to his shoulders, neck, back, wherever I could reach.

This wasn't like any first kiss I'd ever read about or seen in the movies. It was real and messy and...wonderful. If the butterflies in my stomach had anything to say about it, I was sure I'd simply fly away.

Before that could happen, a large book fell to the ground, having been knocked off by one of my elbows, I'm sure, and we both jumped. My hand had somehow ended up on Colton's chest, so I knew he was just as affected as I was. His eyes, though, looked guarded as he walked backward, putting some space between us.

"Well," he said then had to clear his throat. Twice. "That was...yeah."

I nodded. "Mmm-hmm."

"I think we can cross that one off the list."

"Yep," was all I could manage.

Colton rolled his shoulders back, looking up at the ceiling. If I didn't know better, I'd say that his cheeks looked a little flushed. "We should probably meet tonight to see if we can get anything else done. It's only a month, so we should get on that. I'll see you at your house around seven?"

"Okay," I squeaked, thinking about the other "kissing" items I had written down. Was he talking about those or something else? More important: Did I *want* him to be talking about those?

His next words shut down any musings on that subject.

"And you know, we should find you another guy," Colton said. His eyes met mine. "For the kissing parts. I mean, this was convenient, but I don't think we should keep kissing each other. Kyle wouldn't like it."

I blinked, not sure what to say. "Convenient" would not have been the word I would've used to describe that kiss. Amazing, incendiary, passionate. Those were more accurate.

"Or...we could do those, too, if you'd like."

"No!" I said way too loud for the library. Lowering my voice, I repeated, "No, you're right. We should find someone else. Yeah, of course, we should find another guy. I can't even believe we did it the first time."

Colton cocked his head, eyebrow raised. "I would've never guessed that was your first kiss, Sadie. You seemed really into it."

My eyes narrowed at that. "I don't think I was the only one who was into it."

"Yeah, you're right," he said, surprising the heck out of me, and ran a hand down the back of his neck. "I'm just glad I could make it good for you."

I was blushing again, couldn't help it. When he said unexpected things like that, what was I supposed to do? And had he really just admitted to enjoying the kiss, too?

"Yeah umm...thanks for that," I mumbled. Thanking Colton Bishop was not something I had much practice with; I'd have to work on it.

"No need to thank me, Sadie," he said. "It's all for the bet, remember?"

Of course, I remembered the bet. How could I forget? It had just felt right to thank him for some reason.

As he left, I thought it over and realized that my brain really had been muddled by that kiss. I won't lie. I loved every second. Colton had been telling the truth when he said he would deliver. My first kiss had been explosive and right in every way imaginable. Even though he was my enemy, I couldn't get enough of his lips, his tongue, his hands.

But I couldn't forget that he was Colton Bishop, the guy who loved to get under my skin and push my buttons. But now he was also Colton Bishop, the guy who'd helped me check off the first (and so far, the only) item of my "Carpe Diem List."

Even if Colton said the kiss didn't change anything, I was pretty sure it changed everything. For the first time in my life, I was looking forward to seeing him again. And if I was being honest with myself…that terrified me a little.

That anticipation died a quick death the next time I did see Colton.

It wasn't pretty.

After I'd had a chance to recover from the kiss-induced fog, I remembered I couldn't meet Colton at seven because I'd be visiting Betty. We had a standing appointment on Mondays, and I couldn't flake out on her—even if she had set this whole crazy scheme in motion. So, after school, I'd gone in search of Colton…only to find him standing in the parking lot with a split lip and his latest victim.

The parking lot was crowded after school. But as I made my way to Colton's car, through the people that had gathered around it, I saw Shawn Henley, a junior and one of our football team's offensive line, sporting a bloody nose and a shiner on his left eye. Colton had him pushed up against a tree in a threatening position. His hair was a mess, his arms a bit scraped up in addition to the split lip, but Colton looked okay all things considered. And by "okay," I meant openly hostile. He was glaring at Shawn with a satisfied expression on his face. The sad part was this was nothing new.

If I needed proof that Colton Bishop was a bully with too much testosterone, I didn't have to look any further than his inability to stay out of fights. If it wasn't Shawn, it was someone else. This happened at least once a month. It had been happening since we were in middle school. Sometimes the guys were bigger (like Shawn), sometimes smaller, but it didn't matter. Colton would and did fight anyone.

I'd never understood his need to use fists instead of his words to solve an argument.

I was glad when Kyle stepped in and broke the two apart.

"Hey, Colt," he said, "what's this about?"

"Nothing," Colton said and shot a look at Shawn before backing away from him. "We had a disagreement, but we're good now. Isn't that right, Henley?"

"Yeah," Shawn said, spitting to the side. "We're good."

As he rolled his eyes and walked away, Colton stared him down until he was out of sight, then he turned to Kyle and me like nothing had happened.

"How'd you do on that chem exam?" he asked his twin. "I didn't study, so I'm thinking I failed."

Kyle shook his head, unwilling to let the matter go. "You really need to stop all this fighting crap. Mom's going to ream you if you get suspended again. What happened this time?"

Colton laughed. "Chill out, Kyle. The idiot was saying some things in the locker room that I didn't like, so I decided to shut him up."

"Jesus, Colt, do you hear yourself?"

"What? I asked nicely first."

I snorted at that, and the two looked to me. "Sorry, it was funny—but I'm with Kyle on this. You should try talking it out next time, Colton."

"Why, Sadie Day," Colton said, a smile in his voice, completely ignoring my suggestion. "I didn't think I'd see you till tonight."

"Tonight?" Kyle asked. "What's happening tonight?"

"We're going to cross off more of the stuff on her list."

Kyle's eyes widened as he looked between me and his

brother. "More? You've already started the list? Whoa, that was fast."

Colton raised a brow. "It started slow, but yeah, it definitely got faster there at the end. And hot, very hot. Wouldn't you say, Sadie?"

Despite the heat rising in my cheeks, at the challenge in his voice, I said, "That sounds like an accurate representation. Although, I would say it got a little sloppy toward the end."

"Sloppy?" Colton repeated, eyes narrowing to slits.

"Mmm," I agreed, though it was hard not to laugh. Colton looked so insulted. Yes, I'd just lied through my teeth and knocked his kissing technique. It was what he deserved for bringing this up in front of Kyle. Take that, Mr. I-Always-Deliver.

"What the heck are you guys talking about?" Kyle said. "I feel like I'm missing something."

Colton shook his head. "Nah, it was nothing."

My heart deflated a bit. Nothing, huh? I wouldn't have called our kiss nothing, but I guess that was Colton's way of lashing out—or maybe he really thought that. Either way, his comment met its mark.

"We just got one thing crossed off," he said, "which means, so far I'm winning."

"Yeah right," Kyle said. "You've still got a ton more to do. But did you really start, Sadie?"

"Yeah," I said, shaking myself out of it. "Carpe Diem, right, Kyle? Like Colton said, we'd planned to do more, and that's why I came over. I'm meeting Betty, so I'll be at Shady Grove until around 7:00 pm."

"Okay," Colton said. "I'll see you there."

That brought me up short. "Really?"

"Yeah," he said. "I'm not afraid of that Betty woman. We'll start after you're finished. Kyle, you coming?"

Yes, please, I thought. I hadn't wanted Kyle there before—honestly, I'd probably chicken out if he was—but it might help keep my mind straight about his brother.

"Can't. I'm working on a project with Humphries," Kyle said.

"Yuck. How'd that happen?" I asked.

"We got paired up in lit."

"Well, good luck, Kyle. Zayne's awful."

"He's actually not all bad." I stared at him in disbelief. Kyle and Zayne had never gotten along—in fact, they disliked each other almost as much as Colton and me. If my eyes got any wider, I was sure they'd fall right out of my head, but Kyle just laughed. "Plus, you already said you'd feel uncomfortable doing some of the stuff in front of me. Right, Sadie?"

"Yeah," I said. "But now that I think about it…Colton, maybe I don't need your help after all. I'm sure I could do the rest on my own. You—"

"Sadie," Colton interrupted. "A bet's a bet. We're doing this together."

I swallowed.

"I'm going to be the best coach you've ever had." His blue eyes were locked on me even as he said, "My brother's going down, and he knows it. He's not coming because the odds aren't in his favor."

Kyle crossed his arms, a smile on his lips. "I think you guys are full of crap."

"You just keep thinking that"—Colton opened the car door, got inside and closed it—"and be ready to hand over the money when I beat your ass." Turning to me, he said, "I'll see you later. Don't forget to bring your naughty list."

As he pulled out of the lot, Kyle grinned. "Naughty list? That's classic."

"Hey, whose side are you on?" I said as I bumped his shoulder with my own.

"When it comes to you and my brother, I'm neutral," Kyle said as he began walking backwards to his car. "Go out and have fun. Just remember what I said. Remember who Colton is, and you'll be fine."

Sure, I thought. No problem. Colton was the guy who got into fights and loved to provoke me. The guy who'd been so concerned about making my first kiss "good" for me and then turned around and called it "nothing."

At this point, I had one question: Would the real Colton Bishop please stand up?

CHAPTER 7

Betty had no shame. Even after I'd expressed my deep displeasure at how she'd approached Colton behind my back, she couldn't have been prouder of herself. We girls were sitting in the Shady Grove activities room, drinking our five o'clock tea, dishing about our days when I finally admitted her plan had worked.

"I knew he was the one!" she crowed, hands clapping in delight. "When I saw the two of you together, I thought to myself, now there's a young man who'd be a great guide."

I rolled my eyes, but she kept going.

"A young Richard Gere in the making. He was such a gentleman as he led me around the dance floor," she said. "A little tense, but I could tell he was nervous. And oh, the chemistry!"

"Good Lord," Cora said, "chemistry? From what I saw, Betty, that boy could be your great grandson."

Betty sniffed. "I wasn't talking about me, you ninny. I was talking about Sadie and the boy."

I choked, nearly spitting tea everywhere. "Me and Colton? You've got to be kidding. Betty, there's absolutely no chemistry. We hate each other. We always have."

"Ah," Cora sighed. "Sometimes hate can turn to like, and like turns to love. He must like you, Sadie, if he agreed to help."

"He agreed to help because Betty told him she was dying," I said flatly.

Cora gasped, her eyes bright with laughter. "You didn't?"

"I did," Betty confirmed. "And I have to say, I regret nothing because now Sadie has a coach who will show her the ways of the world."

"Oh, you are good, my friend," Cora said. "Devious and brilliant at the same time. I only wish I could've gotten a better look at him."

"He was beyond gorgeous, a perfect match for our girl. I'd love to see him again as well." Betty turned to me. "Do you think he might come by the studio sometime?"

I mumbled into my tea, hoping they wouldn't press.

"What was that?" she asked.

"He's coming by later," I said and winced at their too-bright smiles. "It doesn't mean anything, though. We're just doing more of the list."

"Ooh, how fun," Cora said. "Wish I could come with you."

"Me, too," Betty said. "What are you going to do?"

I shrugged. "Not sure. Colton didn't say."

Betty tapped her fingernail against her cup. "If I recall correctly, there were a lot of fantastic things on your list. Maybe he'll take you out dancing."

"Doubtful," I said. Colton hadn't seemed big on dancing the one time he'd been to Corner Street Ballroom. I didn't want to tell Betty that, afraid I'd hurt her feelings.

"What about that tattoo?" Cora said. "I'm sure he'd know just where to go. Have you decided yet what you're going to get"—she waggled her eyebrows at me—"or where you'd like it?"

I laughed. "No, not yet. But I've got it narrowed down to a few choices."

"Cora's right." Betty smiled. "Colton did say he has a tattoo and multiple piercings—though he wouldn't tell me how many which vexed me greatly. I mean, how am I supposed to find out more about him if he's so closed off?"

"Oh, I know!" Cora said, a glint in her eye. "It's got to be a kiss. There were a few on the list about kissing, right?"

I could feel my cheeks heat and knew even before she said anything that I'd given myself away. Betty had told me once when we'd been playing cards that my poker face was non-existent. The blush betrayed me every time.

"Well," Betty said, her voice filled with excitement, "something tells me there's already been a bit of kissing going on. I think our Sadie's been holding out on us, Cora."

"Sadie," Cora said sternly, "tell the truth now. Did you kiss this Colton fella?"

"Yes," I said quietly.

"Good Lord, girl, you've been here nearly an hour, and we're just now getting to the good stuff."

Betty nodded. "Her first kiss, too. Oh my goodness, Sadie, I can't wait to hear all about it. Okay, how did it happen? Did he kiss you, or did you kiss him? Was it in the library like you'd always wanted or somewhere else? Did you enjoy it? Or was it terrible? Did you remember to wear the lip gloss I bought you?"

Cora lifted her brows as Betty stopped to take a breath. "I think you better tell us Sadie before she combusts."

So, I told them.

I told them all the details of my first kiss: how it happened at school in the library, how Colton had been the one to suggest it (at which point Betty and Cora exchanged a significant look), how I'd been nervous but that had quickly disappeared because of his expert guidance/kissing skills, how I hadn't remembered the lip gloss…but it had been wonderful anyway.

"It was for the bet," I added at the end. The two ladies were completely enthralled by the tale, hearts in their eyes and everything, but I didn't want them to get the wrong impression. "I think Colton really wants to beat Kyle and vice versa. They take their bets seriously."

Cora scoffed, and Betty did a not-so-discreet eyeroll as she took a sip of tea.

"Hey, no need for that," I said. "It was only a kiss. Colton even said it meant nothing to him."

"I'll just bet he did," Betty mumbled. "Sadie, most men aren't as in touch with their feelings as we women are. A lot of times they have to be shown the light."

"It's fine. I don't like him anyway."

Betty frowned. "Really? Why not?"

"Apart from him insulting and teasing me every chance he can get," I said, "Colton just isn't my type. He's arrogant and cocky, thinks every girl wants him. Just because he's a good kisser doesn't make him a good person. I mean, he's so immature he still gets into fights at school."

"Why?" Cora said.

I tilted my head at her question.

"Have you ever asked him why he gets into those fights?"

"No," I said slowly, realizing I hadn't even thought about it. The fights had been happening so long that, at some point, I'd just come to accept them. Kyle had asked about the fight today, but Colton hadn't given a real answer. He'd just laughed it off like it was no big deal.

Cora shrugged one shoulder. "Maybe he has a good reason."

I wouldn't hold my breath on that one, but it was a moot point. Colton wasn't here to ask, and even if he was, he probably wouldn't answer. Time to change the subject.

"Enough about that," I said, smiling and pulling out the romance book we'd started on Saturday. "It looks like it's time for our story. Are you ladies ready to hear more about the dangerously handsome Laird Blackwood?"

"I'd rather hear more about you and the very real Colton Bishop," Betty sighed, "but I'll settle for fictional romance if I must."

I laughed and so did Cora. Betty could be such a drama queen. As the rest of the Shady Grove residents gathered around, I cleared my throat to start reading. This was truly one of the best parts of my day. I got to hang out with my girls, and no one expected anything from me. I didn't have to know which college I was going to or what I was going to major in. I didn't have to think about my list and all the things I'd always wanted to do but had never done. There was no confusion here at Shady Grove. All I had to do was read to them, and we could all escape reality for a little while.

I had no idea how long I'd been reading. It couldn't have been that long because I'd only finished a chapter. Typically, we got to two before either my voice got tired or the residents left to watch their TV shows. We'd reached a particularly juicy scene, one of the many love scenes in the book, when I became aware of a new disturbance in the room. It was nothing I could put my finger on, but…something made me pause. Laird Blackwood had just offered to teach Lady Pippa how to seduce a man. There'd been a lot of back and forth flirtation, thinly veiled innuendos, and now he had her pressed up against the door of his study—but for some reason, I couldn't concentrate.

Catching sight of movement at the back of the room, I looked up and—

Oh. My. Gosh.

He wasn't supposed to be here yet! The clock on the back wall read 6:44 pm, not 7:00 pm, and I was mortified. Colton was early. How long had he been standing there? The look of amusement on his face, the brightness in those eyes, told me it had been a while. Even as my jaw dropped, I couldn't look away.

"Well, don't stop now," Betty said, voice hushed. Apparently, no one else had noticed our new visitor. They were so into the story. "We're finally at the good part."

Colton sat at the back of the room, making himself right at home on a floral sofa, and then he lifted that brow, the pierced one. I couldn't be sure, but the move was so perfect, so challenging, I wondered if he practiced it in a mirror.

"Yeah, come on, girl," this from George Trask, a man who was nice enough but could be a pill if anything interrupted his daily schedule. "Jeopardy starts in few minutes, and I can't miss my show."

"You can't leave us hanging like this," Cora added.

She was right. They all were. Why should I care what Colton thought anyway? These people depended on me, and there was no way I was going to be intimidated. Lifting my chin to where Colton sat, in a cool tone, I said, "If you'd be willing to wait, we're almost done here."

"Oh, hello, Colton dear," Betty called to him like he was a long-lost friend. "You'll wait, won't you? This is a very important scene."

Colton held up his hands. "Hey, I've got no problem with that. I want to see what happens with Blackwood and his girl as much as anyone else."

Of course, he did, I thought as he shot me a grin.

Clearing my throat, I took a deep breath then picked up where we had left off.

Pippa's breathing was erratic. Her heart pounded in her breast as Laird Blackwood's hand made the slow journey up her thigh to cup her backside, a place no other man had ever touched.

"Wrap your legs around me, lass," Laird Blackwood said, voice rough and heated.

Just like that, her legs wound themselves around him seemingly of their own accord. They had begun to weaken some time ago, and now they rested high on Laird Blackwood's hips. The man groaned at her easy acquiescence.

"Good girl," he growled.

"Oh," Pippa cried out as he buried his head into her neck, leaving kisses and little bites up and down the column of her throat. "Laird Blackwood, please!"

His hips thrust up once in response, making both of them moan.

"Tell me what you want, lass."

She hardly knew. Even if Pippa did know what she wanted, she was sure she wouldn't be able to ask him for it. Not out loud, not here in his study surrounded by his amazing collection of books. It was improper. It went against everything she had ever been taught growing up. Libraries were sacred and no place for such dalliances.

I stuttered on that last bit and definitely did not look at Colton. I could feel his grin from across the room, but I decided to do the smart thing and kept my eyes to myself. Looking back down, I kept reading.

Laird Blackwood had no clue where her thoughts had wandered. If he had, he might not have spoken so rashly or so honestly. As it was, his mind so addled by passion and the heady feel of her warmth around him, he said exactly what he had been thinking.

"Your arse is lovely." He gave it a squeeze, causing Pippa to gasp in affronted delight. "Your body is so responsive." His lips pressed against her fluttering pulse. "Most days I walk around hard, and it's all because of you."

I gulped. That last part was bad enough, but did I seriously have to say this next bit? Yes, I thought. Yes, you do have to read it Sadie Day because you are not a goody-two-shoes. You are not too nice, and you are definitely not a coward.

I plunged into the last section, again, keeping my eyes on

the words in front of me.

Pippa clutched the back of his neck, forcing him to look up at her. When she looked into his sable brown eyes, she saw hunger and strength and a fierceness she had come to associate with the brash Scottish highlander. It awakened something inside of her, and she could remain silent no longer.

"Take me, Laird Blackwood," she breathed. "I have an ache inside, and I believe you are the only man who can ease it. Will you help me? Please?"

"Aye, lass," he said, taking her mouth once more in a fierce kiss. "I've got you."

My voice cracked on the last word. *Why me?* I asked not for the first time this week. Was it possible to die of embarrassment? I'd have to Google that later.

When I looked up, the Shady Grove residents hadn't moved a muscle. Their eyes were glued on me (or heads turned in my general direction for those who could no longer see). Even George Trask, the grumpy curmudgeon that he was, had his good ear turned my way. I guess they were waiting for what happened next, but we were done for the day. So done.

"That's the end of the chapter," I mumbled. "We'll pick up here next time."

George was the first to start moving, grumbling about "missing the first part of Jeopardy," the others not far behind. Many of them were talking about the book as they walked/wheeled toward their rooms. Some of them even thanked me for reading which was so nice but completely unnecessary. I hadn't checked to see if Colton had moved yet, hadn't even glanced his way. It like seemed the safest course of action.

Betty fanned herself. "Well...that was some finish. Now, I'm just dying to read the next chapter."

"Me, too," Cora said. "That Quinn Phillips sure does know

how to write a racy scene."

As Colton walked up to us, I kept my eyes averted. "And you? What did you think?"

"I liked the part about the library."

My eyes shot straight to his at that. There was nothing innocent about the look in those baby blues.

"I never realized that was something girls were into," Colton said. "But I'm starting to see the appeal."

I could not believe he'd just said that.

"Oh yes," Betty said, a matching gleam in her eyes. "It's a bookworm thing, I think. A library, the nooks and shadowy corners, all those books looking on, it's the perfect place for romance. Don't you think so, Cora?"

"I do," Cora said. "And I'm sure most book lovers would agree."

I had to break up this little conversation before it went any more off the rails. "The author, Mrs. Phillips, wouldn't take that view," I said. "Even in the heat of the moment, the heroine questions herself and if that was the right place to do...what they were doing."

Colton lifted his eyebrows. "Yeah, but she also wrote that scene. I think it's safe to say she knows it can feel good to be bad."

"Hear, hear!" Betty said. It was a good thing she'd jumped in because I had no comeback. "So, Colton, I see you took what we spoke about to heart. What do you and Sadie have planned for tonight?"

"It's a secret," he said, leaning in conspiratorially, "but I can tell you it has to do with her list."

"Say no more." Betty held up her hands and took Cora's elbow, helping the other woman stand from her chair. Cora may have been ninety-two, I thought, but she moved faster at that moment than I'd ever seen her. "Have a great time. We won't keep you—but I will say one thing."

The two older ladies stepped up to Colton, and standing there, they looked tiny in comparison to his six-foot-two height.

"You're a lovely boy, Colton," Betty said, looking up into his eyes. "I have a lot of faith in you as I've already said. Don't let our Sadie get hurt. If you do...well, let's just say my third husband taught me how to shoot a bullseye at a hundred paces. I have a shotgun under my bed, and my favorite movie is *Misery*."

Colton's face was frozen, and my jaw had dropped during her little speech. Betty had delivered her threat without flinching, but I knew a least some of her statement was false. The only things under her bed were several pairs of fabulous shoes, a box of old records and three hatboxes of love letters from her fans. And her favorite movie wasn't *Misery*. Betty's favorite movie was the same as mine: *Pride and Prejudice*, the BBC version with Colin Firth. I couldn't help but laugh at the look on Colton's face.

"She's kidding," I said.

He nodded but didn't look like he totally believed me.

"You just take care of our Sadie," Betty said.

"Or else," Cora added and sent him an overly flirty wink. The two of them left, cackling as they walked down the hall to their rooms.

Once they'd turned the corner, Colton looked at me and said, "You have some crazy friends."

"Hey," I sniffed, "they're wonderful, and I love them. You're just jealous."

"Whatever. You ready to go?" he said, shuddering. "We can talk about the list in my car. This place gives me the creeps."

I laughed, couldn't help it.

"Aw Colton," I said, leading him out, "don't worry. I'll

protect you from the scary senior citizens."

He shook his head again, and we didn't speak until we were in his car. Colton drove a pristine white Camaro; it was only a few years old, so not vintage, but still a very pretty vehicle. It was mid-sized with two doors, two font seats and a smallish backseat. As I sat on the passenger side, him in the driver's seat, Colton turned on the engine to let the car heat up. It was November and chilly by North Carolina standards.

"So, what are we doing?" I asked.

"I figured we should set some ground rules," he said, pulling something out of his pocket and unfolding it. "Since there's money and my pride on the line, this isn't really just about you anymore."

He handed the paper to me, and my eyes widened as I read aloud.

"I, **Sadie Day**, hereby promise to do whatever my coach, **Colton Bishop**, says for the next 30 days or until all 22 of the items on the attached Carpe Diem List have been completed—with the exception of items #1 and #2." I stopped here to shoot him a glare. "What the heck is this?"

Colton crossed his arms, sitting back in his seat. "It's a contract."

"A contract?" I repeated. "Are you serious? I already told you I'm not doing anything you say. You must be crazy if you think I'd be dumb enough to sign this."

"Keep reading," Colton said. "We both have something to lose now. If we're doing this, Sadie, it's important that we trust each other. This will keep us on track."

Trust him? Ha!

"You said you wanted to complete your list."

Rolling my eyes, I looked down and kept reading. "I promise to help Colton Bishop win the bet against his brother, Kyle

Bishop, at all costs. And I will not, under any circumstances, lose on purpose (aka not complete certain tasks just to let Kyle win)." My cheeks reddened, remembering Kyle's request to do just that, though I knew he'd been joking. "Colton, I would never cheat! How could you even—"

"Keep reading, Sadie," he said.

"In return, Colton Bishop promises not to abuse his power and will only use his authority over Sadie to help her complete her list," I finished in a rush, having to go back and read a second time to really understand the meaning. "Wait," I said, "does this mean I only have to do what you say when it's to help my cause?"

Colton gave an exaggerated slow nod and said, "Finally, she gets it. Give the girl a prize or something. There's one final provision, and I suggest you read it carefully."

Right there, below where I'd stopped, was one final sentence. It was bold and underlined.

It read (and I'm being completely serious): **I promise NOT to fall in love with Colton Bishop—no matter how hot and irresistible he is.**

I snorted a laugh. "Fall for *you*? Irresistible? As if."

"I notice you didn't dispute the 'hot' part," Colton said.

"I do dispute it," I said. "I totally dispute the 'hot' part."

"Too late," he said. "The fact that you think I'm hot isn't a problem, Sadie. Falling for me would be, though, and it's been known to happen. Especially when the girls are as innocent and naïve as you."

I ignored that last dig, chose not to argue—Colton Bishop was hot, *so* hot, and the worst part was…he knew it. Instead I focused on his signature at the bottom. His name was written in close, slanted cursive. There was a line right next to it where my name was supposed to go—if I signed.

"Okay, let's say I go along with this," I said. "Let's say I believe that you're not just in this for yourself and the money. What happens if we don't complete the list?"

"We will."

"But what if we don't?"

"If we don't, then after 30 days, we forget about the list, and I pay Kyle." Colton grimaced, his eyes hard. "But that's not going to happen."

"How can you sound so confident?" I asked. "It's taken me months to even do that first thing, and we still have a lot more left."

"Back then you didn't have me in your corner," he said, and there was the arrogant side of Colton that I knew so well. "I never lose, Sadie. I'm not losing this either."

"Did you even read my list?" I asked.

"Yeah, a few times," he said, a grin forming as I flushed. "It's an entertaining read. We need to work our way from the easiest up to the hardest. I think that's the best way to go."

Could I really sign this? I thought. Everything seemed to be on the up and up, but Colton was a sneaky little bugger. If I gave him this power, would he use it to make me say or do stupid things? He said he wanted to help, and I wanted to believe him. Like he pointed out, he would lose something, too, if I failed. More than anything, though, I really, *really* wanted to seize the freaking day…

Before I could think too much about it, I signed my name above his.

"Good choice," he said, taking the paper, placing it in his pocket.

"Where did you get the idea for a contract anyway?" I asked.

Colton shrugged. *"Fifty Shades of Grey."*

"Seriously?" I choked on air. "Colton that is so messed up."

"Sadie, please," he said, "as if you have room to talk after the reading you did for those horny old people. How often do you do that anyway?"

"It's romance." I sat there shaking my head. "And they pick the books, not me."

Colton's lips tilted upward. "Sure, they do."

"They do," I insisted. Though there was no denying, I did love a good romance. "I just read what they like."

"Okay, I believe you," he said. "No need to get upset. It's not like you care what I think anyway. Right?"

"Right," I said, crossing my arms. "It was just a shock. That's all."

"What was?"

"The fact that you can read," I said sweetly.

"Nice," he said, though I couldn't tell if he was offended or amused. "Now, let's get serious. Your list. Are you ready to start?"

"Sure."

"Okay." He nodded. "For your first task, I'm going to need you to grab my stick."

My eyes went saucer-wide. Did he really just say… "Wh-what?"

"Damn." Colton laughed quietly. "Get your mind out of the gutter, Sadie."

As I spluttered, he pulled the paper back out of his pocket and flipped to the second page which was a printed copy of my list. I noticed that the one about my first kiss (#14) had been crossed off. Also, right under "Carpe Diem List," Colton had written "S's Naughty List." I bet he'd gotten a real kick out of that.

"Right there," he said, pointing about a third of the way

down the page, "number 10, learn to drive a stick shift. It's not that hard. Just grab on, and I'll show you how to handle a stick."

His eyes were laughing at me as I placed my hand on the gear shift and muttered under my breath.

I had a feeling it was going to be a long 30 days.

CHAPTER 8

"Just so you know, Colt said you're banned from ever driving his car again." Kyle looked far too happy about this as we walked to lunch together. In fact, he was practically skipping. "Good going, Sadie. I think you permanently scarred him with your non-existent driving skills."

"Hey," I said, "I'm an awesome driver. You know I always go the speed limit and stop on yellows."

"Yeah, it's incredibly annoying," Kyle said.

I bumped him with my shoulder.

"Colt said he was in fear for his life."

"Yeah well, he distracted me," I muttered.

"How'd he do that?"

Oh, I don't know, I thought. *It could've been how he just had to comment on every single thing I did. Or how he kept jumping, grabbing the sides of his seat when I shifted to another gear. Or how he kept staring at me with this look of horror on his face.* I mean, yes, it had taken me a little while to get used to it (I'd never fully gotten the hang of the whole clutch-shift-then-gas-as-you-come-off-the-clutch rhythm), but by the end, I was able to drive around the block three times with only a few minor hiccups.

"He was being so dramatic," I said. "Like we were going to die every time I had to shift, or we stalled out. It wasn't like I was going off the road or anything. We were totally safe."

"I heard you got pulled over," he said back.

I rolled my eyes. "Yeah, because I didn't have my lights on, and it was after seven. The officer let us off with a warning." *Because I'd cried like a baby*, I mentally added. I'd never gotten pulled over before, and I hoped it would never happen again. "It wasn't too bad."

"I heard you cried a lot."

Of course, Colton had to tell him that.

"Yeah, it was definitely an ugly cry moment," I said. "But it could've been worse."

"Did my brother act like a jerk?" Kyle asked.

I shook my head, remembering how Colton had pulled a clean rag out of his center console and offered it to me without saying a word. He'd let me cry for a good five minutes until I was ready to drive again. He hadn't even said anything when I'd almost taken out one of the mailboxes on the street.

"Colton was…surprisingly decent," I admitted. "He didn't make fun of me—which was weird but in a good way."

"Yeah, Colt's a good guy even if he tries to bury it sometimes." Kyle smiled. "So, I assume you got that one marked off the list?"

"Yeah," I said, smiling back. "I'll never buy a car like that, but at least now I know how to drive stick."

A chuckle came from behind us as Colton stepped up to my side.

"Yeah, she can drive stick," he said—then frowned. "But not in my car. Never again, Sadie Day. Never. Again."

"Calm the heck down, Colton," I said. "It's not like I want to drive your car anyway."

He nodded as if I'd just confirmed something. "I'll see you after school. Meet me in the library."

"The library? Why?" I asked, my mind shifting straight to the last time we'd been in the library together. It wasn't like

I could forget our kiss, but I had tried to repress it. I'd done a pretty good job (if you didn't count all those dreams I kept having) until that moment. The memories came on quick then, escaping one by one, as if a dam had been opened. Colton didn't help matters. He sighed and stopped me with a hand on my arm.

"Sadie," he said, "I'm your coach. You said you'd do what I say without question. Remember the contract you signed?"

Little tingles were going up and down my arm from where we touched, so I shook him off. I didn't understand why he was having this kind of effect on me. The memories were unwelcome and so were the feelings associated with them.

I tried not to show any of this on my face.

"I never promised not to question," I said, rubbing the tingles away. "And I didn't say I wouldn't meet you. I just want to know what we'll be doing."

Colton looked at Kyle then back to me. "I can't speak of it in front of the adversary," he said.

Kyle laughed and held up his hands, backing away. "Okay, okay, I can see when I'm not wanted. I'll save you guys a seat inside."

As he left, I had the strong urge to call him back but didn't.

Instead I faced Colton and gestured for him to go on. "Okay, now tell me what's up."

"We need to work on your vocabulary," he said simply.

"My vocabulary?" I repeated.

"You got a problem with that?"

"No, I love words and learning new things."

Colton hung his head on a sigh. "Wow…Sadie, you're an odd bird, you know that?"

I shrugged. "People have been saying that my whole life."

"Then I'll see you after school?"

"Okay," I said.

Colton nodded, but there was something in his eyes I couldn't place. It felt like there had to be more to it. Yet, I had agreed to meet with him anyway. Working on my vocabulary sounded innocent enough, and he was right. I had signed the contract. After three more periods, during which I couldn't concentrate worth a lick, the final bell rang. I went to my locker to get all of my books then walked to the library in search of Colton. I wasn't sure where he'd be; he hadn't said where exactly to meet him. I scanned the seating areas in the front first, but when I saw no sign of Colton, I made my way back to my secret spot in the stacks.

Sure enough, there he was.

And he had stolen my favorite chair.

Ugh.

Setting my bag down on the table with a thump, I placed my hands on my hips and gave him a look. My glare was completely wasted, of course, because Colton didn't look up. He was reading a book, and as I peered closer, I saw that the cover was gray and had a close-up of a man kissing a woman's neck. *It looked like a...romance novel*, I thought in surprise. And there was no barcode on the side, so he must've brought it from home. I hadn't even known Colton kept books in his room—not that I'd been there or anything. But I knew Kyle only liked to read non-fiction, so it couldn't be one of his.

"What are you reading?" I asked.

He shut the book with a snap then put it on the table face down.

"You're not ready for that yet," he said. "But with my help, maybe you will be one day."

I rolled my eyes, shooting a look at the chair—*my chair*—that he was sitting in with a leg propped up on one of the arms. "Are you comfortable?"

"Sure am," he said, burrowing further into the plush seat. It was one of those old fashioned, over-stuffed library chairs with a high back. I'd sat right there a million times to study, read, watch YouTube, you name it. And now Colton had the nerve to steal my spot. "This chair is like sitting on a cloud. I can't believe you were selfish enough to keep it all to yourself, Sadie."

"Hey, someone put it back here and just forgot about it," I said. "Plus, I saw it first."

Colton raised a brow. "Are you saying you want your chair back?"

I nodded. "Yes, if you don't mind."

"I do mind," he said. "You can sit in that fold out chair over there—or in my lap if you want. Either way, I'm not moving."

"You're disgusting," I said with a huff and plopped into the metal seat across from him. It was cold, uncomfortable, and so un-like my library chair I could cry. Crossing my arms, I wiggled around, trying to find a comfortable position—but it was impossible.

Colton shook his head, and catching sight of his frown, I stopped moving.

"What?" I snapped.

"You going to pout the whole time?" he asked. "Because I really don't want to listen to you whine about this."

"I'm not pouting."

"Yeah, you are."

I wiggled again then sighed.

"Okay, fine," Colton said, jumping to his feet. "If it's so important, you can have your stupid chair back."

Giving Colton a strange look, I stayed seated. "Why do you suddenly want to switch?" I asked.

He blinked.

"Did you do something to it?" I eyed the once loved seat

with newfound distrust. "Plant a whoopee cushion under there or loosen one of the legs so the chair will break right when I sit down?"

He shook his head, running a hand down his neck. "That was in the fifth grade, and it was one time. Could you get over it already?"

No, I couldn't. Colton had pranked me in front of our entire class on Valentine's Day, and when I'd gone to sit at my desk, carrying a pan full of homemade cupcakes, not only had the cupcakes gone flying. Frosting got on my dress, in my hair. The cupcakes had been ruined, and it had all happened in front of Kyle—who I'd had (and still did have) a major crush on. He'd laughed it off, of course, but I'd been scarred.

"No," I said. "I can't even eat cupcakes anymore because of you."

"Well, my hair was blue for weeks because of you," he said back. "It's not like you're a saint, Sadie. You put that hair dye in my shampoo to get back at me. Hell, I couldn't leave the house."

"Did you think I'd let you get away with it?" I laughed, remembering his blue do. It actually had looked good on him—playing off his eyes and giving him kind of a punk-rock vibe—which annoyed me to no end. I'd done it over the holidays, so he wouldn't have to miss any school, and they could change it back to normal before the end of the break. "You deserved it after what you did."

"I said I was sorry," Colton said.

I looked up at him. "I don't remember that."

"Well, I'm saying it now, okay? I'm sorry, Sadie. For the cupcakes, for the prank, all of it. Will you switch seats with me and take your stupid chair back now?"

I got up slowly and sat down even slower, releasing a breath of contentment, eyes falling closed, as the cushions hugged me like an old friend.

"Happy?" he asked.

I opened my eyes to see Colton sitting in the too-small-for-anyone-but-waaay-too-small-for-him fold out chair.

"Yes. Thank you," I said.

"Yeah well," he muttered. "Maybe next time you won't question it if I do something nice for you."

I scoffed at that, and he grinned in response.

"Yeah, you're right. Doing nice things doesn't sound like me," he said. "Bad things, however, are right up my alley."

Reaching beneath his book, he slid a notecard across the table.

"Take a look at that, and let's get to work."

I took the notecard, flipped it over and noticed that it was filled with bad words written in Colton's handwriting. "What do you expect me to do with this? It's full of profanity."

"I know," he said. "Just think of it as a vocabulary lesson. I'm about to teach you the art of talking dirty."

With wide eyes, I looked at the card again. "You actually want me to say this stuff? Right now, out loud?"

"Yes," Colton said as he sprawled his legs out, placed his elbows on his knees and looked straight at me. "It's time to put a few dents in that good girl image, Sadie. We'll start with the basics. There are only 10 words on there, and most of them are four-letters or less. No big deal."

I couldn't tell if he was joking. He probably wasn't. There was a definite taunt in his voice, but he looked like he expected me to do it. And yes, they were mostly four-letter words…but I'd never said any of them.

"I'm telling you to do it as your coach," he said, perhaps sensing my hesitation. "Come on, let's mark this one off the list. If you need it, I give you permission to say anything on that list."

"I don't need anyone's permission but my own," I growled.

"Well, what the hell are you waiting on, Christmas?"

I rolled my eyes. "Not all of us have been cursing since we were in elementary school, okay? Some of us have to work up to it."

"Ah, the good old days of naps and recess," he sighed. "But seriously, it's just the two of us. I'm sure you've wanted to say all those words—probably to me—at some point."

True, I thought. And yet I couldn't get my mouth to work.

"Okay, I'll go first," Colton said then gestured to the card. "What's the first word?"

"It starts with a 'd' and beavers make them," I answered, feeling all kinds of stupid.

Colton nodded, drumming his fingers on his forearms. "Ah, okay. I must've been trying to start you out easy. Damn, that was a damn good idea. Don't you think so, Sadie?"

I bit my lip and nodded.

"Damn right, it was," he said. "Now, you say it."

I did, but it came out whisper-soft.

"What was that? I couldn't hear a damn thing."

Rolling my eyes, I said it louder. "Damn."

Colton whooped and then leaned forward to see the card.

"Okay," he said, "next word. Ass. It's one of my favorites."

"Of course, it is," I muttered.

Colton suddenly groaned, eyes squeezing tight as he gripped his hip with a frown. It looked like he was in a lot of pain.

"Are you okay?" I asked in concern. Maybe he was having a cramp or something. "Colton, you don't look so good."

"No, I'm not okay," he said, opening one eye to peer back at me. "My ass hurts from sitting in this damn uncomfortable chair."

A surprised laugh escaped me as he sat back up with a grin.

"You think that's funny, huh?"

"A little," I said.

"No need to be an ass about it, Sadie," he said.

"I wasn't trying to be an ass," I said back, but as Colton smiled, I grew unnerved. "What?"

He raised his hand for a high-five. "Congrats. You just used one of your vocabulary words in a sentence."

"I did, didn't I?"

"You did. And you didn't even blush once."

I gave him a high-five, felt the tingles run up my arm again as my palm connected with his, and quickly pulled back my hand.

"Let's keep going," I said. "The next word starts with a sound you make when things are too loud."

"Shhh," he said, holding a hand out to me and looking around, "shit, Sadie, keep it down, would you? We're in the library."

I couldn't remember ever having smiled so much in Colton's presence.

When we were through, I'd said all 10 words and used them all in sentences—even the big one, the one that starts with 'f' and sounds like hockey puck. I didn't know if I'd ever actually be able to say that one again. Out of all of them, that word was just...*so bad*. But Colton assured me although some people loved to drop the f-bomb whenever possible, even he didn't say it very much.

"I reserve that one for special occasions." Colton shrugged, his lip piercing glinting as it caught the light. "The f-bomb makes more of an impact if you only use it when you really mean it."

To drive home our "lesson," though, he had me read a passage from the book he'd brought with him.

"It shouldn't be a problem since you read stuff like this to those old people. But I'm warning you, Sadie," Colton said as he handed me the book. "As far as dirty talk goes, the Warden is the best I've ever read. If you can read this out loud, then there's no question you can mark it off the list."

I read the pages he'd indicated out loud, and though I hated to admit it, Colton was absolutely right. The books I'd read at Shady Grove were tame in comparison to the sexy, intense paranormal/urban fantasy romance in front of me.

By the time I was finished even Colton was pink in the cheeks.

"Are you blushing?" I asked. I almost never got to tease him about anything, so I couldn't pass up this chance.

"Yeah right," he said as he got up and turned to put the book in his bookbag. "That's your problem, not mine."

"I don't know." I followed him, raising a finger to his cheek but not touching it. "Your face is warm, and you look kind of pink through here."

Colton caught my hand and held it a moment, meeting my eyes, before letting go.

"You want to cross it off or should I?" he asked after a beat.

Looking down, I noticed he'd brought out his copy of the list. My list.

"I'll do it," I said, taking a pen and drawing a line through **#4 Talk Dirty**. My heart lifted as I made that one small stroke. It felt like a giant leap for good girls everywhere. I was smiling again, couldn't help it.

"Did that feel good?" Colton asked.

"Damn good," I said.

Shrugging on his backpack, Colton shook his head and then, in a completely surprising move, he reached out and placed a hand on my cheek. I couldn't be certain, but I thought his eyes had dipped to my lips for a moment. For some unknown reason, this caused my breaths to shorten, my heart beating faster.

"You should watch that dirty mouth of yours, Sadie," he said…then leaned closer.

I couldn't look away even if I'd wanted to.

He put his lips right next to my ear and in a hushed voice said, "Who's the one blushing now?"

When he removed his hand and stepped back, I swayed forward. The movement was totally unintentional. I wanted to slap myself for it as I noticed Colton's grin. He walked right by me and didn't say another word. After he'd gone, I sank back into my favorite chair and let out a curse. It was one of the new words I'd learned today which seemed to fit my mood perfectly.

Yeah, what he'd said was true. I was blushing. That was nothing new. The new part was it was Colton who was making me blush.

I wasn't sure when this new development had started. What I did know was that it needed to stop. Immediately. If not for my own sanity, then for the sake of our partnership. Colton was my coach. He was helping me with my list, and that was it.

I needed to remember that for next time.

CHAPTER 9

Turns out, the next few days were Colton-free—which should've made me happy.

But it didn't.

Confusion, irritation and a tiny bit of disappointment were what I felt most, but luckily, my mind was on other things at the moment.

It was midnight on Friday, and I was in the middle of choreographing a new dance. My room had a full-length mirror propped against one wall which allowed me to see the lines and shapes I created, my iPod playing music on the nightstand. I got some of my best ideas at night. My mind would start going right as I tried to fall asleep, and I would have to get up and get it all out before I lost it. This was one of those nights when creativity struck.

And thank goodness for that.

Not only did it take my mind off Colton, but with another round coming up for *Dancer's Edge*, I knew I had to start choreography if I wanted to finish and make the deadline in a few weeks. The hard part wasn't coming up with ideas either. It was coming up with *good ideas*.

I had journal after journal filled with concepts, and I never knew which ones were creative, unique and difficult enough. Which to pursue and which to leave behind. I mean, when did you know your work was good? Was it when someone else said so? Or did it only matter what you thought? But wasn't the goal of creating something to share it with others and have an impact?

Well, that was my goal anyway.

Ironically, the scariest part of sharing my work...was sharing my work. It was taking that first step. I knew only too well that I couldn't control how people reacted to the things I created. And I was interested in everything: drawing, photography, dance, poetry, even video games. I'd only ever managed to share a few of my gaming ideas and my dances—but even if I was completely in love with a piece, the *Dancer's Edge* people still might hate it.

I looked to the memory board across from my bed. My rejections letters, all seven of them, were there, printed out and placed where I could see them every day. *Too sweet. No edge. Lacks life experience.* I was reminded every day of what I needed to work on. But it wasn't as masochistic as it sounds. The rejections also meant that I'd given it a shot, that I was reaching for my dreams.

And I couldn't regret that.

The new dance I was working on was a mix of styles. Ballroom-meets-Contemporary with a bit of theater thrown in for good measure. And it definitely wasn't "nice." One of the things I always tried to do was tell a story. A wise woman once said: A dance should tell the story of the music. My aunt had said those words to me, and I'd never forgotten. I had no idea if this particular idea would work, but I'd found a song that I hadn't been able to get out of my head. It made me think of light and dark, softness and intensity, a push and pull between two opposites. It was sensual and aggressive...and there was so much *passion*.

In my head, I pictured a woman being torn by her feelings for two men.

Ooh yes, I thought, moving through the song as the idea bloomed fully to life.

One woman.

Two men.

Their fierce battle to win her affections.

Neither of them knowing that she's the one in control the whole time.

Now, if I could tell that story through movements, I felt like I might really have something.

I re-started the song, sat on my bed to take some more notes—but when I opened the journal, my list fell out. The lopsided daisy teased me. I frowned, tried to concentrate harder on my choreo, but it was no use.

Colton had flaked out on me. He'd avoided me all day at school Wednesday and again on Thursday. When Friday rolled around, I'd finally caught up to him, and he said he was working at the garage again tonight—I hadn't even known he had a job, but apparently, he'd been doing it for three months. He was supposed to call when he was done so we could work on the list.

But guess what?

He didn't call.

Surprise, surprise.

Guy promises to call and doesn't. Girl waits and waits and waits. Girl finally gives up and feels disappointed even though she should've never put her faith in Guy in the first place. Tale as old as time.

When I'd called Kyle to see if he wanted to hang out, he said he had to work on a big project for school—which sucked because I felt like I hadn't seen my best friend in forever.

Guess I'd be spending another Friday night at home.

I frowned harder. So, what? I thought. Because the twins weren't here, I couldn't move forward without them? Just because Colton and I had checked off three items didn't mean we had to do everything together. Ever since that kiss, my mind hadn't been right where Colton was concerned.

It was time for me to take back control of my list—and my life.

With a nod, I wrote the last of my choreography notes then shifted my focus, opening my list and skimming the paper. There had to be something on here that I could do right now. I spotted it almost immediately.

9) *Sneak out of the house.*

My eyes shot to my window, and I bit my lip. Mom was in her room, probably reading, far enough away that she wouldn't hear anything. It was a small neighborhood and late enough that I shouldn't run into anyone outside. Tree climbing was not a skill I'd mastered—but I'd seen it done a ton of times in movies. Peter Parker (aka Spiderman) made climbing things look easy. And he did it wearing a spandex unitard. If I was careful, I was sure I could make it from the second story to the ground.

Pulling on a cardigan and my Corner Street Ballroom jacket, I put my phone in my pocket (after I checked my messages one last time. No, Colton hadn't called. I kinda hated myself for checking.) and opened my window.

Man, it was dark out there.

Kinda cold, too.

And had the second floor always been this high up?

But Spiderman wouldn't let that stop him, and I didn't either. Swinging both feet over the ledge, I eyed the tree that'd always been just outside my window, took a deep breath—and jumped. Or at least I tried to jump. To be honest, it was more like a controlled chest/belly bump with the wood, and all of the air left my lungs in a whoosh.

Okay, so yeah, tree climbing? Not as easy as it looks.

I was gripping the trunk of the tree with my hands, feet, thighs, and I was sprawled out like a great big X, going nowhere fast. Basically, I looked like a sloth. Just not as cute. It took me forever to even move, but my muscles were starting to ache. Inch by tortuous inch, I made my way down. It was slow going. The worst part was when my foot slipped near the bottom. I fell the last three feet to the ground, and I gasped, stumbling to regain my balance.

"Holy smokes," I breathed, looking back up to my room as I fished the paper out of my pocket. I couldn't believe I'd done it. It hadn't been graceful at all, but still. I couldn't believe how awesome it felt to mark off another item on my "Carpe Diem List." One I'd completed all by myself, thank you very much.

The sound of applause had me whipping around.

"Wow," Colton said grinning, appearing seemingly out of thin air. With one final clap, he put his hands in his pockets. "That was awkward as hell, Sadie. What did that tree ever do to you?"

"What are you doing here?" I asked.

"I told you I'd call when I was done. I was about to text when I saw you leap from your window." He cough-laughed. "It seemed like a bad time. You were struggling, and I didn't want to startle you."

He was right on that one. If Colton had texted me as I was shimmying down that tree, I would've probably ended up on the local news: *Good girl, Sadie Day, tries to sneak out, breaks tailbone instead, leaving her mother heartbroken. A witness, Colton Bishop, says it was the funniest thing he'd ever seen.*

"Humph," I said, crossing my arms. "So, you're telling me you just got finished with your so-called 'job' at the garage? It's after midnight."

"Yeah," he said, brows contracting. "We had to get all the

cars done by Saturday, so it was all hands on deck."

"Oh," I said. He didn't sound like he was lying. It was a legitimate excuse, but he still should've called. "I didn't appreciate waiting around all night with no word."

"I didn't know we were going to be this late."

"And you couldn't have called?"

Colton looked like he was gritting his teeth. "I would've if I'd known spending quality time with me was so important to you."

I stayed silent. Jerk.

"Sorry," he said after a beat. "You're right. I should've called."

"It's fine," I said with a sniff. "Turns out I didn't need you anyway. I snuck out of the house all by myself."

Colton nodded. "I saw. Now, are you going to stay pissed at me, or do you want to go mark something else off?"

Ignoring the way his lips twitched, I shrugged. "I guess that would be alright. It's midnight, though, so not a lot of things will be open. What did you have in mind?"

"Sadie, it's the weekend," Colton said, tugging on my hand and leading me to his car. "Everything's open. The night is young."

Rolling my eyes, I got into his car and pulled out my phone.

"Who are you calling?" Colton asked as he settled in beside me.

"My mom," I said, and as Colton sputtered, Mom picked up. "Hey Mom, is it okay if I go out?"

"Sure," she said, and I could hear her surprise through the phone. "But Sadie, do you know what time it is? I trust you. You know that. But I wouldn't be a good parent if I didn't ask where you're going, and who you're going with."

"I'm with Colton Bishop, Mom, and I just snuck out of the house."

"Excuse me? Did you say you just snuck out of the house?"

Colton groaned beside me, but I ignored him. "Yeah, I did. We're in his car now, parked out front, and I don't know where we're going, but I'm sure it'll be okay. I...I trust him, Mom."

Mom laughed on the other end of the line, and I saw her blinds shift as she looked out from her window on the opposite side of the house.

"So, this is it, huh?" she said almost to herself. "You decided to become a wild teenager, and now I'm going to sit up worrying all night."

"You don't have to do that, Mom. I'll be fine."

"Wait, did you just say Colton Bishop? I thought you two hated each other."

"We did. I mean, we do," I said then sighed. I could feel Colton watching me, but I refused to look at him. That would just make this ten times harder. "It's complicated, okay? But I'm going out, and I just wanted to let you know."

There was a beat then. "You be safe, Sadie, and have your phone on at all times. I want you to be able to call if you need me."

"I will, Mom."

"Call if you need anything, okay? Anything at all. Do you have on a jacket? It's cold out."

I smiled, my heart filling at the concern in her voice, but I didn't want her to worry. "Yes, and I promise to call if I need anything. I love you, Mom. Don't wait up."

"Oh Lord," she said on a heavy exhale. "You sounded just like me for a second. I love you, too, Sadie. Have fun and be safe. I want to hear all about it when you get back."

"Alright. Bye, Mom."

"Bye, Baby."

I hit end and waved to her in the window, smiling as she

waved back. I couldn't be sure from this distance, but it looked like her eyes might've been a bit misty.

When I finally turned to Colton, he was staring at me with an odd expression.

"What?" I asked.

"Did you just…call your mom to tell her you snuck out of the house?" he said slowly.

I nodded as I pulled on my seatbelt and clicked it into place. "Of course. I didn't want her to worry."

"You know that's not how it's usually done, right? The whole point of sneaking out is so your parents won't know and get on your case about it."

"Yeah, but my mom's cool. We have an understanding."

Colton shook his head in amazement. "You're something else, Sadie Day."

I shrugged, starting to feel self-conscious as he continued to stare. "Can we get going now?"

"Sure thing," he said, then with a shake of his head, we were off.

It was quiet in the car, too quiet. The silence made me all too aware of the boy sitting next to me. Colton seemed cool as a cucumber over there, occasionally drumming his fingers against the steering wheel, making shifting gears look effortless—which I now knew for a fact it was not. But I was a jumble of nerves. If I was going to get through tonight, I needed a distraction ASAP.

"Can we turn on the radio or something?" I asked.

Without saying a word, Colton pressed a button and music filled the car. It was a song I'd never heard, sounded like an indie rock band, and I found myself beginning to relax right away.

Music really did make things better.

"You good with this?" he said.

"Yeah, thanks," I said. "I've never heard this song before, but I like it."

"What do you like about it?"

Hmm, I thought for a minute. "The lyrics and the singer's voice are nice, and that bass is killing it. It sounds kind of like The Killers meets Bruce Springsteen"

Colton chuckled. "Glad I have your approval."

I glanced at him. "So...where are we going?"

"Eric's parents are out of town, so he's throwing a party tonight," he said. "I thought we'd go crash it. Get that one done and maybe a few other list items while we're there."

I swallowed thickly. "You mean, Eric Greene?"

"Yeah, and don't worry, Sadie," he added, shooting a grin my way. "Eric's parties never end at twelve o'clock. That's usually when the fun starts."

Oh, I'd heard all about Eric Greene's infamous parties. *Everyone* in school knew about them. I had no idea where they went, but it seemed like his parents were always gone, traveling to one place or another. This left Eric free to do whatever he wanted, and all he seemed to want to do was party. The last time I'd been to his house I'd been there to pick up my drunk best friend, who by night's end had puked on me. Thank you for that, Kyle. Ugh. Even the word "party" made my eye twitch, but I wanted to experience a real high school party at least once before I graduated which was why I'd written it on my list.

"Awesome," I said, though I didn't mean it.

"Don't sound so excited," he said on a laugh.

"I guess it's a good thing I learned how to drive stick," I said. "In case you get drunk, I can drive your car home."

Colton's laughter dried up quick after that. "No way," he

said. "You're never driving my car again, Sadie. And for the record, I've only been drunk once in my life."

"Seriously?" I asked.

"I'll try not to feel insulted by your tone of surprise."

"Sorry, I just thought…" I trailed off because what I'd been about to say would've been an insult. I had thought Colton was one of those party boys, like Eric, who loved to get wasted on the weekends. He went to so many parties. It was a valid assumption.

"It only took me one hangover to know that drinking to excess wasn't for me. Not everybody goes to parties to get drunk," he said. "Though a lot of them do, so watch your back. Drunk guys'll hit on anything that moves."

I sniffed. "I'll try not to feel insulted by that."

"Don't," Colton said. "Despite the hair and your clothes, you're not too bad to look at."

I could feel myself blushing. Was that his way of saying I was pretty? If so, there was only one appropriate response.

"That was the worst compliment I've ever heard," I said, trying to play it off. "I don't get it. Do girls really fall for that, Colton?"

"Only when I want them to" was his response.

I turned up the volume, and we listened to a few more songs without speaking. They were just as good as the first one, and I found myself trying to memorize the lyrics, so I could look them up later. I also tried not to think about how Colton's crappy compliment was still running through my head. How pathetic was that?

"We're here," Colton said a few minutes later.

We're not the only ones, I thought, noticing all the cars. They were parked up and down the street and driveway, several people standing outside, some in bathing suits—and was that a slip n' slide on the front lawn? Geez.

Getting out of the car, I was nearly nailed with a water balloon. It sailed mere inches above my head and landed with a splat somewhere on the street. The game was fierce, balloons flying everywhere. To get out of the line of fire, I met Colton at the front of his car, and we walked up to the front door.

"It'll be okay, Sadie," he said. "There's no need to look so freaked."

"I don't know what you're talking about," I said. "I'm fine."

He shrugged but didn't call me on my lie.

When we walked in, I took in the scene. Everyone was carrying one of those red Solo cups, several of which littered the floor and every available flat surface, so I was betting at least half of the party population was already tipsy. I saw a lot of people I recognized but no one I would really call a friend (which proved how much of an introverted social outcast I was, I guess). Girls and guys were talking, kissing and/or grinding on the dance floor. My eardrums were probably going to explode from how high they had the music playing.

Which was something George Trask from Sandy Grove would've said.

Dang, I had been born 80, I thought. Le sigh.

"What do you think?" Colton asked loudly.

"I think my eardrums might burst," I said back.

"What?"

Instead of trying to yell over the music, I led him away from the living room (and the twerking) and into the kitchen (with the alcohol) which was somewhat quieter, but not by much. There was some kind of drinking game going on, and every time someone landed a ball in a cup a loud cheer would arise. I saw a girl with mint green streaks bounce two balls off the table, one after the other, so that they dropped perfectly into cups, which earned her wild applause. Had to admit it was pretty impressive. She laughed, telling another person to drink up.

"I said I think my eardrums might burst," I repeated to Colton.

"Nah," Colton said and lifted a strand of my hair. "All that hair would act as a buffer."

"Ha ha," I said, shaking my curls out of his reach. "Is this all there is? Twerking, drinking, making out and a slip n' slide? Honestly, I feel disappointed."

"Pretty much," he said. "But hey, there's probably someone upstairs smoking weed, and then there's always the prank later. It's usually pretty fun."

That got my attention. "Prank?"

"Yeah," Colton said, "Eric and some of the guys were talking about pulling a senior prank on Principal Wexler. You in, Sadie?"

"Heck yeah," I said in excitement. That was #20 on my list! "I've always wanted to pull a prank on someone. What are they going to do?"

"They're going to TP his house. No big deal."

I frowned. "Won't that take a long time to clean up? And who'd want to waste all that toilet paper?"

Colton stared. "Are you the toilet paper police?"

"No, but—"

"There's nothing wrong with what we're doing, Sadie. Calm down, okay? It happens every year. The principal knows about it, so there's no need to be so uptight."

I tilted my head. "Huh. Well, if he knows about it, I guess it's alright then. Although I do feel bad about him having to clean up later."

"You're hopeless," Colton sighed, but as another cheer rose from the drinking game he smiled. "Hey, there's someone I want you to meet. Athena!"

At the sound of her name, the girl with mint green streaks looked our way and walked over to hug Colton. She embraced him smoothly, looking edgy and cool with her tattoos and nose piercing. Her makeup was perfection, too, eyeliner applied just right to give her a cat-eye look.

"Hey, Colton," she said with a smile. "How's it going?"

"Not too bad." He gestured to me. "Athena, this is Sadie. She's Kyle's best friend and my...pupil. I'm teaching her how to be bad and brought her because she wanted to see what a real party is like."

I did a mental eyeroll at his explanation, but Colton looked pleased with himself. Each of Athena's fingers had a ring on it I noticed as she reached out to take my hand.

"Hi Sadie," she said. "Good to meet you."

"Hey, you, too," I said, and unable to help myself, I nodded to her nose. "Did that hurt?"

"Only for a second—and a little after because it got infected. But not nearly as much as when I had my back or nipples pierced. Now, that shit hurt."

I gulped, keeping my eyes firmly on her face, but she laughed as she released my hand.

"TMI?" she asked. "Sorry, I'm really bad about that."

"I just didn't expect it," I said. For some reason, I felt comfortable around this girl and liked her instantly. "Is that a dragon tattoo on your arm? That is so awesome, reminds me of Harry Potter."

She grinned. "Yeah, I drew that one myself. J.K. Rowling changed my life."

"Me, too, and wow, you're talented," I said, meaning it. "Hogwarts forever."

"You know it," she said, and we did a fist bump.

Colton rolled his eyes, hands on his hips. "If you two are

done with this little nerdy love fest, I had a favor to ask you, Athena."

"Sure, Colton, what do you need?" she said.

"Sadie wants to get something pierced, and I thought you could help us out."

"Sure," Athena said again then looked to me. "I do it all the time at the tattoo parlor where I work. But where do you want it?"

"Ears," I squeaked. Even if I liked her, after the conversation we'd just had, there was nowhere else I wanted to be pierced. Ever. "That's what I want."

Colton grinned, lifting that dang pierced eyebrow. "You sure? I thought since you're trying to be more edgy you might want to get it somewhere more risqué."

"Just my ears," I growled, and Colton laughed. "Don't even think about any of the risky bits."

"Too late," he said.

I gave him the squinty eye. "You know, if I wasn't contractually obligated, I would fire you as my coach, and hire Athena instead."

"No, you wouldn't. Face it, Sadie, you like having me around."

"I like watching you walk away," I retorted. "Far, far away."

"Because you think I have a nice ass?" Colton said. "Thanks."

I huffed. "It has nothing to do with you having a nice ass, you idiot. I just like it when you stop being irritating and leave me be."

Colton looked triumphant. "You just said 'ass'. My job here is done. Athena, take care of her while I go say hi to some of the guys, will you?"

Athena laughed and gave him a little salute. "Will do."

Once he was gone, she sat me down at the table and came

back a few minutes later with a myriad of items: bowl of ice, cottons swabs, some hydrogen peroxide, a cork, lighter and needle she'd pulled out of her purse. It wasn't too long, but it looked sharp. She asked me to pull my hair back, and I did, hoping my hair would cooperate. I tugged it up, around and in, securing it with a big clip I carried in my bag.

"Since my earring gun's back at the shop," she said, "we'll have to do it the old-fashioned way. Or if you want to wait…"

"No." That needle did make me nervous, but I wasn't backing out. "If you're willing, I'd like to do it now."

"Okay, I have silver studs or faux diamonds," she said, holding up the two packages. "I always carry a few from work. Which would you like?"

"Diamonds, please," I said, not even having to think about it.

"These are going to look awesome." I watched as she poured the hydrogen peroxide on a cotton swab. "And really, I've done this loads of times. I mean, I get paid to do it, and I've done it for friends, too. Take this and rub it over your ear for me."

I did. "I really appreciate it, Athena. And I will pay—"

"It's no problem," she said and waved me off. Flicking on the lighter, she held the needle above the flame. After about 15 seconds, she let the needle cool for a bit then poured some hydrogen peroxide over the entire length. "Colton's a friend, so it's all good."

"How do you and Colton know each other?" I asked.

"We used to go out," she said, and I nearly dropped the cotton ball. Athena laughed at my expression. "Is that hard to believe?"

"No," I said, looking at her streaks and piercings again in a new light. It wasn't hard at all for me to believe Colton would be interested in her. They would look perfect on a cover for punk rock *Vogue*. "But I mean, you're just so cool. And Colton is…

well, he drives me nuts most of the time."

"We weren't together long," she said, setting aside the needle and pressing an ice cube against my ear. "It wasn't anything serious, and we figured out pretty fast that we're better off friends."

Colton Bishop, friends with a girl—and not just any girl but this cool chick sitting before me? I never thought I'd see the day.

"Don't get me wrong. It was hot." Athena looked at me and grinned. "But it was nothing on the heat I see between the two of you."

I snorted. "Oh please, we can't stand each other."

She shook her head. "Didn't look that way to me. I could see sparks shooting from your eyes and his."

"I loathe him, Athena, and I assure you, the feeling is totally mutual," I laughed.

"Why are you guys here together then?"

I blinked. "Like I said, he's my coach. Colton's helping me with some things I wanted to do before graduation."

Athena tilted her head. "Did he offer to help?"

"Only after being forced into it," I said, thinking about Betty and the bet with Kyle.

"I know Colton," she said. "He doesn't get forced into anything. If he does something, it's because he wants to."

"I've known him since we were kids, and he's always despised me," I said. "There's nothing going on between us."

"Whatever you say." She still sounded dubious, and I wanted to argue—but I forgot about that as she moved the cork and needle into place. "Are you ready?"

I took a deep breath and clenched my fists.

"As ready as I'll ever be."

CHAPTER 10

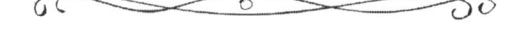

A few minutes later, the little diamond studs were in my ears, shining in the light of the kitchen, and I couldn't stop staring at them in the mirror. Yeah, it had hurt, but I was loving the results.

"They look fantastic," I said, turning my head one way then the other. "I've wanted pierced ears since I was a little girl but never actually did it. Thank you so much, Athena."

"My pleasure," she said as she put away all of her things. "Just don't forget what I told you, Sadie, about keeping them clean. Trust me, peroxide is your friend, and infections suck big time."

I nodded. I definitely wouldn't forget about that, wasn't going to do anything to screw this up. This was one of the coolest things I'd ever done. It made me feel like I'd taken complete control of my body. The power and adrenaline coursing through me were heady.

"So, you did it," Colton said as he walked up to us.

Putting down the mirror, I said, "Yeah, what do you think? I love them."

"They look good," he said, studying me with a frown. "But…"

"But what?" I asked.

"Something's not right."

Colton stared at me a second longer then reached a hand up

to grip the hair clip. In one swift motion, he removed it, and my riotous curls came tumbling down around my shoulders.

"Ah, that's better," he said. "You look more like you."

I didn't know what to say. Colton had always teased me, and one of his favorite things he loved to hound me about was my hair. The comment was so un-Colton like. I felt as if I'd been blindsided by his niceness.

And then he had to go and ruin it.

"I almost didn't recognize you without the crazy lion's mane, Sadie. You can't just alter your appearance like that," he added. "It throws people off."

"It's my hair," I said and crossed my arms. "I can do what I want with it."

"Yeah," Athena said. "And to be honest, I like your hair."

"Thanks, Athena," I said. "I like yours, too."

"No problem." She smiled at me then looked to Colton. "I'm glad you brought her. If you need anything else done, Sadie, piercings or tattoos, let me know."

I smiled. "I may take you up on that."

"Sounds good," she said. "I'll see you guys later. And Colton, try not to be such a dick, would you?"

"Hey!" Colton shook his head as she walked away. "I take it you girls bonded while I was gone?"

I shrugged, moving past him and into the living room. Athena had gotten it right. How could he be so nice one minute and such a jerk the next? It literally gave me whiplash. His comment about my hair made my chest hurt, and I didn't want to examine that too closely.

Taking a seat on the couch, I hoped Colton wouldn't follow—but of course, he did. There was a couple making out at the other end, so Colton ended up sitting much closer to me than I would've preferred. Someone must've turned down the music, too, because it wasn't as loud as it had been when we first arrived.

"What'd you two talk about all that time?" he asked. "What a douche I was? That seems like something you could both agree on."

"We didn't talk about you much at all," I said. "Athena just told me how to take care of my piercings."

"We can leave, you know," he said after a beat. "If your ears hurt."

"What do you care?" I said.

"Hey, I care."

I snorted.

"What's that about?" he said and had the audacity to sound offended. "All I've done tonight is be the best coach ever. We marked three things off your list. You should be happy right now."

I rolled my eyes then looked at him. "Seriously? You insult me in front of your ex-girlfriend, who's beautiful and cool and way too amazing for you by the way, and I should be happy about it? Yeah, no."

"I thought you didn't care what I think."

"Well, apparently, I care a little bit," I said, throwing up my hands. "What is so wrong with my hair?" He opened his mouth, but I wasn't done. "I mean, I know my curls are big and poufy—and that's on a good day. And I know, guys prefer straight, sleek hair like Athena's. But why do you always have to be so dang rude about it?"

"Sadie, I think your hair is great."

"Yeah," I laughed, "that's good. Tell me another one, liar."

"I'm serious," Colton said.

I stared at him.

"And just so you know, most guys would like it, too."

"Colton, don't mess with me," I said.

"I'm not." I sucked in a breath as Colton threaded a hand into my curls, being careful of my newly pierced ears, looking like he was deep in thought. "It's the kind of hair you want to grip onto, run your fingers through, gives men wild thoughts."

"Does it do that to you?" I asked, stunned by his serious tone.

"Oh yeah, all the time."

"But...all these years you've made fun of me for it. And when Athena was here, you said—"

Colton shook his head. "Didn't mean it."

"Oh."

As if coming out of a trance, Colton took his hand back and grinned. "Don't worry, though, Sadie. I've had plenty of practice controlling my masculine urges, and we fight so much it doesn't matter anyway."

I nodded, though despite what he said, it felt like it mattered. A lot. I couldn't believe what he'd revealed. Colton Bishop liked my hair. It gave him wild thoughts. That thought was enough to make my head spin and give my feminine ego a much needed boost.

"Speaking of which," he said, rubbing his hands together, "I think it's time we look for your substitute kissing partner."

"My what?" I asked.

"Your guy. The one you want to do the other kissing parts of your list with," he said. ""I figure now's as good a time as any. There are plenty of guys here."

The way he changed topics so quickly was a godsend because that meant I didn't have to think about my hair and how only seconds ago it'd been between his fingertips. But for some reason what he wanted to discuss made my stomach drop.

"Oh, I'd forgotten about that," I mumbled.

"That's why I'm a great coach," Colton said. "My head's always in the game. Just look around. See anyone you like?"

I glanced around the room, taking in the space and the people in it. Colton was right. There were a lot of guys here, some I knew from school and some that I didn't. Many of them were already paired up with girls, but there were several who were just standing together, hanging out with other guys. I couldn't deny that a lot of them were attractive, but...

"I don't know," I said. "Something about kissing some random guy just feels wrong."

Colton shrugged. "You kissed me."

"Yeah, but I know you."

"And you hate me," he pointed out.

"I don't hate you, Colton," I said.

"You don't?"

I shook my head. "You annoy the crap out of me. You get on my last nerve. You...confuse me at times. But no, I don't hate you. Not really."

He looked surprised, shocked even, but if he could be honest so could I.

After a moment, he said, "Well, isn't there anyone here you want to kiss?"

My eyes fell to his lips on the word "kiss," and I forced myself to look away, pretending to search the room again while inside I was tied up in knots. It was the strangest thing, but the only person I could contemplate kissing was Colton. And holy smokes had I contemplated it. The number of times I'd thought about our library kiss was positively indecent. My stomach rolled again at the thought of kissing a stranger. As much as I wanted to complete my list, as obsessed as I was with kissing and wanted to experience more kisses, I wasn't sure I could do that.

"Maybe we can revisit this subject?" I said. "I need some time to think about it."

Colton nodded slowly. "Okay, that sounds good."

My stomach unclenched, the relief a palpable thing.

"In the meantime, let's focus on your list," he said. "Did you like the idea of approaching it from easiest to hardest?"

"Sounds like a good plan," I said.

"I know. That's why I came up with it." He grinned in that self-assured way of his while I gave a mental eyeroll. "I've done most of the things on your list, but the one that I haven't done is going to be difficult. The third one about *Dancer's Edge*."

I gulped. So, he really had put some thought into this.

"The whole video of the month thing. It's all about their opinion, and we have no control over that. Have you thought of a concept yet?"

"Actually, yes," I said. "I started choreographing tonight and can probably have it finished in a couple days. I feel like the idea is really strong."

"Great," he said. "Is it sexy?"

I felt my cheeks heat up. "There's a lot of passion."

"Passion's good, too. I watched all the dances they pick, and do you know the one thing they have in common?"

I shook my head.

"Sex," he said simply. "They're all sexy and have a unique angle. What makes your dance unique?"

"It's ballroom," I said, trying not to get flustered by all the questions, "which they've never featured before—which is just crazy since it's been around since the 16th century. Ballroom actually comes from the Latin *ballare* which, of course, means 'to dance' and—"

Colton groaned. "That's so boring."

I sat up straighter. He hadn't even let me get to the two

guys/one girl aspect of my new piece, but that was beside the point now. "Excuse me, but ballroom is *not* boring."

He didn't look convinced. "There wasn't anything hot about the 16th Century, Sadie."

"The Latin styles are some of the hottest around," I retorted. "And you would know that if you weren't so dance educationally challenged. That's why my piece for *Dancer's Edge* is going to be a tango."

"Tango," Colton repeated. "Really?"

"Yeah. Tim, my old dance partner, is supposed to be here this weekend. We used to compete together. Maybe you should come by Shady Grove tomorrow and check it out. We're performing for the residents."

"Maybe I will," he said.

"Fine," I said.

"Fine." Colton licked his lips, and my eyes shot right to his lip ring. I hadn't realized how close our faces had gotten until that moment. "Tim, huh? Maybe he could be your new kissing partner."

"Maybe," I said, though I knew it was impossible. Tim would rather kiss Colton than me. The thought had me grinning before Eric Greene came over and squeezed between the two of us. He smelled like a six-pack mixed with the grapefruit bubblegum he always chewed.

"Hey, Colt," he said, throwing his arms over the couch. "You about ready to go? It's prank time, my brother."

"Yeah," Colton said, "are you riding with me? Gotta warn you, there's not much room in the back."

Eric scoffed. "My trunk's filled with toilet paper, man, and Henry's driving it with the rest of the boys, all six of them. So yeah, I'm riding with you."

"Sadie?" Colton asked.

"I'm in," I said, meeting Colton's questioning stare. If he thought I was going to chicken out now, he didn't know me at all.

Eric turned to me and squinted. "Do I know you?"

"Yeah, Eric," I said, trying to be nice because he was obviously drunk as a skunk. "We've gone to school together since sixth grade."

"Are you sure?"

Colton was being no help whatsoever, but I smiled. "Yeah, I'm sure."

"What's your name again?"

"Sadie Day."

"Ooh!" Eric said, pointing a finger too close to my face. "Sister Sadie! The nun, right? How the hell are you, girl?"

"Not bad," I sighed.

Colton laughed and pushed Eric's finger away. "Alright, now that everyone's acquainted, let's go."

Eric whooped and jumped to his feet while Colton and I followed close behind. Once we were in the car, trailing Eric's black SUV, it took us about 10 minutes to get to Principal Wexler's house. We parked a street away, but as we walked closer, I could see the lights were off in the house. There were several trees in the front yard that would make it perfect to TP. The excitement was almost too much, and Colton turned to me, stopping me with a hand on my wrist.

"Are you sure you want to do this?" he asked.

I watched as the other boys continued toward the house, rolls of toilet paper in hand, then looked up to him.

"Yeah," I said, feeling how bright my eyes were, how my hands tingled. "I can't explain it. Even though I know the principal is okay with it, it still feels like we're doing something illegal. Not bad illegal but fun illegal, you know?"

Colton snorted at that. "Fun illegal? I've never heard that before."

"Glad I amuse you. Now, can we go? I don't want to miss it."

Colton nodded, and we joined the others. Decorating Principal Wexler's front lawn was such a rush. As the toilet paper sailed from my fingers through the air, I couldn't contain my smile. The other guys were having a great time as well, soundlessly jogging around, hefting the rolls up, letting them fly over and over again. Colton caught my eye at one point, his smile as wide as mine. And I could totally understand why the principal would let us do this. The paper was like streamers at a birthday party. The effect of all that white on the pitch-black backdrop of the sky was beautiful like art. We were done in few minutes, but it was fun and illicit and awesome. I felt the overwhelming need to thank Principal Wexler for giving me this moment that I would remember forever, so I scrawled a quick note and left it in his mailbox.

Colton drove Eric home first and dropped me off last.

"Did you have fun?" he asked as we parked outside my house.

"The most fun," I said back, still feeling the excitement running through my veins. "Is this how you feel all time?"

"What do you mean?"

"I feel so energized. So alive."

Colton grinned. "That's what happens when you break the rules. Congratulations Sadie, you are officially woke."

"What are we doing tomorrow?" I asked.

"I had a few ideas. I'll come over early."

"Can't wait," I said then not thinking about it, just doing what I felt, I leaned over and kissed him on the cheek. "Thanks, Coach."

Colton stared back at me, his face unreadable. "No problem."

"I'll see you later."

As I hopped out of the car, walked to the house, I saw that Mom's light was still on, shining from her window. She'd stayed up like she promised, and I couldn't wait to tell her everything. It had been the most exciting night of my life. I wanted to share it with her. Once I was in the house and had locked the door, I looked back, noticing Colton's car was still there. He had waited for me to get inside before driving away.

Yep, definitely the most exciting night of my life.

CHAPTER 11

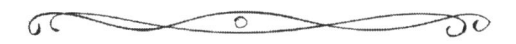

When the doorbell rang at 7:15am the next day, I was surprised to find Kyle standing on my doorstep. He was carrying a box of Krispy Kreme doughnuts and an armful of DVDs.

"Hey stranger," I said sleepily, "where've you been?"

Kyle put a hand on his hip. "I think I should be the one asking that question. My brother told me all about it, and I can't believe you didn't call me last night."

"Sorry," I said unable to hold back a yawn.

It was nearly 4:00am when Mom and I had finished talking—she'd listened to all the details of my night, and I'd enjoyed reliving every second of them. But after that, I'd crashed. Hard. I was still in my pajamas, for goodness sakes, and my hair gave new meaning to the term bedhead.

"I didn't know if you'd have time to talk after working so hard on your project."

"I can't tell if you're being sarcastic or not," he said.

"It was twenty percent sarcasm, eighty percent exhaustion. I'm going on less than four hours of sleep, Kyle. And besides school, I haven't seen you almost all week."

"I know," he said, holding up the doughnut box and DVDs. "And because I've been such a crappy BFF, I brought a peace offering."

I crossed my arms. "Those better be fresh."

He opened the box, and I got a whiff of sugary doughy goodness.

"Was the light on when you got them?"

"Bright red, and I got original glazed."

My favorite.

"Okay, well what else do you have there?" I asked, mostly of curiosity. Kyle had me at "original glazed," but I kept a straight face, wanting to see what he was planning. We used to have BFF days all the time, but with his project taking up so much of his time and me doing my list with Colton, we hadn't had one in a while.

"Dance movies," he said as if it was obvious. "I know how you love a good dance movie, Sadie."

"What's not to love? The sappy plots, the characters who never seem to see that they're perfect for each other, the amazing final dance scene." I could feel myself smiling. "There better be a lot of shirtless Channing Tatum in those movies."

"Oh, you know it," he said.

"Well, come on in then," I said, and Kyle walked inside, making himself right at home.

"Those diamonds look incredible in your ears by the way."

"Thanks, Kyle," I said, glad that he'd noticed.

We'd already started attacking the doughnuts, had just sat down and were about to put in our first movie when the doorbell rang again. With a shrug to Kyle and my second doughnut in hand, I made my way back to the door.

This time it was Colton.

"Hi," I said in surprise. "What are you doing here?"

"I told you I was coming early," Colton said back, eyeing me up and down. I did the same to him. He hadn't put in his piercings today, and though I knew he had to be as sleep deprived as I was, he looked fresh as a daisy in a plain white tee and jeans.

How did guys do that? Colton's lips twitched as he stared at my hair. "I'm guessing you forgot."

"I didn't forget. I just got up."

"Obviously." He was grinning now.

I tried not to squirm under his appraisal but failed miserably.

I went to run a hand through my hair but remembered the doughnut just in time. That's all I needed, I thought, bits of frosting in my hair, the perfect accessory to complete my morning ensemble.

"Looks like you already have some, but I brought breakfast," Colton said, holding up a grocery bag. "Eggs, milk, flour, the whole nine. Everything you need to make pancakes is in here."

My throat closed up a bit. "Pancakes?"

He nodded.

"That's on my list," I said.

"I know," Colton said. "I don't get why you'd want to make your own pancakes when you can buy a mix, but hey. If that's what you want, Coach Colton is here to deliver."

When Dad used to live with us, he'd always made them from scratch each morning, and no mix could ever compare, I thought but didn't say. I was still trying to get it through my brain. *Colton Bishop brought me breakfast. The world must've turned upside down over night.*

"Hey, is Kyle here? I saw his car out front."

Before I could answer, Kyle was stepping past me, pulling Colton into a one-armed guy hug.

"Colt," Kyle said. "What brings you to the Day residence?"

"I brought breakfast," Colton repeated.

"Me, too." Kyle's eyes narrowed, zeroing in on the bag in Colton's hand. "So, let me get this straight. You got up before noon on a Saturday to bring Sadie breakfast?"

There was an odd note to his voice.

"Yeah," Colton said. "Is that a problem?"

Kyle shook his head. "I don't know if it's a problem or not, but you have to admit, it is freaking weird."

"It's on my list, Kyle," I said to clear up any confusion. "Making pancakes from scratch is #21."

Kyle still looked suspicious. Suspicious of what I wasn't exactly sure, but I didn't like the frown on his normally happy face.

"He's just being a good coach," I added.

Colton leaned over to his brother. "She means the best coach."

I rolled my eyes but smiled.

"And now, she's smiling at you," Kyle sighed. "My God, what have I done? I feel like I'm on a different planet or something."

"I'm not smiling at him," I retorted. "I'm smiling at the pancakes."

Colton leaned in again. "She was smiling at me. I've totally replaced you as Sadie's favorite."

Kyle elbowed his brother in the stomach for that one, and Colton grunted out a laugh.

"Hey man, I was kidding," Colton said. "What were you guys doing before I got here?"

"We were about to sit down and watch a bunch of highly underrated dance movies," Kyle said, smiling at Colton's grimace. "Did you want to watch, too?"

"I don't know," Colton said. "Dance movies aren't really my thing."

"You should stay," I said.

As both pairs of eyes flew to me, I realized how odd that sounded, coming from my mouth, directed at Colton. Honestly, I realized it even as I'd said the words but hadn't been able to stop them.

"After we make the pancakes, there's going to be a ton of

food. There's still a bunch of doughnuts left," I rambled on. "Kyle and I couldn't possibly eat all that. And even when Mom wakes up, she doesn't like eating a lot for breakfast. So…like I said, you should stay, Colton. If you want."

Kyle was looking at me like I was nuts. Colton looked like he was trying not to laugh. And I felt my cheeks begin to redden as I stood there.

"I'll stay," Colton said. "Thanks for the invite, Sadie."

Once he had walked past us into the house, I turned to Kyle, who was still staring at me with a what-the-heck-was-that expression.

"Hey," I said, patting him on the arm. "There's enough room for doughnuts and pancakes in my life, Kyle. Stop looking so stressed."

"Sadie, we talked about this," he said. "I don't want to see you get hurt."

"I won't."

"Colt's just doing this for the bet. You get that right?"

"Yes, and I'm just doing it for my list," I said. "It's no big deal. We used to hang out all the time as kids anyway before Colton got too cool for school. Although, he didn't seem to like it much when I was around."

Kyle laughed. "He didn't like it because I hogged all your attention."

"Oh whatever," I scoffed.

"It's true," he said. "Colt would probably kill me for telling you though."

That made literally no sense whatsoever. Kyle was so off base, and I was about to tell him that when Colton reappeared in the doorway.

"Are you two coming or am I making these pancakes alone?" he said.

And with that, the three of us went inside, and I learned how to make my very first batch of pancakes. They turned out well—not as good as my dad's, but not too shabby. When Mom woke up, she even ate a couple. Kyle and I were in a Channing-induced coma of love while Colton scoffed and grumbled under his breath. We'd watched *Step Up*, *Step Up 2: The Streets* and were currently watching the opening credits for *Magic Mike* when the doorbell rang for the third time today. I figured it was the postman dropping off a package for Mom until she called my name. *Must be for me*, I thought.

Turned out it was for me.

But it wasn't a package.

The first thing I noticed was the police officer's uniform and how Mom stood so stiffly beside the door. The second thing was the cruiser parked at the curb.

"What's up, Mom?" I asked, coming to stand next to her.

"This officer's here to see you, baby," she said.

Her voice sounded strained, and I could completely understand why. When the cops came to your house, asking for your child, it was never a good thing. At least, it was never good in the movies or on TV. I had no real-life experience. Until now.

"Me?" I asked. "Why would he want to see me?"

"Are you Sadie Day?" the officer asked, and I realized it was the same man who had pulled me and Colton over that time for the lights.

"Yes, sir," I said. "And I remember you. Officer Hilliard, right?"

"That's right."

"Nice to see you again," I said without thinking. "Just so you know, I haven't forgotten to turn on my lights at night. Not once."

"Good to hear, Miss Day. Good to hear," he said then got to

the real reason for his visit. "I'm here because I received a call from a Stanley Wexler about someone TPing his front yard last night. Would you happen to know anything about that?"

"Yes," I said. "I was there."

Kyle came over at that point and stood behind me.

"What's going on? Everything alright?" Kyle asked.

Officer Hilliard squinted, examining Kyle closely. "Colton Bishop, is that you? Good Lord, I should've known you'd be involved in this."

Colton walked over then, standing on my other side.

"Nope, that's my brother, Kyle," Colton said, and despite the circumstances, he seemed relaxed. "How's it hanging, Hilliard? Are you keeping criminals and truants off the streets?"

"You have a twin," Officer Hilliard muttered, shaking his head, looking from Colton to Kyle and back again. "Damn, the resemblance is uncanny."

"It really is," my mom said. "I've known them since they were little kids and still have trouble telling the two apart."

"Don't feel bad, Mrs. Day," Kyle patted her shoulder. "Even our mom has that problem sometimes."

"Yeah, only seven days out of the week," Colton mumbled then lifted his chin toward the officer. "What brings you here anyway, Hilliard?"

"Somebody TP'd Wexler's house again last night. Know anything about that, Colton?"

"I might," he said. "Or I might not. That still doesn't answer why you're here. Sounds like you don't know who did it."

"Oh, I know who did it," Officer Hilliard said.

"How? Did someone see something?"

Officer Hilliard shook his head, a smile playing on his lips. "Nope. Miss Day, here, left a note."

"A what?"

Colton's eyes widened as Officer Hilliard flashed us the note I'd left in the principal's mailbox last night.

"'Dear Principal Wexler,'" Kyle read aloud. "'Thank you so much for allowing us to TP your house. I've always wanted to be a part of a prank, and I had a wonderful time. If you need help cleaning up, please let me know.'"

Colton groaned as Kyle laughed and kept reading.

"'I wouldn't feel right if I didn't at least offer. You are the best. Sincerely, Sadie Day.'"

When he finished, Kyle turned to me with a grin and said, "Nice penmanship."

I rolled my eyes. Yes, I'd included a smiley-face at the end, but only the one. That was progress, right?

"You left a note?" Colton asked in disbelief, turning to me.

"Yeah," I said as he closed his eyes. "What? I wanted Principal Wexler to know how much fun we had. Was that wrong?"

Officer Hilliard still had that amused look on his face. "Were you aware, Miss Day, that the fine for littering in the state of North Carolina is anywhere between $250 and $1,000?"

"No," I breathed. Holy smokes, that was a lot of cash.

"I didn't think so," he said. "No property was damaged, but the TPing is bad enough. Lucky for you all, Wexler has a good sense of humor."

"But I thought Principal Wexler said it was okay, that he allowed it."

The officer gave me a pitying look. "He'd have to be a saint to allow something like that."

"Colton?" I turned to him, a pit of dread opening in my stomach as I saw his dire expression. The implications of my actions were just starting to hit, and I had a feeling I already knew the answer to my next question. "He said it was okay, right?"

Colton just shook his head. "I can't believe you left a note.

Who does that?"

"Oh my God," I gasped in horror. That meant I'd committed a crime, an actual real crime. I was a criminal. The cops had come to my house, were at our door, and I was having a hard time not freaking out. Kyle put an arm around my shoulders to offer his support, but I hardly felt it.

"Baby, calm down," Mom said, seeing my distress. "It'll be okay. What happens now, Officer?"

Colton stepped in front of me before he could answer and said, "I'll pay the fine, Hilliard. Whatever it is I'll pay. It was my fault, not Sadie's. She didn't know all the details."

"I gathered that," Officer Hilliard said blandly.

"But I wanted to do the prank," I said. I was still miffed at Colton for lying, for withholding vital info, but I'd been just as much a part of last night as he was.

"But I tricked you into it, so it's my fault," Colton insisted.

"No," I said, "*I* was the one who told *you* I wanted to do a prank, so I'm guilty, too."

Colton shot me a glare. "I'm trying to do the right thing here, Sadie."

I glared right back. "I don't need you to stand up for me."

"Well, I am anyway," he said and turned back to the officer. "Tell me what the fine is, and I'll pay it."

Officer Hilliard seemed like he wanted to laugh but was trying to keep it professional.

"Well Colton," he said, "as much as I enjoyed that, it looks like there's no need for your heroics. Wexler's decided not to press any charges. Like I said, the man was amused by that note. He would like to take Miss Day up on her offer to clean his lawn though."

"Of course," I said quickly. "I'd love to."

Officer Hilliard nodded. "I'm going to need you three kids

to come with me."

"Hold up," Kyle said, "Just for the record, I didn't do anything. I wasn't even there. But I'll come help"—he shot his brother a smile—"Colt's not the only hero in the family."

"Sounds good," Officer Hilliard said. "More hands will make the work go faster. Follow me, please." He spoke to my mom. "I'll bring them back when the job's done. Shouldn't take more than an hour."

She nodded. "Could I have a minute first?"

"Yes, ma'am, just send them over when you're through."

"I will."

As Officer Hilliard walked away, Mom stared at the three of us, not saying a word, her face blank slate. It was impossible to tell what she was thinking. I was the first to crack under the pressure of that stare, but Colton wasn't far behind.

"I'm so sorry, Mom," I said. "Please don't be mad."

"Sadie…I'm not mad," she said finally. "I'm just surprised. You never do anything wrong, so this is new territory for us."

"I'm sorry," I said again, feeling my eyes fill with unshed tears. If there was one thing I hated, it was disappointing her.

"Mrs. Day," Colton said, "this one's on me. Like you said, Sadie doesn't do anything wrong. I'm the troublemaker—just ask Hilliard. I messed up and got Sadie in trouble, and I'm sorry for that."

Mom looked to Colton. "According to my daughter, you also gave her one of the best nights of her life. She told me everything."

Colton looked to me. "She did?"

"Yes," Mom said, "and you're not a troublemaker, Colton. You made a mistake, and we all do that. Lord knows, I've made a ton of them. Next time, just tell Sadie all the facts and let her decide what she wants to do."

"I'll do that," he said, putting his hands into his pockets. "Thanks, Mrs. Day."

Mom's gaze met mine.

"Okay then," she said as if she'd decided something. "Okay. Sadie, since this is your first time getting into any sort of trouble and you appear to be sincerely repentant, I don't see any need for more punishment."

"You don't?" I said.

She shook her head. "You're going to have to clean up the mess you made at the principal's house—which you volunteered to do in the first place. I think you've learned your lesson."

I threw my arms around her, burying my head in her neck. "Thank you so much, Mom. I love you."

"I love you, too, baby," she said and hugged me back. "Promise me I won't see you riding in the back of any more police cars."

"Promise," I said.

We walked to the curb in a silent row. Officer Hilliard was waiting and had opened the door for us. Colton looked resigned, and Kyle looked stunned as we piled into the police car.

"Someone tell me how I got roped into this again?" Kyle asked.

"You're my best friend," I said, ducking into the car after Colton, ending up in the middle seat between him and Kyle. The police car was compact and the metal cage separating the front from the backseats reminded me of all those *Blue Bloods* re-runs I used to watch. "We stick together through thick and thin."

"And toilet paper," Kyle mumbled.

As Officer Hilliard closed the door, Colton let his head fall back on the seat, closed his eyes and chuckled.

"What?" I asked.

"I still can't believe you left Principal Wexler a thank you note," Colton said.

"I didn't know what we were doing was illegal."

He opened one eye to look at me. "Fun illegal or bad illegal?"

I rolled my eyes as he chuckled again, and Officer Hilliard got in on the driver's side, started the car. We pulled away from my house, began the drive to Principal Wexler's. Things were quiet in the car for several minutes until Colton broke the silence.

"For real though, Sadie, I'm sorry," Colton said. "For not telling you—"

"It's okay," I cut in. He didn't need to apologize again. "Honestly? Besides wishing Principal Wexler would've been in on the prank, I wouldn't change last night for anything."

Kyle glanced at me. "Well, I would. I wouldn't have left a signed note, pointing the finger at myself. That's just crazy."

Colton grinned at that. "No, that's something only Sadie would do."

"Agreed," Kyle laughed.

Officer Hilliard was silent during the drive, but every now and then he would adjust the rearview mirror. He couldn't seem to stop glancing at the brothers and shaking his head.

"There something on your mind, Hilliard?" Colton asked.

"I just can't believe there are two of you," the officer said. "I may have to start pulling double shifts. How do people even tell the difference?"

"I'm the good-looking one," Kyle said with a smile.

"And I'm the better-looking one," Colton said.

Officer Hilliard scoffed, used the mirror again to look from one brother to the other. After a moment, he clucked his tongue.

"Twins," he said. "I don't know what you're talking about. You look the same to me."

"Don't feel bad," Kyle said. "Hardly no one can tell us apart."

"Yeah," Colton said. "That's why they call it identical."

Officer Hilliard addressed me next. "What do you think, Miss Day?"

I shrugged. "I don't have trouble telling them apart."

What I thought was this: Kyle and Colton, though twins, couldn't be more different if they tried. It was nothing specific, just an expression here or there, a way of moving, talking, personality. Without his piercings, Colton and Kyle really were identical, but even when we were kids, I'd always been able to tell the difference. Always.

Turns out cleaning up after a prank wasn't nearly as exciting as the prank itself.

It took us 45 minutes to de-TP the principal's yard. It would've been less, but Kyle and Colton thought it'd be fun to have a snowball fight with the toilet paper. Boys. Ugh. Thank goodness, Principal Wexler was so cool about the whole thing. He'd watched as we cleaned, talking with Officer Hilliard the whole time, and when I apologized, he said in his Southern drawl, "No harm done, Sadie. You're a good girl, always have been. Me and my wife had a good laugh about that letter of yours."

I was never going to live that one down.

And as far as the "good girl" part went?

Well, I was working on it.

CHAPTER 12

I was currently at Corner Street Ballroom, sitting in one of the foldout chairs, taking a break from my practice with Tim. My old dance partner was just as excited about performing tonight as I was. We'd needed the practice, but after an hour, our routine was looking good.

I took a sip of water and opened my Carpe Diem List, took out a pen to do what was becoming one of my favorite things.

Marking off the items on my list.

6) See the inside of a police car.

Been there done that. I couldn't remember why I'd even added it in the first place. Moving farther down, I went ahead and marked off another.

21) Learn how to make pancakes.

I closed my eyes, remembering how awesome it had been making pancakes with the guys, how unexpected it was to see Colton on my doorstep. At the time, I'd thought it was incredibly thoughtful—until I remembered it was for a bet. Still…Colton really was a great coach, I thought, skimming my list again. It was the end of the first week, and we'd already done almost half the items. Just like he'd said in the library.

Before our kiss.

Which was for the bet.

The memory of which shouldn't make my chest clench like it was doing right now.

I sighed, tucking my list away, as Tim came back into the room and took a seat.

"Now, that sounds like love to me," Tim said, throwing an arm around my shoulders. "What's been going on since I last saw you, Sadie? Don't be shy. Tell Big Tim all about it."

"Love?" I scoffed before resting my head against his shoulder. I'd been 11, and he was 12 when we found each other. Though he'd lived an hour away, we had paired up and competed for years before he graduated last year and retired from the sport of competitive ballroom to pursue a degree in computer science. We hadn't seen each other in a while, but talking to him was easy, a much-needed release. "Yeah, right. You know my situation, Tim. Unrequited love is the name of the game for this girl."

Tim smoothed my hair until it wasn't in his face then settled his arm more fully around me.

"So, this is about Kyle?" he asked.

I laughed. "Funnily enough, no. It's actually about his brother."

"Brother?" Tim asked, instantly becoming alert. "You never mentioned a brother."

"A twin actually," I said.

"So, he's hot, too?"

"Oh yeah."

"Hmm," he said, sounding thoughtful. "I say your unrequited love has lasted long enough. I've never actually met Kyle—or his twin—but if he doesn't appreciate your wonderful self, perhaps it's time to move on." Tim bounced his eyebrows. "Maybe to his equally hot brother."

I shrugged. "I'm not interested in Colton. I love Kyle. Always have."

Tim gave me a long look, and I lifted my head. "Are you sure?"

"Yes," I said, rolling my eyes. "I love Kyle."

"Why?" he asked.

"What kind of question is that?"

"If you love him, it's an easy one."

I blinked, not believing he'd had the audacity to ask me this.

"Well?" Tim said.

"Kyle is…nice and well-mannered," I said. "He's loyal, easy to be around, makes me laugh."

Tim nodded. "Excellent qualities. You could also attribute them to a favorite pet, but who cares, right?"

My jaw dropped. "I can't believe you. Kyle's my best friend, not a puppy. Although, puppies are perfect in every way. They literally make people less stressed and happier. It's a scientifically proven fact."

"I'm not even going to touch that about the puppies," he said. "I've always said you watch way too many of those dog videos online."

I crossed my arms. "They're therapeutic. And you know what, I've always said you take way too much time on your hair. I mean, an hour Tim? Really?"

"It needs time to breathe and set up."

"But an hour?"

"Perfection takes time." Tim rolled his eyes. "Anyway, back to the point. How does Kyle make you feel?"

"What do you mean?"

"When he looks at you, does your heart feel like it's about to leap out of your chest?" Tim gripped my shoulders, hands gentle but firm. "When he touches you, do you feel like you're burning on the inside? Whenever you see him, do you just want to walk up to him and kiss his face off?"

I laughed out loud at that, couldn't help it. "Kiss his face off? Now, that's romantic."

"Whatever. Does Kyle make you feel that way? It's a simple question, Sadie."

I thought about it and my laughter stopped as quickly as it had started. If I was being honest, I couldn't say yes to his questions. I wasn't sure if I'd ever felt those things about Kyle. We'd always had more of a warm relationship, comforting and safe like a soft blanket, familiar like slipping into your favorite sweater. It wasn't the burning Tim described, but...

"I love him, Tim," I said with conviction. "I do."

"Okay, if you say so." Tim's tone was skeptical as he began examining his nails, and I nearly growled. Why wasn't he listening? "I just thought Colton would be a better option. Help you get over the other brother, give your love life a pick-me-up."

"Hate to burst your imaginary bubble, but Colton doesn't want me either."

"He's a moron then," Tim said, looking me straight in the eye. "They both are."

"Not morons," I sighed. "Just not interested."

I'd never told anyone Kyle's secret, so Tim had no idea that Kyle, being gay, could never be interested in me in a romantic way. Even if he was straight, let's face it. Chances were good that he still wouldn't be into me. Take Colton, for example. He was straight as a freaking arrow.

"Enough about me," I said, needing a change of subject. "How's Little Tim? Is the gaming industry clamoring for you guys yet? Because they should be."

"Ah, Little Tim." He smiled like he did whenever he talked about his long-time boyfriend/soulmate. "He's amazing, as usual, told me to tell you 'hello.' The guy can't do his laundry to save his life, but I don't know what I'd do without him."

"Sounds like you guys are happy," I said.

"We are, Sadie." Tim's smile turned sly like he had a secret.

"And you'll be happy to know that, as of yesterday, we're in talks with a company who's interested in one of our games."

"Oh my gosh! Which one?"

"Just a little game called 'Her Majesty's Revenge.'" Tim laughed as I gasped and hugged him, surprised and elated. "Yes, your idea, sweetie. It drew their attention."

"Wow, that's awesome, Tim! Congratulations!"

"Thanks," he said, hugging me back. "Speaking of ideas, you still trying to get your dance videos out there?"

"Yeah," I said, "but the rejections are piling up."

"Stuck-up charlatans." Tim frowned as we pulled away. "If you had more followers, your dances would've already been picked. It's about who you know, Sadie, how many likes and views you get. *Dancer's Edge* likes to take people who make it big on their own and then pretend they 'discovered' them first. Such a scam."

"I'm trying a new tango piece this time," I said, cutting in. Tim had no love for *Dancer's Edge*. In addition to seeing how devastated I'd been when the rejections first started rolling in, Tim was a believer in free internet and open sourcing, and he'd never been a fan of big business. "It's different than my usual pieces, more risqué. I'd need two guys and a girl, but I have a really good feeling about this one."

"A little tango never hurt nobody," he said and smiled. "Let me know if there's anything I can do to help. As a lowly game designer/college student, you know I love sticking it to the man."

"Will do," I said back.

"Have you decided where you're going for college yet?"

"Not yet."

"Well, you better hurry, girl. Time's a ticking."

I tried to keep my smile just as bright. I hated that question, hated how it made me feel like such a loser for not knowing where I was going in life. Whenever someone asked me that, a spike of fear rose up inside my chest.

Shaking it off, I said, "We should run the dance a few more times so we're ready for tonight."

"Sure." Cutting me a challenging glance, he added, "I wasn't going to say anything, but you were a little rusty."

"Ha," I said, "you're the one who's rusty, college boy."

"We'll see about that."

The nerves were new.

Performing in front of people had never been a problem for me. I'd grown up dancing, doing choreography that I'd run a hundred times, getting lost in the music, feeding off the energy of the crowd. It was what I loved. That's why I'd been doing it for years. Tonight, though, I didn't know why, but I was feeling nervous.

It could've been that crack Tim made about me being "rusty."

Total crap, of course.

I was at the top of my game. He was the one who'd struggled at first—which was understandable since he'd been gaming more than practicing his closed hold and gauchos. Still, we'd always moved well together and were more than ready for this.

It could've been that I hadn't performed in a few months.

My focus lately had been more on choreography. But again, it was old hat. I knew how to work a crowd, and the Shady Grove residents loved this kind of thing. Twelve of them had shown up to watch us perform. Tim and I were filling in for my parents, who'd arranged the whole thing but had ended up having to miss it because they'd been called up to judge a ballroom competition a few towns away. Betty and Cora, my #1 fans, were catcalling from the front-and-center seats they'd managed to grab.

So, lack of support wasn't a problem.

Then there was the fact that Kyle and Colton had walked in a minute ago.

I guessed it could've been that.

My stomach clenched as they started walking my way, and I thought, yep. The nervous, nauseous feeling twisting my stomach up in knots? Totally because of their presence. I should've expected this. Although Kyle was my best friend, he'd never seen me dance live, let alone Colton. I'd kept this part of myself separate from the rest of my life. Dance was like my secret. I could be anyone I wanted during those few minutes. I felt every emotion and lived it on the dance floor. Besides competitions (which were with fellow dancers) and dancing at the studio (which again was with people who took dance), my videos for *Dancer's Edge* had been my only effort to put my dancing out there. Ballroom and my real life had been two mutually exclusive entities—until tonight.

My stomach gave another roll, and sensing my unease, Tim turned to me, rested a hand on my back.

"Hey Sadie, you okay?" he asked.

The twins stopped in front of us, then Kyle let out a low whistle.

"Dang Sadie, that sweet-heart neckline and those heels?" he said. "Perfection."

"Thanks, Kyle," I said.

"Seriously, the dress is gorgeous. Red was always your color—but why do you look like you're going to be sick?"

"I'm fine," I mumbled, but to be honest, my attention was elsewhere.

Colton's eyes traveled the length of my body, appraising and intense, and I couldn't help but watch for his reaction. His gaze stopped on Tim's hand on my back, stayed there a moment, before coming up to meet my eyes.

"No cardigan tonight?" he said.

"It's not usually what you wear to tango," I said.

"I noticed that."

"I noticed you noticing."

Colton's lips twitched, but he didn't deny it.

"If you stared any harder, I thought my dress might catch fire," I added, having to tease him. He'd been caught staring, and he knew it.

Colton raised an eyebrow. "Are you saying I make you hot?"

"No," I said, blushing fiercely. How had he managed to flip this on me?

"Because that's a natural reaction, Sadie. You shouldn't feel ashamed about it."

"I'm not ashamed. I just don't feel anything but annoyance," I said through gritted teeth.

"Sure, you don't," he said.

Tim cleared his throat which ended our stare down.

"Well, well," he said, looking between me, Colton and Kyle like he was watching some kind of soap opera or reality show. He sent me a significant glance. "Sadie, aren't you going to introduce me to your friends?"

I didn't know what that look meant. It made me a little wary, but his syrupy sweet tone was what really put me on my guard.

"Sure," I said slowly. "Tim, this is Kyle and Colton. Guys, this is my former dance partner, Big Tim."

"Hey, I'm Kyle. Nice to meet you," Kyle said.

"The pleasure's all mine, I assure you," Tim said as he shook Kyle's hand and held his eyes until my best friend blushed, looked away. Dear God, I knew Tim was attractive.

Objectively-speaking, with his confident air, his deep brown eyes and fantastic hair, he could've made most girls—or guys—swoon. But he must've had some serious mojo to get Kyle blushing after a simple handshake. "I've heard a lot about you, both of you, from Sadie."

Colton scoffed low. "I'm betting it was less than flattering."

"You might be surprised," Tim said and took Colton's hand. For some reason, their handshake looked a lot less cordial, more intense. "Good to meet you, Colton."

"You, too," he said, looking Tim in the eyes, not releasing his hand. "Is there a reason they call you 'Big Tim?' You don't look so big to me."

Tim flashed a full smile. "I guess you're not looking in the right place then."

"Guess not," Colton said while Kyle cough-laughed.

"I'm actually the perfect height to partner Sadie," Tim said, looking the twins over. "You and your brother would be, too. What are you six-foot-one? Maybe a little taller?"

Colton shook his head. "Yeah, but I don't dance."

"Too bad," Tim said.

"And why's that?"

"It's sad when a man isn't confident enough in his masculinity to dance."

Colton shot him a grin. "Trust me, confidence isn't a problem."

"I can see that," Tim said.

"We've never even seen Sadie dance," Kyle put in. "Besides her videos. She's my best friend, and I'm trying not to be offended that, the one time she did invite me, Colton got the invite as well."

I was hoping Kyle wouldn't notice that, but of course, he did.

"I wanted to come to one of her competitions, but she'd never let me," Kyle said in a whisper to Tim. "Threatened to shave off my eyebrows more than once. Sadie's always been weird about dancing in front of me."

"You're exaggerating," I countered, though he was right on the money. If Kyle had come to see me dance, if he hadn't liked it, I would've been crushed, absolutely annihilated. I hadn't wanted to take that chance—and I knew how much Kyle cared about his eyebrows, so it'd been the perfect means to keep him away. "And hey, like you said, I invited you tonight."

"So, you guys came to support Sadie," Tim said. "That's nice."

"Yeah," Colton laughed, finally releasing Tim's hand and backing away. "We're here to see some of that sexy 16th Century ballroom dancing she told me about. Right, Sadie?"

I sniffed, giving a small nod. "I have a point to prove."

"Yeah, you do," Colton said. "There somewhere you want us to sit?"

Before I could answer, Betty raised her hand, waving to get Colton's attention. He frowned slightly when he saw who it was flagging him down, and I smiled.

"Looks like there are some seats right over there," I said sweetly. "You wouldn't want to keep Betty waiting."

Kyle laughed. "So, that's Betty? Oh, I can't wait to meet her."

"And I'm sure she wants to meet you. She absolutely adores Colton," I added.

"Of course, she does." Colton turned to me and shrugged. "Why wouldn't she? Let's go, Kyle."

"Good luck, Sadie," Kyle said and nodded to Tim.

As the twins walked off together, Betty looked pleased as punch to see them, gathering them both into a hug once they were close enough. Tim waited until they were out of earshot then pulled me to face him, eyes bright like he was on a sugar high, smiling like a kid in a candy store who'd just found the chocolate aisle.

"Sadie, why didn't you tell me?" he said, voice full of excitement.

"Tell you what?" I asked.

"Well, for one, that Kyle's gay."

I blinked. "I don't know what you're talking about."

Tim rolled his eyes. "Oh come on, the boy may be in the closet, but he's gay as gay can be. No wonder he's never gone for you. I hit him and his brother with my come-hither stare, and Kyle reacted like a moth drawn to a flame."

"I—"

"And the brother! Oh my God, I can't believe you never said anything about the brother."

"What about Colton?" I asked.

"He's into you, Sadie." He nodded as I shook my head. "Oh yes. Didn't you see how he was staring at you? And how he got all jealous when he thought we were together? It was hot."

I had to laugh at that. "Tim, you are so incredibly wrong."

"I'm so incredibly right," he countered. "There were definite sparks, and he was eating you up with his eyes. FYI, you were eating him up, too."

"I did not look at him that way."

Tim crossed his arms. "You look at him like you've kissed him, and you can't wait to do it again."

My face flamed up like a freaking forest fire.

"Oh my God," he said, eyes widening, "have you kissed him? You have, haven't you? Sadie!"

"Okay, okay," I said as Tim wore me down, "yes, we kissed. Once. And I can't stop thinking about it, which is really frustrating and confusing as heck. But it's just because it was my first kiss, not because I have any weird repressed attraction to Colton."

"Really? Because I'm positive there was some repressed attraction there."

I gave him a look.

"So, you're saying you're confused about the kiss with Colton, and that's why you may or may not have been looking at him with I-hate-you-even-though-I-want-you eyes?"

I shrugged. "If you want to put it that way, I guess."

"Then you know what this means right, Sadie?"

I shook my head.

"You have to kiss him again."

CHAPTER 13

Kiss him again.
Kiss him again.
Kiss him again.

The words replayed through my head again and again during my performance with Tim. To be honest, I didn't know how I managed to get through it without tripping, let alone stay on beat. My brain was so discombobulated. Besides those words echoing in my ears, the way Colton and Kyle's eyes followed us across the dance floor made my heart race. Were they impressed? Did they like it? Hate it? Oh God, please don't let them hate it.

Though the dance was only a minute and thirty seconds, by the end I was sweating. And it wasn't because of my curves or a lack of stamina.

Oh no.

It had everything to do with the two guys in the front row and the pair of eyes that I couldn't seem to stop meeting even as I'd been dancing with Tim. Surprisingly, those eyes hadn't belonged to Kyle. The applause was deafening as we came out of our final dip, so we must've done a decent job. But if you'd asked me what'd happened in those 90 seconds, I wouldn't have been able to tell you a thing.

After we finished, some of the residents got up to dance while others remained seated just enjoying the music, and Kyle came over and grabbed me up in a hug.

"Holy wow, Sadie," Kyle said. "Why didn't you ever let me see you dance? That was awesome!"

The relief I felt almost brought me to my knees. "Really? You liked it?"

"Are you crazy?" he said, taking a step back. "You were incredible!"

"You have no idea how much that means to me, Kyle. Thank you," I said as Colton joined us. For some reason I couldn't explain, I wanted to hear his opinion—even if it scared the crap out of me. "What about you, Colton? You said ballroom couldn't be sexy. Do you still think that, or did we change your mind?"

Colton shook his head, and I braced myself.

"I stand corrected," he said and met my eyes. "You were amazing."

"Thanks," I said unable to look away, my heart skipping for some reason. What the heck was that about?

"You were good, too, Big Tim," Colton added.

Tim did a little bow. "Why thank you."

"Man, I wish I could do that," Kyle said. "You know, when we were younger, my mom put Colton and me in dance class for a few years."

My eyes widened in disbelief. "What? I never knew that!"

"That's because we promised never to speak of it again," Colton muttered. "Seriously, what the hell, Kyle?"

"What kind of dancing was it?" I asked still stunned.

"Ballet and tap," Kyle said and shoved his hands into his pockets, ignoring Colton's glare. "This was before I even knew you, Sadie. We did it from kindergarten to fourth. I was decent, but Colton was actually pretty good."

My eyes shot to Colton. *"You* took ballet?"

"And I hated every second," Colton said.

"Aw, come on, you were good," Kyle said.

"I still hated it. Are we done talking about this?"

I shook my head. "I can't believe you took ballet. And tap! I'm having a hard time picturing it."

"Don't," Colton said. "Stop trying to picture it right now. That's an official order as your coach."

Eyes closed, I held up a hand. "Wait, wait, I almost have it—"

"Sadie," Colton practically growled. This was too much fun.

"He was good," Kyle said, and I could hear the smile in his voice. "The girls were too scared to talk to him, though, because he looked miserable. So, they talked to me instead. I think most of them had a crush on one or both of us."

I could picture it so clearly. Kyle, loving it, drinking up all the attention, and Colton, grumpy as all get out, waiting for it to be over.

"Miss Patricia used to always say, ‚You Bishop boys both have rhythm, but Colton is a natural.'"

At Colton's sigh, I opened my eyes. "Thanks," I said. "I have the perfect mental image now. But honestly, Colton, I don't see what you're so embarrassed about. Dance is awesome."

"Yeah well, not everyone thinks so," he said.

I didn't really understand what he meant, but Tim nodded like he got it. To Colton, he said, "Was it the ballet belt, the classical music, or all the crap you caught from other guys that turned you off?"

"It was everything," Colton said deadpan. "Those were dark times."

"Ah well," Tim said, "kids can be jerks. That's why no one at my school knew I did ballroom. But at least the teacher said you can move."

"I'll believe that when I see it," I mumbled.

I'd made the comment mostly under my breath, but from

the way Colton's eyes narrowed, he must've heard. Wonderful.

"Hey, Sadie," Tim said, which gave me an excuse to look away from Colton. Bless Tim and his perfect timing.

"Yeah?" I asked.

"Don't you always say there's nothing more attractive than a guy who can dance?"

If Tim's tone was innocent, his eyes were anything but. They were shining with mirth as my mouth fell open. I take it back. My ex-dance partner had the most awful timing imaginable.

"I—well I…did say that," I sputtered. Of course, I had said that. And yes, I truly believed it. When a guy knew how to move his body, there was nothing more appealing—except maybe a guy who loved to read. The truth was I'd take a man who could move over a football jock any day of the week. I just didn't necessarily want to own up to it in the presence of certain bad boys with already humongous egos.

"While you two talk, Kyle and I will be just over here going through the finer points of ballroom," Tim said as he whisked my best friend away. Kyle followed all-too-willingly, and I was suddenly left alone with Colton. He was looking at me with this calculating gleam in his eye that I didn't trust for a second.

"So, dancing," Colton said finally. "That's what does it for you?"

"It might," I said, crossing my arms over my chest.

"I'll keep that in mind."

My eyes widened, my brain grinding to a halt. Did he really just say…? Before I could think too long on it, Colton's next words stunned me again.

"By the way, have you given any more thought to the kissing?"

"What?" I squeaked, my eyes shooting to Tim. Had he said something to Colton when I wasn't looking? Tim *had* been the one who was all gung-ho about me kissing Colton again…but no, he couldn't have. I'd been here the whole time, and it hadn't come up.

"Kissing," Colton said again. "Have you thought any more about it?"

"Not really," I said, the lie tripping easily from my tongue, but I was pretty sure my blush gave me away. The library, his lips, my lips. Meeting in a first kiss to end all first kisses. Was he crazy? *Of course*, I'd thought about it.

Colton frowned, the metal in his lip catching the light. "Listen, Sadie, I can't be the only one thinking about these things. You've got to do your part, too."

"Y-you've thought about it?" I asked in disbelief. "The kissing?"

"Well yeah, only like every day."

"Wait, wait…what exactly are you saying?"

Colton stared at me a beat then said slowly, "We need to find you a new kissing partner. There's no way we can complete your list without one. I thought we were on the same page about this."

I exhaled a laugh. "Oh, of course! Yes, I completely agree. Couldn't agree more actually."

"What did you think I was talking about?" he asked.

"The kissing partner thing," I said, my tone bright. "I was just making sure you knew what we were talking about. You know, sometimes I like to test you, Colton, just to make sure you're paying attention."

"Trust me," he said, "with you, I'm always paying attention."

"Well that's…nice."

"No, it's not," Colton grinned. "I'm your coach, so it's my job."

I guess when he put it like that…

"So, you wanna go out tonight?" My jaw dropped, and Colton laughed at my expression. "Ah, don't get overexcited, Sadie. It's just so we can cross off a few more things on your list and find you some guy to kiss. No big deal."

"Oh," I said, unsure what I felt right then. There was definitely relief, but something else was mixed in there. Something I chose not to examine too closely. "Yeah, that sounds good."

"Think your mom will let you go?"

I thought about it a second then nodded. "She won't be home until tomorrow actually. But I'll call her, and she'll be okay with it. I'm about 99 percent sure. Mom trusts me."

"Of course, she does." He shook his head. "Such a good girl."

I rolled my eyes at that as Colton turned to look at his brother. Following his gaze, it seemed like Tim really had shown Kyle some basic ballroom steps. I felt my lips turn up at the corners. My BFF was smiling, enjoying himself, and it was obvious the two were having a good time. Curiously, I didn't feel even a hint of jealousy. I'd long ago accepted the fact that Kyle would never be mine. I just hoped Big Tim had mentioned Little Tim. If he'd led my best friend on...well, ex-ballroom partner or not, we would be having some serious words.

"Hey Sadie."

I turned my attention to Colton, only to find his eyes already on me.

In a completely serious tone, he said, "Be ready at eleven, and bring your naughty list."

No matter how many times I asked, Colton wouldn't tell me what we were doing tonight. He refused to give even the tiniest of details. It was frustrating. *He* was frustrating. But to be honest, I wasn't really worried. And *that*—the fact that I wasn't worried—worried me.

I sighed as I glanced over at my cell. I'd gotten off the phone with my mom a couple hours ago, and the conversation had gone like this:

Mom: "Well of course, you can go, Sadie. But where are you going?"

Me: "I'm not sure. Colton wouldn't tell me, said it was a surprise."

Mom: "Colton." A long pause and then, "You're going out with Colton Bishop again?"

Me: "We're not going out, Mom. He's just helping me with a project."

Mom: "A project? For what class?"

That one had given me a moment's pause, but I'd finally come up with a great and (mostly) truthful answer.

Me: "Life Sciences. It's due soon and requires some work we can only do at night."

She'd been thinking it over—I could practically hear the gears turning in her mind—when suddenly my father was on the phone.

Dad: "Sadie, it's Dad."

Me (laughs): "Yeah, I know. Hi Dad, how's it going?"

Dad: "Going fine. Now, is this the Colton Bishop who removed the screws from your chair in fifth grade and ruined your cupcakes?"

Me: "Yes."

Dad: "The Colton Bishop who filled our mailbox with Swedish Fish that summer?"

Me: "I'd forgotten about that."

Dad: "And wasn't he the kid who punched Sherriff Molina's

son and nearly got expelled? This is the boy you're going out with tonight? If you ask me, I don't think it's a good idea."

There was movement on the other end of the line, and I heard Mom and Dad arguing, but it was muffled. Someone must've remembered to cover the receiver. My bet was on Mom. A minute later, she was back on the line.

Mom: "You still there, Sadie? Your dad had to be reminded that Colton was not the only boy in history to nearly be expelled for fighting."

Me: "Yes, I'm here. And Mom, I know Colton may have done all those things. But he's really trying to help me."

Mom: "I know, baby, but your dad and I just worry. It's the norm, the universal condition of parents everywhere to be concerned."

Dad (in the background): "Especially when their baby girl decides to date a guy like Colton Bishop."

Me: "Ugh. Please tell Dad this is not a date."

Mom: "You sure about that, baby?"

Me: "One hundred percent."

Mom: "Hmm. Well, I think it's fine if you go, date or not. Your dad and I trust you. Isn't that right, David?"

I could hear Dad's muttered, "Yeah…it's him I don't trust."

Mom (whispering): "No TP'ing tonight, right? You'll text when you get home?"

Me: "No, none of that, and I will definitely text when I get home."

Mom: "Okay, then." She was smiling; I could hear it over the phone. "Have fun, be safe, and I love you."

Me: "I will. I love you, Mom. Tell Dad I love him, too."

It hadn't been the worst conversation, though I wasn't loving the fact that I'd caused them to argue. And I could totally understand why they were concerned—but to be honest? I was more concerned with the state of my list. Specifically, the kissing parts.

15) Kiss in the rain.
16) Kiss in the car.
17) Kiss in public.
18) Kiss in my bedroom.

No matter how many times I went over it I kept coming to the same conclusion. I just had no idea how I was going to tell my coach my thoughts while keeping my pride and dignity intact. Sighing, I checked the clock again. Five more minutes, and Colton would officially be late. I was debating the pros and cons of him not showing up when there was a knock at the door.

I went to answer, and there he was. Colton Bishop, on my doorstep, right on time.

My stomach was in knots, and I couldn't tell if it was from fear or excitement.

"You changed," he said, looking me over from head to toe. "What happened to the dress?"

I shrugged, stepping out and shutting the door, feeling a lot more like myself in my cardigan and jeans. "I wanted to be comfortable," I said as I pulled on my Corner Street Ballroom jacket. "Plus, somebody wouldn't say what we're doing tonight, so I didn't know what to wear."

"Okay." Colton gave a small nod, turned and walked away, expecting me to follow.

Which I did.

Ugh.

When we were both in the car and on the road, I'd finally had enough.

"Will you just tell me where we're going?" I said exasperated.

"There's this club just outside of Durham called *Shots*. I've been there a few times," Colton said, drumming his hands on the steering wheel. "We're going to check that off your list—but I'm telling you now, Sadie, I don't dance. You're on your own for that part."

Colton said it so easily, but at the word "club," my body tensed. Social dancing was something outside of my comfort zone. Going to an actual club with a ton of people I didn't know, doing steps that had no rhyme or reason was kinda daunting. Oh, who was I kidding? I was shaking in my sneakers—which was why I'd added it to my list in the first place. I'd wanted to conquer that fear.

"Oh," I said, "that sounds like fun."

Colton must've sensed something because he said, "You scared, Sadie? Don't be. It'll be fine."

"I know." I took a deep breath. "I've just never been to a club before. Kinda nervous is all."

"Is it the clothes?" he said, shooting a look of disdain at my jacket, cardigan and jeans ensemble. "Because if you want, we can always go back and get that dress."

I rolled my eyes. "I happen to like the way I look, Colton."

"Even the hair?" he asked dubiously.

My eyes narrowed to slits, the fear of going to a club forgotten for the moment. "There is nothing wrong with my hair. If I remember correctly, you even mentioned something about it giving men ‚wild thoughts.'"

"Hmm…did I? I don't recall the instance to which you're referring, Sadie."

"Do you enjoy irritating me?" I asked.

"Sometimes," he said with a grin. "Maybe it's just me, but it feels like there's something missing from my day if I don't see the look of derision in your eyes."

"It's hate-fire," I said simply. "My eyes spit hate-fire whenever

I'm around high levels of arrogance."

"If that's a *Pitch Perfect* reference, I approve."

I crossed my arms, secretly impressed.

"Does that make me Bumper and you Fat Amy?"

My eyes shot to his. "If you even think of calling me fat at any point tonight, we're done here."

"Wasn't going to," Colton said, holding up a palm, his eyes creasing when he glanced my way. "And ah, there it is again. The hate-fire I love to see. My day is now complete."

"You're an idiot," I huffed.

"Acca-scuse me?" he said.

I closed my eyes, shook my head, trying desperately not to laugh. Colton Bishop was not funny. Not at all. He was a jerk, I reminded myself, and there was no way I could be amused by someone I found so insanely annoying.

We didn't talk again until we got to Durham—which was probably for the best. If we'd kept the conversation going, there was a fifty-fifty chance Colton wouldn't have made it to the club alive. And then my list would never be complete because I'd killed my coach and was in jail for 25 to life. Le sigh.

I met Colton in front of the car, and he said, "Just let me do the talking."

"I can speak for myself, thanks," I said back.

Colton shook his head and handed me a card.

"What's this?" I asked, holding it up to catch the light.

"It's your ID," he said, pulling my hand back down. "The one that says your 21 and old enough to do whatever you want once we get in there."

My jaw dropped as I looked at…well, me. It was a picture from last Halloween when I'd gone as a blonde Bellatrix LeStrange—hence the heavy makeup. I wasn't sure if it made me look 21, but I definitely looked older.

"Wow," I said, "did you do this? When did you make it?"

Colton lifted a brow. "A couple nights ago. Now, are we done with the questions?"

"Sure." I shrugged, fluffing my hair a bit, grateful I hadn't taken off my makeup. I'd gone a bit heavier for the performance today. "I'm just kind of impressed."

"Really?" he said, waving as he caught the eye of the bouncer. The big guy smiled and lifted his chin. It looked like they knew each other.

"No," I said. "I'll be impressed if we get in there and you show me this natural rhythm you supposedly have."

Colton shook his head, looked me dead in the eye. "Not gonna happen, Sadie."

I patted his arm. "Okay, Coach. Let's do this."

It turned out Colton did know the bouncer. He was Eric Greene's cousin (of course), and he'd let us in with a handshake and a smile. Well that, and I couldn't be sure, but I thought Colton might've slipped him a twenty.

The music was loud. There were a ton of people—college kids liked to party. Who knew? Most of the girls weren't wearing much, and everyone who wasn't out there gyrating seemed to have a drink in their hand. I took a sip of my water. Fake ID or not, getting drunk wasn't on my list. Also, after I'd watched one girl get into a fight with another girl who'd accidentally stepped on her toes, complete with hissing and hairpulling? Yeah, no drinking for me, thanks.

"You having a good time?"

I looked at Colton—he was drinking water, too, I noticed. I didn't know if it was to make me feel more comfortable, but for some reason it did. "It's okay, basically what I expected. Not really my scene though."

"Yeah," Colton said. "Once you've been to one, you'll feel like you've been to them all."

"Hmm," I nodded, not really knowing what else to say.

Was this it? Why did people go to places like this? The music wasn't even that good, and all those strangers dancing in that massive swarm of bodies? I shivered.

"You planning to go out there anytime soon," Colton said with a knowing grin.

"I'm working myself up to it," I sniffed.

"Really?" he said. "Because we've been here about an hour and you haven't made a move toward the dance floor."

"I know," I said. "I'm just trying to find my happy place in my mind, so when I go out there, I won't make a fool out of myself."

"Sadie, look around." Colton gestured with a hand. "Who're you afraid of embarrassing yourself in front of? No one's even looking at you."

"You are," I said quietly, but was glad he couldn't hear over the loud music.

Colton frowned, leaning forward. "What was that?"

"Nothing," I said. "Maybe we could do something else on the list while I build up my courage."

"Okay," he said and looked over the crowd. "Have you seen any guys who strike your fancy?"

"My fancy?" I laughed. "Why Colton, how positively old school of you."

"Whatever, you know what I mean. Do you see anyone you find attractive?"

I nodded. "I have to admit, there are a lot of hot guys here."

Colton let out a grunt. "Yeah, like who?"

"Well," I said, my gaze landing on a blond guy a few booths away. "He's kinda cute."

With no discretion whatsoever, Colton swung around to look.

"*That* guy?" Colton said, thrusting his thumb in the guy's direction as my eyes widened. Could he be any more obvious? Geez. "You think he's cute? Sadie, he probably spent an hour on his hair and looks about twelve."

I shrugged. "His face is cute. That's all I'm saying."

Colton shook his head. "And he probably kisses ‚cute.' Is that what you want? A ‚cute' kisser, someone who's so hesitant you don't even know you've been kissed? Try again."

"Okaaay," I said and lifted my chin. "What about him?"

Colton sighed as his eyes landed on my second choice. "Really, Sadie? He's carrying a man purse. Next."

"What about the guy over there? The one leaning against the wall."

My third choice was a brunette who was on the other side of the room. He had his hands in his pockets, was tapping his foot to the music, and from here, I thought he was good-looking. Guy #3 got a scowl from Colton.

"He's wearing a UNC jersey."

"And?" I said. "So are half the guys in here."

"That shirt probably means he's a frat boy," Colton mumbled before taking a long pull on his water.

"I think a lot of them are, judging by the number of jerseys."

"Didn't take you for a jock chaser, but okay, if that's what you want. He'll probably kiss you—if he's not too busy staring at his own pretty boy reflection."

"First of all, who said anything about kissing?" I shook my head at him. "And second, have you ever heard of the pot calling the kettle black?"

Colton tsked. "I have, but it doesn't apply. Unlike him, I woke up like this, no mirror time needed."

"And you're so humble, too," I said sarcastically.

"Who needs humble when you've got a face and body like this?"

I couldn't help but laugh. Colton's tone was serious, but I knew it was a joke. The small smile he wore while I laughed said as much.

Once I'd stopped, I asked, "So, what next?"

"Just go introduce yourself, and get to the kissing," Colton said then cleared his throat. "Who knows what the guy may be carrying—those jocks get around—but hell, you need somebody for your list, right?"

I hadn't wanted to tell Colton, but I'd actually already made up my mind. About my list, I mean, and more precisely about the kissing parts. There'd been a lot of time to think while I'd waited for him to pick me up tonight. I just didn't know what I'd do if he turned me down.

"Colton?" I said.

"Yeah?"

Okay, deep breath, Sadie. You can do this. Time to swallow your pride and carpe freaking diem.

"I was hoping you might want to be my kissing partner."

CHAPTER 14

"Come again?" Colton's face had frozen at my words, but now his forehead creased in a frown. "I must've misheard. I thought you just asked me to be your kissing partner."

I closed my eyes on a sigh. "Please don't make me say it again."

"But…we talked about this. I thought you wanted someone else."

And here was the hard part.

"Believe me, I've thought about it a lot since then," I said. "It just has to be you. Okay?"

Colton ran a hand through his hair. "But you don't even like me. I know it can be confusing with the twin thing. Sadie, I'm not Kyle. This is Colton Bishop you're talking to, in case you forgot."

Okay, I was starting to get a little angry now. "Thanks, Colton, but I can tell the difference. Even at his worst, Kyle never gets on my nerves as much as you do."

"Oh, I get it," he laughed. "Kyle pissed you off, and you want to get back at him. Why didn't you just say so?"

"That's not it."

"Then what is it, Sadie? I'm drawing a blank here."

"Holy smokes." I threw up my hands. "I know you, Colton. Alright? I know about your expertise in this area, and I've basically known you my whole life. Crazy as it sounds, I don't think

I'm the type of girl who can just kiss someone I don't know."

Colton looked stunned, so I decided to spell it out for him.

"I want you to kiss me," I said.

"What?" he said.

"I want you to kiss me, Colton," I repeated louder. "Not some random guy I met at a club called Shots. Not a stranger. You."

"Sorry, can you say that again? I didn't hear you."

It was then I noticed his grin, and my cheeks heated up like a furnace, my entire body burning with embarrassment.

"Oh, ha ha," I said and crossed my arms. "Real funny, Colton. I hope you got a good laugh out of that."

"No really," he said, moving around to my side of the booth. "I think I need to hear it again to know this isn't a dream. *The Sadie Day needs my help? My*"—he lowered his voice—"*kissing expertise? I'm shocked.*"

I rolled my eyes, feeling all of the humiliation the words had cost me.

"Never mind," I said, scooting farther away from him. "Just forget I asked."

"Never," Colton said. "That's not something a guy forgets."

I shook my head, looking anywhere but at him. "I can't believe I just said that. God, I am so pathetic, asking something like that of my best friend's brother."

I felt Colton's body tense beside me, but the words just kept coming.

"And seriously, you're like the most arrogant person on the planet. This'll probably inflate your ego even more, but I still can't believe the first time went so well. The kiss, I mean, in the library. And yes, I've thought about it, okay? I can't deny that. How could a person not think about it when it was their first and only kiss? But even so, when it comes to the rest of my list, a girl would have to be nuts to want to do those things with you. But as you always like to remind me, so many of them *have*. You're the world's biggest player, and I guess I thought you wouldn't mind. I'm just another girl, right? Again, so unbelievably pathetic. What the heck was I thinking?"

I wasn't sure how long I'd been talking, but I didn't think I'd taken a breath the whole time. It felt like something had burst somewhere inside me, all these thoughts and feelings pouring out until I'd completely drenched myself and Colton in an emotional downpour.

It was then I noticed Colton staring.

"Why are you looking at me like that?" I asked.

"I'm thinking about something," he said.

"What?" I asked, not sure I wanted the answer. His eyes were so intense, the ocean blue clear and focused, unwavering from my face.

His brow furrowed. "Kissing you."

"Why would you be thinking that?" My eyes widened as he leaned closer, and my voice was slightly hysterical, a bit breathless. "Didn't you hear what I just said? You're off the hook."

Colton just shook his head, leaned even closer so that we were breathing the same air.

"Maybe it's the only way to shut you up."

He raised a hand, and I opened my mouth to protest—then shut it again because now that hand was tangled in my curls.

He studied my lips. "Maybe I just have a thing for girls who call me on my shit."

My breath caught as Colton finally met my eyes.

"Maybe…I've been thinking about it for the last week, and I just want to."

Colton kissed me then, and it was like everything else melted away. The way-too-loud music, the smell of cheap beer, the crappy strobe lighting. All of it disappeared. It was just him and me, and this kiss that could erase the world. His lips moved with mine like they'd missed each other and were thrilled to meet again. My hands found their way to his chest. His fingers tightened in my hair, drawing a gasp from me, and he took full advantage. I kissed him back just as fiercely. I couldn't believe I'd even considered doing this with someone else. It just felt so good, so wonderful, so…right with Colton.

The thought had me pulling away fast, and if my heart wasn't already going a mile a minute from the amazing kiss, it was hammering now. But for a completely different reason.

"Something wrong?" he asked.

"No," I said, quickly disentangling myself from him and standing from the booth. Space, I thought. I just needed some space between us to get my mind right. Then maybe the fluttery feeling in my chest would go away. "Nothing's wrong. Why would something be wrong? Everything's great."

Colton gave me a funny look. "You sure? Because you're rambling again."

I nodded probably too fast, fidgeting as I went to take off my jacket. "Sure, I'm awesome. But is it hot in here to you?"

He tried to hide it, but I think he laughed. And why shouldn't he? I was freaking the heck out.

"You wanna go dance?" I asked, deciding this space wasn't quite big enough. We needed a lot more distance between us. "I think I'm ready to go dance now."

"I don't dance," Colton frowned, and bingo, there was my escape.

"Okay, well, I'll see you later then."

I couldn't get away from him fast enough. The thoughts I was having right before ending the kiss…they were trouble. The dangerous kind. My heart was getting confused. This was

Colton, not Kyle. I was in love with Kyle. I'd always been in love with him—but then why was my heart still beating so hard after that kiss with his brother? Ugh, I thought. Don't think about it. What I needed right now was to dance it out.

Without a thought to being embarrassed, I moved to the beat of the Drake song currently blasting through the speakers. I let my hips sway and shook my head side to side, trying to shake it off. So, Colton could kiss. That didn't mean anything. I just had to make sure my heart knew what my mind already did. This was just for the bet. Colton wanted to beat Kyle, and I wanted to complete my list. Period. Keep your dang feelings under control, Sadie Day, and there'd be no problem whatsoever.

I was so caught up in my thoughts I didn't realize someone had come up behind me until he spoke.

"Sadie Elizabeth, what kind of moves are those? I can't tell if it's a weird mating call or you're about to have a seizure."

I felt the guy lean closer, the next words whispered right into my ear.

"And what the hell are you doing in *Shots* when I know your momma wouldn't approve."

Spinning around, I grinned at the speaker.

"Ash Cornelius Stryker," I said, completely dismissing his tone of disapproval and smiling wide. I'd known Ash my entire life, our moms having been best friends forever, so his All-American boy-next-door look didn't fool me. He was sarcastic and cocky and the closest thing I had to a brother, and I was happy as heck to see him. "I haven't seen you in ages, college boy. What are you doing here?"

Ash glared at me, but it just made me want to laugh. Besides, we were both still dancing, so I knew he wasn't really mad.

"I'm here to celebrate a win with my team," Ash said.

"Yours truly scored the game winning goal. But I repeat, why are you here? Does it have anything to do with that douche I saw you kissing earlier?"

Looking back to the booth, I noticed Colton had company. He hadn't moved, but now two girls had joined him at our table. I couldn't see the girls' faces clearly, but even from here, I knew they'd be beautiful. Colton looked perfectly happy with the situation. I winced, feeling the sting of something I'd never felt before yet recognized. Jealousy mixed with more than a dash of disappointment. Should've known, I thought. Garnering attention of the female variety had never been an issue for him. Plus, why shouldn't he go from kissing me to finding his next hookup? It wasn't like we were together. Colton was my coach. Nothing more, nothing less.

Bringing my attention back to Ash, who was still dancing but watching me carefully, I said, voice neutral, "He brought me here, but it's not what you think. We're just friends."

"Friends who kiss?" he frowned. "I don't know if you're old enough to have that kind of friend, Sadie Elizabeth."

"Relax, faux big brother," I said with an eyeroll. "There's nothing going on with me and Colton."

He tilted his head as we danced around each other. "I can hear the disappointment in your voice. If I didn't know better, I'd say you were down about that."

"Nope." I shook my head for emphasis. "He's like you, completely uninterested, and I'm totally okay with that because I'm not either."

"Uninterested, huh? Let's test that theory."

"What do you—"

Before I could finish, Ash had swung us around and pulled me close, like way closer than I'd have allowed anyone else. I scowled up at him. He was lucky I didn't knee him in the junk.

"You're so lucky I don't knee you right now," I hissed.

"Please don't," Ash laughed. "You're like my baby sister. I'm going to have nightmares about this as it is."

"What the heck do you think you're doing?"

"Just testing your boy over there," he said and glanced back. "Oh, and he doesn't look happy. For a guy you say's not interested, he's having a mighty fine reaction."

"Ash, seriously, what the heck?" I said. "What would Snow say about this?"

If I'd thought mentioning his girlfriend's name would deter him, I was mistaken.

"Why don't you ask her?" He lifted his chin, and I spotted his totally awesome/kick-ass girlfriend Snow, the one girl who was his perfect match in every way, sitting at a booth to our right. Snow smiled, nodded our way, and I gave a weak wave in return. "She's the one who told me to come out here and dance with you."

"Ash, I really—"

"Can I cut in?"

Ash released me, and I turned to see Colton standing there, looking like...well, looking like he wanted to punch Ash.

Either oblivious of this or not caring, Ash grinned. "I don't know," he said. "I'm a tough act to follow."

Colton gave him a once over. "If you say so."

"I do," Ash said and thrust out a hand. "I do say so. Don't know if she's told you, but I'm Ash, Sadie's first crush."

Oh my gosh. I couldn't believe he just said that!

"Nah, she never mentioned it," Colton said, gripping his hand. "But I'm Colton, the guy who was her first kiss and her second, so I think I won that round."

Ash had stopped grinning. "You sound a little cocky there."

Instead of backing down, Colton took a step closer, the two

standing nearly chest-to-chest. "Yeah well, I say you're the cocky one."

They stared at each other, and the moment was heated. I wasn't sure what was about to go down, but luckily, Snow was there to save the day.

"Hey, is everything okay?" she said, putting a hand on Ash's biceps, but keeping her eyes on Colton.

"Fine," Ash said, placing a hand over hers but not ending the stare down.

"Great," Colton said back.

"It's cool, just a little too much testosterone," I said, doing my best to draw Colton away. If Snow, a real, honest-to-God ninja, really felt like Ash was in danger? She'd lay Colton out before he could blink. I'd seen her in action before. "They were just introducing themselves."

Two more people joined us which I thought was good. The more people the less aggression, right?

"What's going on over here?"

I recognized the newcomer immediately. The guy was tall with dark brown hair, wearing a jersey like Ash, except his had "KENT" written on the back. You didn't grow up in Chariot not knowing who Becks Kent was. The soccer phenom and current sophomore at UNC had one arm wrapped around his girlfriend, Sally Spitz, who I'd met through Ash. She was wearing a Gryffindor jersey that made me want one of my own—though mine would've been Slytherpuff for sure. I'd taken many tests and had it on good authority that I was a 50/50 split of Slytherin and Hufflepuff.

Ash still didn't take his eyes off Colton. "Hey, Kent. Sadie's friend here just called me cocky."

Becks gave it some thought then said, "Sounds accurate. So Stryker, we gonna keep celebrating our win, or do you two guys want some time alone?"

Sally and I laughed which suddenly broke the tension. Ash backed off with a grin, putting his arm around Snow, who no longer looked ready to take Colton out. Thank goodness. For his part, Colton put a hand on my waist—which made me gasp—and he somehow ended up next to me.

"The only person I want some alone time with is my girl Snow," Ash said. "These two can do whatever they want."

"Yeah man, you go celebrate," Colton said as if he and Ash hadn't been giving each other the death stare a moment ago. "Sadie and I'll stay here."

"Okay, you guys have fun," Snow said, and Ash pointed a finger at us as she led him away. "Just not too much fun," he said. "You hear that, Sadie Elizabeth?"

Becks was shaking his head at his teammate. To his girlfriend, he said, "I still can't believe you're friends with him."

"One" Sally said, "*we* are friends with Ash—even if you refuse to admit it. And two, the Force is strong with him." She smiled as Becks frowned. "Not as strong as it is with you, Baldwin. I've told you before, no one has a Force stronger than yours."

"Baldwin, huh," Becks said, lifting her up as she gasped out a laugh. "Oh, you're going to pay for that one, Sal."

"And I'm sure I'll enjoy it," she said which made me blush for some reason. To Colton and me, she waved, calling out as Becks carried her away, "It was nice seeing you again, Sadie."

"You, too," I said.

And with that, they disappeared into the crowd.

About five seconds later, Colton said, his tone full of disbelief, "Did you actually have a crush on that Ash guy?"

"I did," I said.

"Why?"

"I was young. He was the cutest boy I'd ever seen." I shrugged, turning to face him, never once forgetting his hand was still on my waist. "Our mothers were best friends, even gave birth at the same hospital. It seemed like fate."

"Fate," Colton scoffed. "Only good girl-hopeless romantics believe in stuff like that." I narrowed my eyes as he went on. "And cute? More like cocky as hell."

"Well, at least he can dance," I said, testing out a theory.

Colton scoffed again. "What he was doing just now? You call that dancing?"

I tilted my head. "Unlike some guys, Ash knows how to move."

"Oh really?"

"Yeah," I said. "And you sound a little jealous, Colton."

Colton shook his head, a grin lifting his lips. "I'm not jealous, Sadie. I could dance circles around that guy."

He *was* jealous. And of Ash of all people. The thought made me want to laugh out loud, but I forced my face to remain blank.

"Yeah?" I said, voice thick with sarcasm. "Prove it then."

Colton's eyes flashed as pulled me close. "Fine, I will."

And boy did he.

Throughout the entire next song, Colton's hands never left my body. They started out on my waist—which you might've thought was innocent enough. But it didn't feel that way, not with Colton. Big Tim had been my dance partner forever. I couldn't count the number of times his hands had been in exactly the same place as Colton's were now.

But the way the boy in front of me gripped the curve of my waist...the way his fingers glided up and down my sides...the delicious pressure as his fingers clenched against my hips...it should've been illegal.

I tried not to react, tried to remain indifferent. But the weird thing was our bodies just immediately seemed to sync together. His hips swayed, and mine moved in counterpart. I'd take a step, and Colton was right there with me. Moving with him was as natural as breathing. Though I admit, as he leaned in brushing his cheek against mine, my breath was a bit on the short side.

The feeling of his breath on my neck gave me goosebumps. And still we moved together like a dream.

"How you doing, Sadie?" he said into my ear as our bodies swayed in perfect harmony. "You're breathing a little fast there."

With a swallow, I said, "I thought you said you couldn't dance."

He chuckled, the air hitting my neck as he ducked his head.

When Colton leaned back, it was almost worse because now I could see his eyes, and they bore right into mine, seemingly cool and unaffected. I had no idea what mine revealed, but I hoped it wasn't too much.

"I never said I couldn't dance," he said. "I said I don't. Two completely different things."

"Apparently," I muttered.

It was chemistry.

Pure and simple.

And absolutely terrifying.

Still, despite the fear and all of the mixed emotions, I might've stayed like that in his arms for at least another song (maybe two), but my phone started going off in my pocket. Stepping back, I pulled out my cell and looked at the screen.

"It's my mom," I said, brows furrowed. "I told her I'd text when I got home, and she's checking in to see if I made it alright."

"Well, we better get going then."

My head snapped up, and Colton seemed to be waiting for something, studying my expression.

"Yeah," I said, looking away, trying and failing to fight a blush that shouldn't have been there, one that definitely shouldn't have been brought on by the boy in front of me. "Let's go."

I knew in reality it couldn't have taken longer to get home than it had taken us to get to *Shots*, but the drive seemed to last forever. The uncomfortable silence that had descended ever since we got into the car didn't help. Colton hadn't said a word to me since we left the club. After our totally unexpected yet amazing dance.

I sighed as we finally reached my driveway.

Just as I opened the door and was about to step out of the car, Colton put a hand on my arm, said, "Hey, Sadie."

I looked back, and before I knew it, his lips were on mine.

It wasn't a long kiss by any means or an overly passionate one like our others had been. This kiss was more gentle, warm instead of scorching hot, but my breath caught just the same. When Colton released me and leaned back, his eyes were unreadable. I was sure mine were stunned. *What was that for?* I tried to convey the question with my eyes since my voice was currently incapable of speech.

Colton ran his tongue over his lip ring then said, "Number 16 on your list. Kiss in the car."

I nodded. "Oh yeah, right. Thanks."

I wanted to slap myself as soon as the word was out of my mouth.

Colton just grinned. "You're welcome."

Before I could embarrass myself further, I hopped out of the car and shut the door. I had to put some space between us before I did something else stupid. When I got inside the house, I put my back against the door and tried to calm my breathing.

There is no way you are falling for Colton Bishop, I reminded myself. *You love Kyle, remember? You best friend? The best guy you've ever met? It doesn't matter that he's gay. It doesn't matter that he's unavailable to you. Your heart is true, and you will not waver.*

My phone buzzed in my hand, interrupting my internal mantra.

I looked down and tried to ignore the way my heart jumped at the name on the screen.

Colton Freakin' Bishop: Don't forget to text your mom. Tell her what a great dancer I am ;). See u soon.

I caught myself smiling even before I heard Colton's car drive away—which told me he'd waited for me to get inside before leaving. Which shouldn't have impressed me and definitely didn't mean anything.

"It doesn't mean anything," I said to myself as I texted Mom and walked upstairs to mark a few more items off my list. "Don't think about it anymore because it doesn't mean anything."

If only I could stop replaying that kiss, our dance, the whole night in my mind, I might've believed it.

CHAPTER 15

Needless to say, I got zero sleep.

It was good and bad in a way. Good because my mind was racing, the creative juices flowing, and I got all of my choreography done, completing the dance I planned to submit to *Dancer's Edge*. And it was freaking awesome if I did say so myself. Definitely my best work yet. Bad because…well, I needed two guys, knew exactly who I wanted them to be, but at least one of them was probably—strike that—he was *definitely* going to say hell no.

Shaking my head, I picked up my cell and called the one I knew I could depend on.

Kyle picked up on the first ring.

"Sadie," he said, and I could tell he was smiling. "My long-lost best friend, how are you this fine Sunday morning?"

"Kyle," I sighed. "God, it's good to hear your voice."

"Good to hear yours, too. Is something going on?"

I stiffened. "No. Why do you say that?"

"Well, you sound a little off, and my brother told me—after much prodding—what you guys did last night."

"He did?" I choked.

"Yeah," Kyle said slowly, "he said you guys checked three more things off your list. Colt wouldn't tell me what though… which seemed ominous. You want to tell me what the big secret is?"

"No secret," I said, nearly melting with relief. If Colton hadn't told Kyle, that meant last night wasn't a big deal to him. Our dance, that incredible kiss and the surprise one as I left the car…they meant nothing to him as I'd suspected. I frowned. Why didn't I feel more relieved about that? "It's true. We got three more done. And I kind of needed your help to complete another. It's a big one."

"Oh now, I'm intrigued. Do I smell a Sadie Day project coming on?"

"You do."

Kyle laughed. "Excellent. You know I'm always there for you."

At that, my heart warmed.

"You are so awesome. What's your schedule look like for Monday?" I asked.

"I'm actually busy after school."

"Okay, well, that night I have to work at the studio. What about Tuesday then?"

"Err, kind of busy then, too."

"How about Wednesday?"

"Well…"

"Kyle," I groaned.

"I know, I know," he said. "Sadie, I'm sorry, okay?"

"Does this have anything to do with that guy?"

"It might."

"It seems like you and he are spending a lot of time together," I said, trying not to sound disappointed. I had really hoped we could start the dance this week. "You going to tell me who he is already? I'm starting to feel a little left out."

"Are you going to tell me what you and Colton were doing last night?" he said back.

Looking to my right, I spotted my list and could just make

out the latest items I'd marked off.

5) Stay up and watch the sun rise.

11) Go dancing at a club.

16) Kiss in the car.

17) Kiss in public.

Number five had been an unintended side effect of my sleepless night but...considering two of those items involved kissing and his twin, there was no way I wanted to talk about them with Kyle.

"Yeah, I thought so," he muttered after I'd been silent too long.

"What?" I said. "At least, you've seen my list. I don't even know who this unnamed guy is that you're crushing so hard on."

"I know," Kyle said. "We've just been spending a lot of time together—kind of like you and my brother."

I frowned at his tone. "What's that supposed to mean? You were the one who pushed for Colton to be my coach in the first place. I didn't even want to work with him, remember? Completing this list is important to me, Kyle."

A moment passed...then another....and another.

Kyle sighed then said, "Sadie, just tell me when you want to meet, and I'll make time to be there."

"Don't bother," I said, feeling tears well up in my eyes. "I've got other things to cross off my list anyway. Thanks for your half-assed offer to help though."

"Sadie, wait—did you just say ass?"

I hung up.

So much for being able to depend on my best friend.

Pulling up Colton's name on my phone, I fired off a text.

Me: Want to meet up tomorrow? The forecast says it looks like rain.

His response was immediate.

Colton Freakin' Bishop: Can't wait to kiss me again, huh? When and where?

I rolled my eyes at that but responded anyway.

Me: My house, after school.

Colton Freakin' Bishop: No, your house during last period. #19

I read the text again, not that I really needed to. I knew what he meant. Nineteen on my list was "Skip school," and I had P.E. that period, the same as Kyle and Colton. But I was hesitant about actually skipping a class.

Me: I'm not sure…

Colton Freakin' Bishop: Not asking. Your list is 1st priority. Skip P.E. That's an order from the Greatest Coach Of All Time.

I grinned as I typed out a reply.

Me: Whatever you say, Coach.

My hands were unsteady as I unlocked the door to let us into the house. Colton had followed me home from school. I'd been sure someone was going to stop us before we left the building—a teacher, staff member, security. I'd nearly had a panic attack just walking out the school's front doors. But we didn't run into anyone.

No alarms went off when we got into our cars and left the parking lot.

Mom had gone in early to teach a private lesson, so no one was home.

That meant it was just me and Colton Bishop, who I was sure had skipped school tons of times, some of them quite possibly to go make out with girls. Unlike me, he didn't look perturbed at all. About the skipping or the kissing. He was cool as a freaking cucumber as we walked into the backyard, the grey clouds overhead roiling, ready to open up at any moment.

"So, you skipped school," Colton said, shoving his hands into his pockets. "You're officially a rulebreaker, Sadie. How's it feel?"

I looked up at the darkening sky. "Honestly? It feels like Mother Nature is preparing to strike me down for leaving early."

He chuckled then said, "What's the deal with that anyway? The rain? I get that you're kiss-obsessed or something. But why rain?"

"It's romantic." I shrugged as I sat in one of the lawn chairs we had outside. Colton took the chair opposite me. "You know Betty?"

He nodded. "She's a hard one to forget."

"Betty would absolutely love hearing you say that," I smiled. "Well, she and I have a thing for movies. One day we made a list of our top 10 favorite movie kisses—"

"You and your lists," he said.

"—and it was awesome. Betty has great tastes. But I mean, seriously, do you know how many of the best kiss scenes happen in the rain?"

Colton sat back, crossed his arms and said, "Enlighten me."

So, I did.

"Of course, the best and most memorable cinematic rain kiss has to be from *The Notebook*." I sighed. "Noah and Allie finally coming together after years apart? Her thinking he moved on and forgot about her, him thinking she ignored the 365 love letters he sent her from the war? All that pent-up passion and desire…"

I looked to Colton—which was a mistake. He wore a grin that made me realize just how silly I must've sounded, rhapsodizing over a kiss in the rain, asking him here to kiss *me* in the rain. Ugh.

"Anyway, it's a great scene," I said quietly, blushing like mad.

"Sounds like it," he said. "Stupid movie, though. They both die in the end. Are there any more?"

"Well...there's that kiss from *Spider-Man* where he was upside down."

Colton shook his head. "Too complicated. I heard water got in his nose, and the guy could hardly breathe."

"I heard that, too." I laughed. "Who wants to die just for a kiss right?"

"It depends on the kiss, I guess," he said.

My jaw dropped. Who was this guy and what had he done with the real Colton Bishop? Seeming amused by my look of wonder, Colton stood and held out a hand.

"Looks like it's about to start coming down," he said—just as lightning struck and a steady rain started to fall. "We better get ready."

"Okay," I mumbled, letting him pull me to my feet.

"You're not going to freak out again. Right?"

"I didn't—" At Colton's look, I stopped, took a deep breath, decided to start again. *This* was the Colton I knew. He wasn't romantic, just freaking annoying. "No, Colton, I won't. I thought about it and decided there's nothing to get freaked out over."

His eyes narrowed. "Care to explain that last bit?"

"Well," I said, "it's true. I enjoy kissing you. I can't deny that—but maybe that's just because I haven't kissed anyone else. Maybe, I just really enjoy the act of kissing."

"You—" Colton tried to interrupt, but I kept going.

"I mean, I figure it's either that or maybe it's how you look so much like Kyle."

The glare he gave me then would've melted the face off a

lesser person.

"Come on, Colton. It's no secret—at least not to you," I said, warming to the topic. I really had thought a lot about this, and there was only one explanation that made the most sense. "We've never gotten along, and I'm in love with Kyle. I have been forever. You look just like him, being his twin and all. So, because of that, of course I would enjoy kissing you."

Colton stepped closer, and my mouth shut instantly. The look in his eyes, the tension in his body said he was done listening. His voice when he spoke was almost too low to hear over the rain now pouring down on us.

"Are you trying to tell me," he said, "that when we kiss... you're thinking of my brother?"

I blinked. "More like your face reminds me of him, and that's what makes it enjoyable. But yeah, in a roundabout way, I guess you could say that."

Colton sounded like he was gritting his teeth. "Good to know."

"Listen, I didn't mean any offense," I said.

"Oh no, why would I be offended?" he said, but it wasn't really a question. "Like you said, Sadie, we've never gotten along. We can't go two seconds without arguing. You annoy the hell out of me."

I sighed with relief. "Exactly, I—"

"And you're not my type," he added. "An uptight, prissy librarian look-a-like, a little miss perfect good girl who's afraid to take risks."

"Hey!"

"I'd agree completely with your assessment." Colton wrapped an arm around my waist and pulled me closer. "Except for one thing."

"Oh?" I swallowed. By this point, both of us were soaked

through from the rain, but strangely, I wasn't cold at all. My skin burned where he ran a hand along my cheek, his thumb sliding against my bottom lip. "And that would be…?"

Colton put his lips near my ear. "You're not in love with my brother."

He backed away an inch to meet my eyes. "If you were, there's no way you'd kiss me like you do."

With no retort to that, I said, breathlessly, "You know, this reminds me of another movie, an almost-kiss that happened in the rain."

"What's an almost-kiss?" Colton murmured.

"In *Pride and Prejudice*—the theatrical version with Keira Knightley and Matthew McFadden?—the rain is falling, Mr. Darcy's just told Elizabeth how much he loves her despite his will, and she's rejected him, but then they have this almost-kiss," I explained. "They're so mad at each other, so overwhelmed by their feelings, that they almost kiss…but stop right at the last second."

Colton's gaze lifted from my lips to meet my eyes.

"It's about control. About wanting," I said, swallowing hard, "but then forcing yourself to resist."

"Where's the fun in that?" Colton said and took my mouth in a kiss that left no doubt about who I was kissing and exactly what he thought about almost-kisses.

I heard a door slam, and then a voice thundered across the lawn.

"What the *hell* is going on here?"

Colton and I sprung apart. And there was Kyle standing on my back porch…right next to Zayne Humphries of all people. I wouldn't have even noticed the other guy, but he made himself known by saying, "Damn, Sister Sadie. I never knew nuns could kiss like that."

"Well?" Kyle said.

He was standing at the foot of the couch in my living room, looking between Colton and me like he wasn't sure who he was more disappointed with. Zayne stood beside him, looking completely out of place and totally amused—which made him the only person in the room who was enjoying himself.

"Somebody better tell me what that was back there," Kyle added. "My mind has gone through all the possibilities, and I don't like any of them."

"It's not a big deal." I shrugged, uncomfortable and red to the tips of my ears. "Colton was just helping me, being a good coach."

"Yeah," Colton said slowly, studying my face, then turned to his brother. "It was all just part of the bet. What else could it be?"

Something inside me tightened at his words, my heart deflating, but I tried to ignore it.

Zayne laughed. "Well, it looked like you two were trying to eat each other's faces off. Not that anyone asked me."

I groaned at the same time Colton shot him a scathing look.

"You're right, Humphries. No one did ask you," Colton said. "Why are you here anyway?"

Kyle held up a hand. "Can we try to stay focused, please? I just caught my best friend and my twin brother kissing in the rain like something out of *The* freaking *Notebook*—"

"Told you it was the best," I mumbled to Colton.

"—There are some things you just can't un-see," Kyle went on. "My eyes cannot simply wash the sight away. Colt, that's my best friend. How could you even think of taking advantage of her like this? And Sadie, what the hell? I thought you weren't going to be one of those girls."

We were all silent a moment, and I didn't think I could sink any farther into the couch, but at Zayne's next words, I did.

"I thought it was hot," Zayne said.

"Seriously? You did not just say that," Kyle said.

"What? He looks like a punked-up version of you," he said. "How am I supposed to be immune to that?"

"Seriously?" Kyle said again.

"Ah, Kyle, no need to be jealous." Zayne smiled, nudging my best friend's shoulder. "You know I prefer the preppy version."

I'd had enough. "For real, Zayne. Why are you in my house? For that matter, why are you and Kyle here together?" Eyes shifting to Kyle, whose cheeks were suspiciously pink, I frowned. "I thought you said you had something after school."

Kyle looked away, and that was when it hit me. They were here. *Together*. And Kyle had blown me off so he could spend time with the guy he was crushing on. Good Lord, did that mean…?

"Oh," I said my gaze flitting from one boy to the other. "But…I thought you guys hated each other."

"Hate's a strong word," Kyle muttered.

"Yeah," Zayne said, eyes roaming over Kyle. "All the insults, the teasing, that was more like foreplay."

"Oh," I said again, not knowing who to look at. "So, Zayne is the guy?"

"Yep," Kyle said. For his part, my best friend's gaze had settled on Colton, waiting for his brother's reaction. "Zayne is the guy. I've actually liked him for a long time. I was shocked to find out the feeling was mutual, but after working together on that project, we just kind of hit it off."

"Wow, I never would've guessed." Looking to Zayne, I said,

"So, you're gay, too?"

"Oh honey," Zayne said, "aren't you sweet with that this or that mentality. I appreciate and welcome all types. No, I'm not gay. I'm Bi."

To say I was stunned would've been an understatement. I could only imagine what Colton was feeling. My eyes went to him, and his face was unreadable. He didn't look angry or upset or even surprised really. But I knew this was a big moment for him and especially for Kyle.

Colton stood up, walked over to stand in front of the two guys, while I held my breath. Placing a hand on Kyle's shoulder, he said, "About time. I was wondering when you were finally going to tell me."

"Finally?" Kyle said, sounding surprised and a little choked. "You mean, you knew? All this time?"

"Of course, I knew," Colton said. "You're my twin."

"And…you don't care? That I'm gay?"

"Kyle," Colton sighed and pulled his brother in for a hug. "What kind of dumbass question is that? I love you. I accept you. I would love and accept you no matter what."

Kyle hugged him back, and I felt tears well-up in my eyes.

"Even if the guy you like is a complete ass," Colton added, making Kyle laugh.

As they broke their embrace, Colton turned to look at Zayne.

"And you," he said. "Gay, straight or bi, if you hurt my brother, I'll make you regret it every day of your life. Understand?"

Zayne lifted his hands up. "Hey, stand down big brother. I'm not planning to hurt anybody, so no need to get all hostile. Though it was kind of hot."

We all groaned, and that was the exact moment Mom chose

to come home.

"Hey," she said, walking into the living room. "I didn't know you were going to have company, Sadie. Want me to go back out and pick you guys up some food?"

"No but thanks, Mom," I said. "I actually needed to talk to Kyle and Colton about something."

Zayne rubbed his hands together. "And I'll take that as my cue to leave. Sadie, Colton, it's been fun. See you later, Kyle."

"Yeah," Kyle said, smiling, "you will."

Zayne waved to my mother as he left, and afterward, I hustled the boys up to my room. Mom might've had a problem with me having Zayne in my room, but since the twins had been coming over for years, she thought nothing of it. Though, I realized after shutting the three of us in, it was the first time in a while that Colton had been here. In my bedroom. The way he was looking around, eyes never missing a thing, made me nervous. Kyle, on the other hand, grabbed Mr. Teddy Wiggles and plopped down onto my bed, looking right at home.

"So, what's the deal with this kissing thing?" he said. "You didn't think you guys were going to get off that easy. Did you?"

I shrugged, took a seat at my desk. "What more is there to say? Colton's been helping me with my list. You've known this all along."

"Yeah," Colton said, still studying my room. Holy smokes. He was now examining my kissing wall (the one I'd added with pictures of kisses from my favorite movies and tv series), and I thought... yeah no, I knew...I wanted to die. Gah, why did he have to see that? "This shouldn't come as some big shock. I told you we've been checking things off left and right, Kyle. There's no way you're winning this bet."

"Oh yeah? Then let me see the list," Kyle said.

"No can do," Colton said. "That would be sharing key intel

with the enemy."

"Ouch. The enemy, really?"

Colton threw a look over his shoulder, cocked an eyebrow. "If the Gucci belt fits, brother."

"At least tell me it was just the one kiss," Kyle laughed as if the thought of more was ludicrous. "I know there were like 5 on Sadie's list. But there's no way, right? You don't even like each other. Imagining you two like that…it's just wrong."

Colton was silent, had finally moved on from the kissing pics—and was now staring at my memo board filled with rejection letters. Perfect. Not only was I crazypants about kissing, but I was also a pathetic reject. Ah, who was I kidding? My girl cave was being invaded by a guy who'd basically said the only reason he would ever kiss me would be to win a bet. Pathetic didn't even begin to cover it.

"Guys?" Kyle said again. "Please tell me that was the only time?"

Colton glanced at me. "You want to take this one, Sadie?"

"Well…" I trailed off, unable to hold his stare while I said this next part, wringing my hands. "There may have been a few others."

"Ugh," Kyle said, "a few? Not even like one or two more, but a few? Sadie, are you insane? Why are you suddenly kissing my brother all the time?"

"It hasn't been all the time," I mumbled.

"Oh God, are you guys together now or something?"

Colton laughed lowly, finally turning to face us, propping his back up against the wall.

"Like you said Kyle, we don't even like each other," he said, but his eyes were on me. "It's not like Sadie wanted to kiss me. She just didn't want to do it with a stranger."

Kyle looked to me for confirmation. "Is that true?"

"Yeah," I said, though something about it felt wrong. The last part about not wanting to kiss a stranger was true, but…ever since that mind-blowing first kiss in the library, I hadn't even considered doing it with anyone else besides Colton.

"And it's not like she's got a crush on me or anything," Colton went on, a gleam in his eye. "She's in love with someone else. Isn't that right, Sadie?"

"Really?" Kyle smiled. "How come I've never heard anything about this? Do I know him?"

"Oh yeah, we both do," Colton said. His words a clear taunt, but I lifted my chin. "He's a great guy, kind of dense, though."

Through gritted teeth, I said, "He's not dense. I'm just really good at hiding my feelings."

"So, you see," Colton said, ignoring my words, "she doesn't actually want to kiss me per se. It was a matter of convenience." I could barely contain my wince. "Speaking of which, the only kiss left is number 18, the one in her bedroom. I guess we could get that crossed off now—though I know she'd love it if I was someone else. What do you say, Sadie?"

"I'll do it," Kyle said suddenly.

I wasn't sure who was more surprised, me, Colton or Kyle.

"What was that?" Colton asked.

"I said I'll do it." Kyle stood and pulled me to my feet. "It's obvious how much you guys despise each other. And I would hate to have to watch two of the people I love most in the world do something they don't want to do. Plus, you said Sadie didn't want to kiss a stranger. I'd be happy to help."

I shook my head, stunned. "But…what would Zayne say?"

"Knowing him, he'd probably say, 'That's hot' then ask to watch," Kyle laughed. "So, what do you think?"

I didn't know what to think. I was currently incapable of that particular brain function.

Not knowing why, I looked to Colton to get his opinion on the matter.

"Colton?" I asked. "What do you think?"

"I think you should do it," he said, his ocean blue eyes going from me to his brother and back again. "You should. It'll be one more thing we can check off the list."

I blinked, trying to figure out why his words made my chest tighten.

"Okay," I said quietly.

"Okay," Kyle said and took a step closer, placing his hands on my waist. "Ready?"

I nodded, closing my eyes as Kyle leaned down, trying to ignore how wrong it all felt. But why did it feel so wrong? I thought. Hadn't I been in love with Kyle forever? Wasn't this what I'd always dreamed about, wanted, hoped for? As my best friend's lips pressed sweetly against my own, moved gently with mine, it was warm and nice and…not at all what I'd come to expect from a kiss. Why wasn't my heart exploding? Why weren't my lips begging his for more? Why wasn't I going off like a shooting star like I did with…?

The next thing I knew it was over. Kyle was standing back up, smiling down at me while I was completely discombobulated.

"Wow," Kyle said, "Sadie, you look completely out of it. I should've warned you ahead of time. I've been told I'm a great kisser."

I couldn't respond. He was right. I was out of it, but it definitely wasn't because Kyle was a great kisser. I mean, he could've been; maybe he was, but I wouldn't know because the entire time I'd been kissing him, I'd been comparing it to the one kiss I actually wanted.

And surprisingly, it wasn't from the boy I'd thought I was in love with since grade school.

When I snuck a glance, Colton was staring at me.

Not in a smug way, not even like he wanted to say, "I told you so"—which at this moment, he totally could. Colton had been right. I wasn't in love with Kyle. My heart was pointing me in a completely different direction, making Colton's quiet stare so much more unnerving.

But he was just staring at me, studying me, probably seeing much more than I wanted him to. Before I could get lost in those ocean blue eyes, before I had to face my true feelings that were becoming increasingly/embarrassingly obvious, I blurted out a request that I knew would shift everyone's focus.

"I need you both to be in a dance I'm choreographing, and I won't take no for an answer."

CHAPTER 16

Getting Kyle to say "yes" had been a piece of cake.

Colton? Not so much.

"But you're my coach," I said, walking beside him—chasing him really—as we moved through the halls between classes. "I need you. Don't you want to win the bet?"

"Yes, I want to win," Colton said, trudging along like I wasn't struggling to keep up. At six-foot-two, his legs were so much longer than my own. "No, I won't dance with you."

"Well, why not?" I asked.

"Because I won't."

Nice. The typical douchebag non-answer.

"But—"

Lorra Shoemaker, one of Colton's cooler exes, stepped in front of us then and halted our progress. Thank goodness. Chances were good that my legs would've given out if we'd kept up the pace much longer.

"Hey Sadie," she said, her bright brown eyes shining almost as much as her smooth black hair. "How's it going?"

"Hey, fine," I said back. "Oh, and congrats on that softball win last week. You girls were killing it out there."

"Thanks, we try," Lorra shrugged, which was something I loved about her. She was always so humble even though her pitching was what led our team to most of their wins. "Hey Colton," she said, shifting her gaze to him. "So, you and Sadie are hanging out now? That's cool."

"Define 'hanging out,'" he said. "And also, Sadie, you're welcome. I'm guessing that's the first time anyone's mentioned your name and 'cool' in the same sentence."

I scowled. Oh, so he had jokes now did he? Awesome, fantastic. But I had to hold my temper in check because I wanted something from him. Namely for him to be one part of the devastatingly fabulous tango trio I'd concocted in my head, so I tried to be nice.

"Ah thanks, Colton." I smiled. "Your jokes are almost as hilarious as your face."

Colton did something really interesting then. His entire face morphed into something between a grimace and a smirk. He girked…smimaced? Anyway, it was an odd expression, and I found myself biting my lip not to laugh.

"You think his face is funny?" Lorra didn't seem to get the joke. "What's so funny about it?"

This had been one of her downfalls, I remembered then with a sigh. She'd never been good at sarcasm. It was one of the reasons Colton had broken up with her if I wasn't mistaken.

"Sadie was just kidding," Colton said. "Being sarcastic."

"Was I though?" I asked in just as innocent a tone. By the confused look on her face, that one sailed right over Lorra's head as well. "Anyway, yeah, Colton's been helping me out with a few things. I'm currently trying to convince him to do a dance with me. But he's kind of being a jerk and refusing to cooperate."

Lorra laughed/wheezed. "Dance? Colton?" she said then laughed again. "I can't even picture it. When we were together, he flat-out refused to dance with me even when I begged him. And that was at my sister's wedding!"

Hmm, I thought. That was interesting if only because I'd gotten him to dance once. At the club—the thought of which still made my skin tingle. I pushed those thoughts to the back of my mind and vowed that I would do it again. Colton would be a part of this trio. I just had to find the right way to convince him.

"I can see why you'd want to break up," I said to which Lorra's mouth dropped and Colton frowned. "Girls love a guy who can dance, one who's willing to stand up with them when it matters."

"Yeah, that's true." Lorra shook her head. "But Sadie, you know, Colton broke up with me, right? If he was single now, I'd probably want him again. No offense. I mean, I know you two are together now. Anyway, I'll see you guys later."

She walked away as the warning bell rang, and I was stunned by her admission—and her assumption—while Colton just looked smug.

"A guilt trip, Sadie? That's the best you've got?" Colton tsked. "I'm disappointed."

"Well, what will work? I've already tried groveling and guilt."

"The groveling was amusing," he said, "but I think you can do better."

Making my eyes soft, voice pleading, I said, "Please, Colton? Please say you'll dance with me?"

"Nice." Colton nodded. "But the answer's still no."

Crossing my arms, I frowned. "How about the truth?"

Colton held out his hand in a go-ahead gesture.

"You said so yourself," I began, laying out my case, "I need something that'll stand out, something hot. And what's hotter than two guys fighting over the same girl? Not just two guys but twins? And not only twins but gorgeous ones dancing a tango."

"Gorgeous?" Colton shook his head. "And I thought flattery was beneath you."

"Nothing is beneath me at this point." I held up my hands.

"Seriously Colton, this is the biggest item on my list, and you and Kyle are my ace in the hole. This is my shot, my chance to finally be accepted to *Dancer's Edge*, not to mention it's essential to you winning the bet."

"You'll just find someone else," he said dismissively. "The idea will still work without me."

"No," I said. "Don't you understand? I need you."

He was silent a moment just looking at me as the final bell rang—and we ignored it, continued to stand right there in the middle of the hall. I was skipping again, and I didn't even have it in me to care. This was that important.

Colton sneezed suddenly (twice) and then said, "You know, Sadie, I've been feeling off lately. I've also got work at the garage that runs late. Seriously, you'll find someone else."

I nodded, accepting defeat. Colton wasn't going to help, and I would never be on *Dancer's Edge*. Thinking again of that night, the way we'd danced together, how natural it had been, all the amazing chemistry, I decided to go out on a limb and try one final thing. It was a longshot, but hey. Colton had already said no about a thousand different ways. What did I have to lose?

"You know, I think you're right," I said, pretending to think it over. "I could probably get another guy. It would have to be someone who can dance. Maybe Tim—but no, he won't have time since he's back in college."

Colton sighed. "See? I told you—"

"Ash would probably do it, though," I said, watching Colton's back stiffen at the name.

"You mean that cocky guy from the club? The one who had his hands all over you?"

"Yeah," I said. "That's actually a great idea. You know, Ash is so good-looking—"

Colton grunted.

"—and I know he would do it in a heartbeat if I asked him."

I knew no such thing.

"And we moved so well together."

Colton cleared his throat. "You know, I don't think that's a good idea."

"Oh?" I asked. "Why not?"

"Like you said, this is about your list, part of the bet. It's a me and you thing, Sadie." My heart thrilled at his words—the fact that Colton and I even had a thing—but I tamped down the emotion. "And that Ash guy? The way he danced with you right in front of his girl? I don't trust him." Colton shook his head, not realizing it had all been Snow's idea in the first place. But I played along, seeing as he was starting to come around. "Plus, what kind of coach would I be if I abandoned you with only a few more items to go?"

I didn't want to come off too eager, pretended to study my nails. "Well, I wouldn't want to put you out. I mean, like I said, Ash would be happy to—"

"No," Colton said. "I'm in."

"You're in?"

"Yeah."

"As in, you'll dance with me?"

"God, what do you need it in blood or something?" He threw his head back. "I said yes, I'm in. No need to call anybody else. Dammit Sadie, I'll dance with you. I'm your guy."

Again, my foolish heart skipped a beat, hearing a hidden meaning behind his words that wasn't there. I shoved the emotion aside, smiling so big it hurt.

"That's all I wanted to hear."

Later that night, I'd reserved the studio, which wasn't hard, of course, since my parents owned it. Kyle was staring at me in amazement while I checked my watch for what felt like the hundredth time. It was supposed to be our first practice—and Colton was already 10 minutes late.

"But how did you convince him?" Kyle asked. "Colton never dances. Ever. He hates it with a passion. Kind of like I hate Physics, man buns, and how Sherlock never ended up with John."

"It should've been Molly Hooper, and you know it. Sholly forever." I shrugged. "And I just asked, and he said okay."

"That's it?"

"I might've annoyed him into it. You know I can be really stubborn."

Kyle shook his head. "I know my brother, Sadie. He's twice as stubborn as you. Colt never does anything without a reason, and I still don't understand why he'd do something he hates so much. Unless..."

"Unless what?" I said, biting my lip. What if Colton didn't show? What would I do then? I had no backup plan, and I was already so committed to this idea. The choreography wouldn't work without Colton. It was him or no one.

"Unless he had a stronger reason to do it," Kyle said.

I nodded. "Yeah, winning the bet. Beating you and two-hundred dollars seem like pretty nice incentives."

"I wasn't talking about—" My best friend took my hand, his eyes meeting mine so like Colton's, but Kyle's touch, as always, was warm and completely friendly. "No bet would make my brother do this. He'd just drop out before it was set in stone. Or as is the case here, he would insist on getting someone else to do the dance. Hell, anyone else."

"I used my powers of persuasion."

"I didn't know you had those," he said, looking impressed.

"Me neither." I grinned. "But it felt kind of good, being bad."

Kyle shook his head in wonder. "Who are you, and where has my clueless best friend Sadie gone?"

I laughed, pushing his shoulder. "I'm still me, Kyle."

"Yeah," he said, "you are. And I'm honestly a little worried. Sadie…tell the truth. Are you falling for my brother?"

I nearly choked on my tongue, the question was such a surprise. It was like someone throwing ice water in your face, and then expecting you to function like a normal human being. Completely impossible.

"I-I…"

"Yeah?" Kyle prompted.

"I don't dislike him as much as I used to think," I said, choosing my words oh-so-carefully. "He's not bad at all really. We've been spending a lot of time together, and…well…"

"And?"

"I think we're becoming…friends," I finished lamely.

Kyle tilted his head, his face a question. "Hmm. My brother doesn't really have girls who are friends. He has exes, and then he has hookups who want to be girlfriends—who usually end up being his exes. That's about it. I'm just worried about you…and him."

"Kyle, it's fine, okay?" I said, feeling my stomach hollow but knowing this was the right thing to say—even if I wished it wasn't true. "Your brother would never like me like that. He said so himself. I'm not his type."

"Yeah, but all the kissing and—"

I forced a laugh though my throat was dry. "Oh that? Those were just for my list, for Colton to win the bet. You know that."

Kyle stared at me, and I knew, through our best friend bond, that he could tell I was lying. His next question proved as much.

"Okay, that's how you think he feels, but what about you. How do you feel? Sadie, I know you. You can't just kiss someone without getting attached."

He'd always been way too perceptive.

"It would be really stupid of me to fall for Colton Bishop," I said finally.

After a beat, Kyle laughed. "And you've never been stupid. Yeah, I guess you're right. You two are so completely different."

"We are different," I said. "It would never work with us. Plus, I don't think I could handle being just another one of Colton's exes."

A laugh sounded from the hallway, leading from the entrance into the studio, and suddenly Colton was there. I hadn't even heard the door open.

"My exes all love me," he said, shrugging out of his work shirt for the garage. It was dirty with oil stains and so were his hands. That left him in a white tee that also had a few stains—but there was nothing he could do about those. Colton's eyes moved to his brother for a moment. They exchanged a look that I couldn't read, and when Colton's eyes came back to me, there was something cold, impassive, like a wall had gone up. "You'd be lucky to be one of them."

My eyes narrowed, but worse, my heart clenched at his harsh words.

"Are we dancing or what?"

I stood and instead of answering said, "Nice of you to show up."

Colton cleared his throat. "I had work. I told you that already."

"You could've at least washed your hands," Kyle said, eyeing the oil stains.

"I did," Colton said. "Three times. Trust me, they're clean."

"Whatever you say," Kyle muttered.

"Hey man, I don't even want to be here, so if you're going to give me grief—"

"No," I said, holding my hands up between them. Our first practice wasn't going well at all. Time to salvage this. "No, it's fine. We're all here now. It's all good. We've got less than two weeks until the video deadline, so let's get started."

Colton coughed, shrugged then dropped into the seat next to Kyle. Twins or not, seeing them side-by-side like this really made their differences undeniable. Colton sat slouched, his arms stretched across the top of the sofa, looking unimpressed, as if he hadn't a care in the world. Kyle, on the other hand, was leaning forward, eyes bright and eager to go.

"So, what's the plan, Sadie?" Kyle asked.

Taking a deep breath, I said, "Well, I feel like the only way I even have a shot at getting picked for *Dancer's Edge* is to create something so strong, so edgy, so passionate they can't deny it. And it has to be unique. That's where you two come in."

Colton sniffed, but Kyle nodded for me to continue.

"I figure there's no way they can overlook the twin aspect," I said, gesturing between the two of them.

"And the gorgeous aspect," Colton inserted, turning to Kyle while my cheeks flamed. "She thinks we're gorgeous. Just thought you should know."

"Who doesn't?" Kyle said.

"Exactly," Colton said with a grin as he and Kyle bumped fists.

"But that's only the start," I said quickly. Ugh, they were so full of themselves—and undeniably gorgeous, I thought, cheeks heating again as their attention came back to me. "The main thing is the tug of war between two opposites, light and dark, two men vying over the same woman, not knowing that she is the one in control, the one with all the power."

"Sounds awesome," Kyle said.

"Yeah, the song is amazing, and the dance I choreographed relies on passion and emotion. We'll have to get the feeling just right, but if we do, there's no way they can say no."

Kyle was smiling and so was I...right up until Colton decided to open his big mouth.

"And what happens if they do?" he said.

"What?" I asked, my face falling.

He looked at me then. "What happens if they say no again? Let's be honest, Sadie. You don't have the best track record with these people."

"Colt, you are such an ass," Kyle sighed.

"No, I'm a realist," he said back. "I just want to know why you're putting all your faith in them instead of yourself." My brow scrunched as he pulled something out of his pocket. His copy of my list, I realized. From it, he read aloud, "Number 3 on Sadie's Naughty List, and I quote, 'Be featured on *Dancer's Edge*—or get a million views LOL whichever comes first.'"

With that, he lowered the paper, his gaze meeting mine.

"I figure we should try for the million views."

I scoffed, couldn't help it, but Colton didn't seem to hear.

"All you have to do is post a video online and go viral," he said. "Easy, right?"

Rolling my eyes, I said, "Oh yeah, super easy. Great idea, Colton. Tell me the part about you being a realist again."

"Do I detect a hint of sarcasm?"

"More than a hint," I said. "Do you know how difficult it is to make a video go viral?"

"It can't be that hard."

I stared at him. Was he really that oblivious? "I've posted

exactly five videos of my dances. Do you know how many followers I have?"

Colton shrugged. "I don't know. 50?"

"Try four," I said as he flinched. "Do you know how many views those videos have gotten?"

"Under a thousand," he said.

"Um, under one hundred—" I waited a beat then added "—combined. Kyle back me up."

Kyle was shaking his head. "She's not lying, Colt. I'm one of the four followers."

"Yes, and the others are my mom, dad, and Betty," I said. "They've always been super supportive."

Colton refolded the paper, put it back in his pocket, then said, "Well, it's a start. And I bet if you tagged the videos, used the metadata or whatever-you-call-it, and let more people know about it, they would watch, and their friends would watch, and it would all take off from there."

I shook my head, arms crossed. "You're crazy."

"It's worth a shot, right?" he said and stood up. "So, which am I? The light or the dark?"

Kyle followed his lead and got to his feet while I gulped. So...we were really doing this. Wonderful.

"You're dark, and Kyle's light," I said and despite my nervousness, I laughed. "Seemed to fit your personalities pretty well."

"Okay, Colt, broody, no fun, dark," Kyle said while his brother rolled his eyes. "Me, awesome, the best, and light. Got it. What next?"

"Well, next you have to get the look down."

"Huh?"

Both guys tilted their head exactly the same way at the same time, and it was so stinking cute, I barely held in a sigh. Getting it back together, I tried to put my thoughts into words.

"The dynamics between us is all about UST," I said, then seeing their blank expressions, I tried again. "You know, unresolved sexual tension? Anyway, the way you look at me needs to convey wanting and aggression. It is a tango after all. And maybe even a hint of frustration."

I finished with a quick intake of breath as Colton took a step closer, his eyes giving me everything I'd just asked for and more. I felt his stare down to my toes.

"That won't be a problem," he said.

"Wanting, aggression, frustration," Kyle repeated. "Got it. What else?"

Rolling my shoulders back, I said, "Then we need to work on the actual choreography and telling the story, of course. A lot of it has to do with proximity. We need to get comfortable being close to each other."

Without me giving them direction, Colton erased the distance between us, stopping inches away from my face, and Kyle moved around to my back.

"This close enough?" Colton murmured, still giving me that look.

"Mmhmm," I breathed. "Now, Kyle put your right hand on my waist."

"Like this?" Kyle asked.

"Yes, and Colton, put your left hand on the other side." I'd had no reaction to Kyle's touch, but I nearly jolted out of my skin as Colton's palm brushed against the curve of my waist. "And I'll take your other hand with my left, put my right hand on your shoulder. Kyle, you put your left hand on my shoulder. And this is—" I cleared my suddenly dry throat "—our starting position. How do you guys feel?"

"Awesome," Kyle said.

Colton's fingers pressed into my side. "It's not awful," he said. "What happens now?"

And so it went.

Our first practice went well despite the rough start. Better than well. It was great actually. Besides Colton's gruff complaints now and again, Kyle's struggle to keep a straight face when he had to give me "the look," and me almost having an asthma attack every time Colton touched me, everything went much better than expected. We spent about three hours learning the first minute of the piece, but the guys were getting it. With their natural rhythm, they caught on quicker than I could've hoped. We'd need a few more practices, but I left feeling good.

Before I went to bed, I checked *Dancer's Edge* to see if they'd added any new videos (they hadn't) then went to check my YouTube Channel. I wasn't expecting anything—it was done completely out of habit—but I noticed something right away.

I had a new follower.

After months and months of being stuck at four, my follower count now read five.

Eyes widening, I checked my notifications and was surprised to see that "Colton247" was now following my videos. It shouldn't have made me smile the way that it did. It definitely shouldn't have had any effect on my chest which felt all fluttery and warm. The conversation I'd had with Kyle before Colton joined us in the studio replayed in my mind, and recalling my words from earlier, I shook my head.

It would be really stupid of me to fall for Colton Bishop.

Yeah, I thought, I would be pretty stupid to fall for Colton Bishop. Unfortunately, my head and heart were not on the same page where he was concerned.

And my heart was a fool.

CHAPTER 17

"How's the life makeover going, Sadie?"

Betty was sitting across from me at one of the many tables here at Shady Grove. We were having our five o'clock tea. Cora was there, too, sipping her Earl Grey. So much had happened that I didn't really know where to start, but I gave it a shot anyway.

"It's going," I said. "There are only four more items left to do, but they won't be easy."

Cora took another sip of tea then said, "Only four? Well, that's just wonderful. And your coach? How's he doing?"

"Yes, dear sweet Colton," Betty smiled. "How is our boy?"

"He's good," I said, trying not to blush. I didn't think Colton would appreciate being called "dear" or "sweet" since he was neither. But Colton could fight his own battles, as he'd proven once again today. "He got into another fight at school, punched a boy right in the face, nearly knocked his teeth out. Though the guy deserved it," I muttered.

"Well now," Betty said, leaning forward, "I must hear more. What was this fight about?"

"Did the other boy get any hits in?" Cora asked.

I shrugged. "He tried. But Colton was upset—and absolutely in the right this time."

Remembering the scene I'd walked in on, I grimaced. Kyle and Zayne were at Kyle's locker—where I'd been headed—and

Billy was there, too. He'd apparently seen something, some sign of affection, between the other two guys and couldn't resist being a jerk.

"Damn Z," Billy said. "If I'd known you swung that way, I would've covered myself up in the shower."

Zayne for his part rolled his eyes. "Not much to cover, my friend."

Kyle grinned at this, but Billy was not amused.

"What are you smiling about queer?" he said to Kyle. "Your brother's not here now. I could jack you up, and even your boyfriend here wouldn't say a word. It's against team policy. Never rat out a teammate."

Zayne slowly shook his head. "I don't know about that. Pretty sure bullying's against team policy, too."

"So, you're taking his side over mine?" Billy scoffed.

"Yeah," Zayne said. "I am."

"You don't have to stick up for me," Kyle said. "I can handle him."

"But you shouldn't have to."

Billy hooted out a laugh, and it wasn't a pretty sound. "You're just gonna stand there and pretend like you didn't make fun of him and his uptight girlfriend along with the rest of us? Wow, Z. That's real big of you."

"Some of us evolve," Zayne said. "And some of us stay assholes forever. Guess which camp you're in, Billy."

"Yeah right." Billy looked to Kyle who seemed to be bracing himself. "Do you know what we used to say about you?"

That was my cue to step in, but before I could make it, Colton said "I got this, Sadie," shot past me and into the fray, placing himself between Billy and the other two.

"What's going on here?" he asked.

"It was a running team joke," Billy said, ignoring Colton,

not taking his eyes off Kyle. "If your brother wasn't always there to defend you, we would've settled it a hundred times over."

"Maybe you need another warning, Billy boy," Colton said menacingly.

Billy either didn't hear or didn't care at this point.

"We always wondered," he said, taking a step forward, "why you two hung out with a girl like Sadie. I mean, she's no prize to look at. She doesn't party or mess around. But then we figured, you and your brother must be hitting that. It was the only thing that made sense."

I gasped, couldn't help it. His words were so vile. Billy glanced from me to Colton, who looked like his head was about to explode. But my mind was having trouble processing it all. So, people had actually been saying this behind our backs? Colton knew, and that was why he… This was why he got in fights all the time? And what did Billy mean first saying I was uptight then implying I would…with both… God, some people really were disgusting.

With a hateful smirk, Billy said, "You want to settle this for us, Colton? You guys take turns or what?"

Colton went at him then, and it was as if someone threw a switch. He wasn't holding back. Billy was on the floor, his mouth a bloody mess, before I could draw my next breath. Colton looked like he wanted to kill him, and I wasn't sure what to do. Kyle and Zayne were frozen, looking on as if they couldn't believe what was happening, watching as the two boys punched and rolled. So, I did the only thing I knew would break up the fight.

"You pulled the fire alarm?" Betty said.

I nodded, taking a much needed and welcome sip of my tea. "It seemed like the only thing I could do."

"Good girl," Betty praised. "That was some quick thinking

on your part. I'm sure Colton would've beaten the daylights out of that despicable Billy, but you did the right thing."

"I don't know," I muttered.

"And then," Cora said, her eyes expectant. "What happened after that?"

What happened after was what made me uncertain.

"They both got written up and sent home," I said. "But it wasn't Colton's fault. He was just defending Kyle and me."

Betty sighed. "I knew I liked him."

"Me, too," Cora agreed.

They weren't the only ones, I thought. The way something inside my chest fluttered whenever I thought of Colton indicated some serious like-age on my part.

"And those four leftover things," Cora asked, shooting Betty a conspiratorial glance, "do they by chance include any of the kissing items, or are those all complete?"

I pretended to be very interested in my tea, and Betty laughed.

"Oh, I'd say by the silent treatment, those were done well indeed," she said knowingly. "I can't even remember the last time I blushed like that. It must've been back when I dated Dean Deville. He was Old Hollywood, Sadie, the up-and-coming director at the time, and oh, one heck of a kisser. Ooh, the lips on that boy. They were full and lush—much like your Colton's."

"Holy smokes," I mumbled, trying desperately not to think of Colton's mouth—and failing. "Can we not talk about this, please?"

"Whatever you'd like, dear."

Cora and Betty tittered while I gathered my wits. Brows furrowed, I said, "Did you say up-and-coming director? Betty, I haven't heard this story yet."

"Oh, I'd wager there's a lot you haven't heard," Cora said.

"Betty had a string of beaus back in the day, and they were all well-known, award-winning, something-or-others. And she helped each and every one of them get there. Her makeup skills were the things of Hollywood legend."

"Really?" I said, intrigued.

Cora nodded. "She basically had her own fan club back then. Bet a lot of them still remember."

"I have kept in touch and do have several of their numbers," Betty said coyly. "It's nice to reminisce with good friends."

"Or past lovers," Cora mumbled to which Betty nudged her side.

"I just loved making whoever it was look their best on camera." Betty held up her tea to me in a toast. "It was my delight."

The conversation made an idea bloom fully in my head. Before I gave it much thought, I heard myself say, "Hey, Betty?"

"Yes, dear?"

"I was hoping to ask you for a favor."

Betty nodded. "Well, go right ahead. Is this about your list? Because you know I would do anything to help you."

"It is," I said. "We're going to be shooting a video, probably next week, of one of my dances, and I was wondering…well, if you wouldn't mind, I know it's not the Oscars or anything…but would you be willing to do my makeup for me?"

Betty put her cup aside, one hand going to her chest, suddenly slumping over in her chair. Not going to lie, I freaked. I was up and beside her in two seconds flat.

"Betty," I said urgently, "are you okay? Should I call a nurse?"

Cora seemed to be holding her breath as well.

But when Betty looked up, she was smiling as bright as the sun.

"Sadie, do you know how long I've been waiting for you to ask me that very question?" she said, voice quivering with elation.

"Geez," I said, "don't scare us like that."

"I wasn't scared," Cora said and took another quick sip of her tea. "I've just been waiting for the old hag to croak so I could finally get a crack at her dress collection."

Betty sniffed. "As if they would fit your tiny frame."

"Oh, I'd make them fit."

"Oh Sadie." Betty's eyes were on me once more. "I'll start drawing up a color palette tonight. Do you know what you're going to wear yet?"

I shook my head.

"Well, let me know when you do. Though with your coloring I'd definitely go with something in the red family. It would look so divine. I'll have to get out all my brushes and eyeshadows, lipsticks, foundations and concealers for sure—"

"Betty, you really don't have to do all that," I said. "I think some blush and a little darker gloss would be just fine."

Betty cut me a swift glance. Her smile was sweet as sugar, but her eyes were steel.

"Sadie, now don't you worry about a thing," she said and gave my hand a pat. "You just leave all the makeup concerns to me, and everything will go right with your production. It will be my finest hour."

Betty's eyes took on a far-off look, and Cora shook her head at me as if to say, "Hey, you asked for it."

Oh my God, I'd created a monster.

Five hours later, I was the one who felt like the monster. I knew he'd be mad. Colton wouldn't have gotten caught—Mrs. Wiggins wouldn't have walked out of her Econ class to find him and Billy duking it out and dashed off to get the principal—if it wasn't for me pulling that alarm.

But I didn't expect him to just skip practice.

Our days were numbered. The deadline for *Dancer's Edge* was coming, and he had to know there wasn't much Kyle and I could do without him.

Okay, so we actually did get a lot done. I'd focused purely on Kyle's part, perfecting what he'd already learned, moving on as much as possible without the entire trio, and Kyle did awesome. But it would've gone better if Colton had been there.

And okay yes, I desperately wanted to apologize.

I felt all kinds of guilty. Although Billy instigated the fight, it was my fault the two got in trouble. The need to speak to Colton, tell him I was sorry, was eating me up inside.

Which was why, after practice, I followed Kyle to their house.

"I'm not sure about this," Kyle said, locking his car as we walked up the driveway.

I rolled my eyes. "Like I said, I'll just apologize to Colton and leave."

"When I got home and knocked on his door, he wouldn't even speak to me."

That wasn't a good sign.

"I'm just trying to prepare you, Sadie. My brother isn't good company when he's in a mood. Case in point: He chucked a Nike at my head once in the eighth grade when I tried to come into his room uninvited."

Rolling my shoulders back, I followed him into the house, ready for anything Colton might throw at me (hopefully not a shoe). Kyle wished me luck then headed back out again to meet up with Zayne (they had a lot to discuss after today) while I made my way up to Colton's bedroom, a place I'd never been. I used to come here back when the boys shared a room, but since they'd grown up and out of their bunk beds, I usually spent all my time in Kyle's. So yeah, this would be a new experience. Taking one last deep breath, I knocked on Colton's door.

"Go 'way."

The voice was muffled, but it definitely belonged to Colton.

"Hey," I said. "It's me, Sadie."

"I said, go away," he said louder this time.

"Listen, I know you're mad," I said to the closed door, feeling like a complete idiot, "and you have every right to be. But... that's no reason to skip practice. I mean, it was kind of a jerk move, don't you think? I just wanted to tell you I'm sorry, and I really wanted to do that to your face. So, could you please open the door?"

I waited a beat.

"Colton?"

Still no answer, no sounds of movement.

"Well, I am sorry," I mumbled. "Jerk."

I was about to leave when the door opened, and Colton stood there, leaning one shoulder against the door with his arms crossed.

"Did you just apologize and call me a jerk in the same breath?" he said. "Nice, Sadie. I didn't think you had it in you."

The first thing I noticed was he was wearing a sweater with pajama pants —which was strange since it was rather warm in the house. The second thing was that his nose was red. It was awful because neither of those things, not the dorky mismatched pajamas or the redness, made Colton look any less attractive. Argh.

"What are you apologizing for anyway?" he said.

"I got you in trouble," I said. "With the fire alarm."

Colton shrugged. "I've had worse."

"But then why didn't you come to the studio?" I asked. "I

thought you were mad since I got you sent home."

"Billy's big mouth was the reason I got sent home," he said, "and I'm not mad at you."

"Is that why you're always getting into fights? To defend Kyle?"

And me, I thought but didn't say.

Colton shrugged. "Someone had to shut him and his stupid friends up. By the way, did you know pulling the fire alarm when there's no fire is a federal offense?" Eyes widening, I gaped, and he laughed, though it sounded more raspy than usual. "Thought so, Little Miss Perfect. I guess you really are becoming a bad girl, huh?"

His eyes were bright, and I was about to tell him off for teasing me—I mean, it's not like he had anything to worry about. He wasn't the one who'd committed a federal-freaking-offense!—but Colton abruptly started coughing. And it wasn't just any cough. You know the cough you get when your throat is tight and swollen? The one that hurts? Yeah, it sounded like that, and I finally got why his nose was so red.

"You're sick?" I asked. "Is that why you weren't at practice?"

"Ding, ding, ding," he said, voice thick with sarcasm even as he swayed unsteadily. "Thank you, Captain Obvious, for your keen observational skills. Now Sadie, please leave me alone."

As his body was wracked by another bout of coughing, I did the exact opposite. Getting underneath his arm, I led him carefully over to his bed.

"What are you doing?" he asked.

"Helping you," I said.

"Why?"

"Because as Betty would say, you look like death warmed over." As he grumbled, collapsing onto his navy blue sheets, I frowned and put my hands on my hips. "Actually, this reminds me of when I had the flu last year. Where's your mom? Did she see you like this?"

"Yeah."

"And she didn't stay home?"

He mumbled, and though half his face was turned into the pillow, I got the gist. "Hospital. Said she had to go because two other nurses called in sick."

I sighed. Mrs. Bishop was a nurse, an awesome one, too. But here was her son, and if I was any judge, he had one heck of a fever. And she'd just left him here to fend for himself?

Shaking my head, I placed my hand against his forehead.

"Ah, trying to cop a feel when I'm sick," he said, eyes closing. "Cheap move. Not that I blame you."

"You wish," I said. "I'm seeing if you have a fever—and yep, you are burning up, buddy. We should try to lower your temp. You should take off that sweater."

Colton groaned as I helped him sit up.

"How long has this been going on anyway?"

"Well, you see," he said, fumbling with the buttons, "there's this girl who made me stand in the rain for something called a 'rain kiss.'"

"No," I said.

"Yes." Colton finally got the last button undone, and as his sweater fell open, I realized my mistake. He wasn't wearing anything underneath. Oh Lord. All that stared back at me was a gloriously toned chest attached to a firm stomach. I felt myself blushing but couldn't look away. "Basically Sadie, you're responsible for all of this."

"Oh my God," I said, reaching out to stop him.

But not quick enough.

His wrists were hot beneath my hands, his sweater off his shoulders, still covering his forearms, but he was naked from the waist up for all intents and purposes. Feeling guilty and a bit fevered myself, I had no idea how to handle this. Colton Bishop was sick, and I was to blame. No one else was here. I had to stay and take care of him—didn't I? Make sure he was okay and…was I seriously ogling his abs when he was ill? Maybe he wouldn't notice.

"With the way you're staring," Colton said, "at least I know I'm still hot even in this state."

And maybe he would.

I spun on my heel and headed for the door.

"You finally going?" he asked.

"Just downstairs to get medicine."

"Mom had me take some already."

"Okay, then I'll bring up water, a cold compress, Ginger Ale and Saltines if you have them," I murmured. "Be right back."

"Just go," Colton groaned, but by then I was determined. I would stay until he went to sleep. It was the right thing to do. He needed me, and I was going to stay, no matter how much he grumbled about it.

Colton groaned.

Again.

It was like the third time in the last five minutes. Sensing he needed a little attention, I turned my head without removing my eyes from the TV. We were both on his bed—and I was trying my best to forget that fact. Me on top of the blankets, sitting up, him under the sheets on his back (which meant his naked chest was covered, thank goodness). We were about ten minutes into the first episode, and it was starting to get good.

"You need something, Colton?" I asked.

"What the hell are you making me watch?" he demanded.

"It's a period drama. One of my favorites."

"A period what-a?"

"It's a period drama, BBC's *Pride and Prejudice*," I sighed, pushing pause then looking at him. "It's a mini-series. What's your problem anyway? I thought you said you were going to ignore me and get some sleep."

"I was trying," he said. "But then all those people started talking in this weird way, keeping me up."

"I can turn the volume down if you want." He frowned, and I shrugged. "Or we can watch it together."

"Just leave already," he said—then coughed in that pained way which made my throat hurt in sympathy. "Won't your mom be worried?"

"I already texted her."

"'Course you did," Colton said. "Go home, Sadie."

I shook my head. "Sorry, no can do. I need to take your temperature again in thirty minutes."

Colton's scowl couldn't have been deeper. He was running a 101-degree fever, and his arms were crossed in the petulant pose kids do when they can't have their way. His forehead was covered by the cool, wet cloth I'd just applied, warning him not to take it off or else. With that, the red nose and messy hair, he looked absolutely adorable.

I wanted to smack myself. Oh geez, I thought, giving myself a mental slap that did absolutely no good. If I could still be attracted to him, even grumpy, disgruntled and sick? It was too late. My feelings were too deep. There was no turning back now. I was a goner.

"*Pride and Prejudice*," he said. "Is this the one with the almost kiss?"

"No, this is a different version." Clearing my throat, I said,

"It's great. You should give it a chance."

"It looks dumb," he said.

"Well, it's not. It's a love story about a rich guy and a poor girl and how their opposite personalities and social statuses should keep them apart, but only end up pushing them together, making them perfect for each other. It's really soothing, and I thought it might help you relax. Plus, it's romance," I said, gesturing around his room. "Don't think I haven't noticed your books. There've got to be at least what? 20 romances? And some of them are very naughty."

Colton's mouth tipped up in a grin. "And how would you know that?"

"Well," I sputtered. He had me there. "I read a few to the Shady Grove residents, and others I picked up because they looked good."

Tempting, I thought, was a better word.

Kind of like the guy beside me when he chuckled that raspy laugh.

"No need to be ashamed, Sadie," he said, patting my thigh, nearly making my heart leap out of my chest. "So, you're saying this period drama is a little naughty? If so, I'm in."

"Umm…"

Nodding to the screen, propping himself up, he said, "Go ahead, push play. I'll try to stay awake."

I re-started the episode, deciding not to tell him there was absolutely zero naughtiness, and the main characters didn't even kiss until the end.

Colton made it through the first two episodes, but his eyes were drifting closed by the third. I couldn't blame him. Despite the appeal of Mr. Darcy and Elizabeth's many misunderstandings and hidden attraction, he was truly not feeling well, the guy's body fighting off what was either a nasty cold or something worse.

Mom had texted to check up on me a moment ago.

Mom: Hey, everything okay?

Me: Yes, Colton's sick, and his mom's at work, so I was helping him.

Mom: Oh no, poor kid :(. Anything I can do?

Me: Nah, I'll be home in a bit.

Mom: Okay, if you or Colton need anything, let me know. Love you, Sadie.

Me: Love you, Mom.

I looked down at Colton, whose breathing had finally evened out. The last time I checked his fever was down to 99.8, and he'd just taken his medicine again 10 minutes ago. The movie had done its job. He was resting peacefully.

It was my cue to leave.

Trying not to disturb him, I turned off the TV, slowly rose from the bed. I was just about to go when I felt a hand on my wrist. Looking over my shoulder, I saw Colton's eyes were still closed.

"Stay," he said quietly.

His grip was light. I could break free so easily, and he'd probably go right back to sleep. In fact, I wasn't even sure he was awake now. The word had been little more than a whisper, and with the fever, he might not have realized what he was saying.

But I wasn't strong enough to go.

Instead, I said, "Okay," sent Mom a quick text to let her know I was staying and got back into bed. I turned away from him, scooting all the way to the edge, but couldn't seem to stay quiet.

"So…what'd you think of the movie?" I asked, wondering if he'd respond or if he really was asleep.

"I don't trust that Wickham guy," he mumbled.

I smiled. So, he was awake, and he'd been paying attention.

"And Darcy's kind of a douche."

"Nah," I said, "it's only a front. Mr. Darcy's a complex guy, one of the most beloved heroes of all time."

Colton grunted.

Looking around his room, unable to hold my tongue, I said, "Can I ask you something real?"

Another grunt.

"Do you know what you want to do after graduation?"

He answered immediately. "Cars," he said.

"I know you love cars," I said, noticing the posters of foreign cars on his wall—the only pictures on display besides a few of him and his brother—and what looked like an engine part on a towel sitting on his desk with a bunch of tools, "but what do you want to do? Go to college and study cars? Engineering?"

"Garage. Own one someday," he mumbled.

Of course, Colton had it all figured out. Sometimes I felt like the only person who didn't.

"Can I tell you a secret?" I said quietly, and when he didn't grunt or respond, I hoped maybe he'd fallen asleep. I'd never confessed this to anyone. But it'd been clawing at me to get out, so with a deep breath, I admitted the ugly truth. "I have no idea what I want to do. After school, I mean."

Again, Colton remained silent, and with my back to him, it was easy to keep talking.

"Part of me wants to go to college. But I have no idea what I'd study," I went on. "I'm interested in so many things, have so many ideas. Part of me thinks if I go to college maybe I'll figure it out. But another part…is terrified that I won't. What if I never know what I want to do with my life? What if I never find the one thing that I'm really meant to do?"

There I'd said it. Confessed my worst fear to what was once my worst enemy, now the guy I was secretly falling for. But he was out like a light, so there was nothing to fear.

"Dance," Colton said out of the blue, making me nearly jump out of my skin.

"You're awake?" I gasped. "I thought you were asleep."

"Dance," he repeated. "You love it. That's what you should do."

Shaking my head, I said, "I do love dance and choreographing. It's always been my dream. But seriously, Colton, I've been rejected seven times already. Maybe it's a sign that I should stop dreaming and try something else." I swallowed a lump in my throat. "Maybe I'm not good enough."

Colton sighed and somehow ended up right behind me. One of his arms curled around my waist, his hand on my stomach and his legs pressed right up against the backs of mine. I was so surprised I stopped breathing for a moment.

"It means you're trying," he said. "God Sadie, do you know how brave you are? You get rejected but keep putting yourself out there. It takes guts to do that."

"Or stupidity," I muttered, having regained my ability to speak.

"You are good enough," Colton said. "Their opinion doesn't matter, only yours does. Do what you love. Smart or stupid, that's always the right choice."

If I hadn't been lying down, that bit of wisdom would've knocked me flat. I couldn't respond no matter how hard I tried. Minutes passed and still, I had nothing. We lay there, Colton at my back with his arm over my stomach, his breaths deepening once again. My mind kept replaying his words, my heart leaning more toward him with every breath.

Colton buried his head in my hair with a sigh.

"Beautiful," he mumbled.

Must be the fever, I thought, half-hoping he'd say it again, half-dreading it because it fed my delusions. No matter how much I wanted him, no matter how much I willed it to be true, Colton would never be mine. Despite what he said, I wasn't brave. I was a coward through and through.

And his was the one rejection I couldn't risk.

CHAPTER 18

Colton was sick for three more days.

Turned out he actually did have the flu. His mom kept him on quarantine, no school, no visitors (except Kyle, of course), no strenuous activity until the fever was gone. The twins thought she was taking extra-good care of him to make up for being away that first night. Kyle called it "babying" and told me Colton was "dying to escape."

This meant I hadn't seen or spoken to Colton in a while. I used the time to take stock.

My feelings were all over the place.

The one thing I knew for sure: I was totally falling for Colton Bishop.

Had fallen.

Fell hard.

As much as I tried to remember my old feelings of dislike and disgust, they just wouldn't come. I didn't see him the same as I used to. He wasn't my arch nemesis anymore. Colton Bishop was now the guy I couldn't get out of my mind, the one I imagined kissing a hundred different ways (in addition to the ones we'd already tried), the one I wanted to talk to about a million different things.

This was totally inconvenient because:

1) He was my best friend's brother. I knew Kyle wouldn't appreciate me crushing on his twin. It'd be weird for him, and he'd

already warned me off once before.

2) I was beginning to realize this was so much more than a crush. I could tell it was more because…even when I'd thought I was in love with Kyle, it never felt like this. When I thought of Colton, something inside my chest would ache then start to soar like a bird terrified of flying but unable to cage itself. I couldn't stop my feelings for him any more than I could make my heart stop beating.

3) Colton was my coach. He was supposed to be guiding the whole life makeover, helping me complete my list—which meant there was no way I could avoid him without it looking totally suspicious.

4) He was only helping me to win the bet and beat Kyle.

5) I was totally aware of this fact, and it still didn't stop me from falling for the guy.

6) There was no way Colton felt the same. He'd probably just grin and shake his head if I told him—which I'd never have the lady balls to do anyway.

7) I had no idea how to hide my feelings.

And that was the real problem.

Unrequited love was nothing new for me (sad but true). With Kyle, disguising my feelings had been easy. He'd never suspected a thing, and maybe part of it was that while I loved Kyle, I'd never really been *in love* with him.

But I was at least a little bit in love with Colton.

I'd just have to fake it, I thought. Shouldn't be hard, right? If he noticed anything, I could pretend it was all in his head. It was the best plan I had. Colton's quarantine was ending today, and Kyle had texted to let me know they were on their way over to the studio. They'd be here any minute.

At five o'clock on the dot, the twins sauntered into Corner Street Ballroom.

"Hi guys," I said, acting as if everything was normal while trying not to look at Colton. "How's it going?"

"Good," Kyle said. He tilted his head toward his brother. "Busted this guy out of the house, and he's eager to do some dancing. Isn't that right, Colt?"

Colton shrugged. "Eager might be a stretch, but I am feeling a hell of a lot better."

"You are?" I said, still avoiding eye contact. "Well, that's good. I'm glad you're feeling better."

"I had a good nurse," he said.

I nodded. "Your mom is pretty awesome."

"She is, but I didn't mean her."

I looked at him then. How could I not? Colton was staring back at me, his eyes clear, lip piercing glinting as his mouth tilted up in a grin. Colton looked good, better than anyone recovering from the flu had a right to. My eyes ate him up like they were starved, savoring the sight of him. But after a moment, I forced myself to look away.

"Well, the flu is no joke. Be sure to take all your medicine, and don't overexert yourself." Looking to Kyle, I pushed my hands into my pockets. He was my buffer, and I locked my eyes on him like a lifeline. "There's a lot of work to do on the dance. The deadline's coming up."

Kyle nodded. "I know."

"Do you remember the choreography?"

"Of course," Kyle said.

"Does he?" I asked.

Colton frowned then stepped forward. "*He* is standing right here. And yeah, I remember the choreography. I was only sick for a few days, Sadie."

"Awesome," I said, turning away, trying to hide the thrill I'd felt when he said my name. "Let's get to work then. I'll start reviewing with Kyle and—"

"Actually," Kyle said, "I've got to go meet Zayne."

Whipping around to face him, I caught his gaze. My buffer was trying to abandon me? This would not do.

"But…we've got practice," I said.

"I figured you and Colt would need to work alone, one-on-one like we did."

"Well…"

"It really helped, Sadie. Plus, like I said, I know my part." Kyle suddenly struck a pose, a dramatic one from the dance. He threw a glance at his brother. "It's this slacker who needs the work."

Colton rolled his eyes. "Please," he said. "I'll be caught up in an hour."

"Then I'll be back in an hour," Kyle said.

"But Kyle," I said desperately, "the dance, our deadline, we—"

He cut me off, placing a hand on my arm. "I'm coming back. Just work with him and see what happens. It won't be that bad."

"Won't it?" I muttered, but no one seemed to hear.

Before I could argue, Colton said, "There are some things me and Sadie need to talk about anyway. Later, Kyle."

Kyle winked at me and left. I didn't know what the wink meant, couldn't tell whether he was just being cute or if he suspected something, but that was beside the point. He was gone, and now I was alone with his brother. And all my freaking feelings for said brother were struggling to break free. I could feel Colton staring even as I avoided his gaze.

"So, what'd you want to talk about?" I asked.

Colton was silent a moment. Then, "Your list. I am your coach, and by my count, we still have three more items to go."

"Two," I said automatically.

"Two?" Colton said.

"Yeah, I didn't know how long you'd be out, so I did one while you were gone." My cheeks flamed. "Plus, we crossed off number 22."

"Ah yes," Colton said, "how could I forget? Number 22, one of my favorites on the naughty list."

Mine, too, I thought but didn't say.

22) Sleep with a guy (Just. Sleep!)

It was something I could hardly believe I'd done, but the memory was imprinted on my mind. Surprisingly, Colton had behaved like a perfect gentleman the whole time I'd been in his bed. I frowned. I wasn't sure if I was happy or disappointed by this fact.

"Sadly, I don't remember much," he said.

My eyes snapped to his. "Really? You don't remember?"

You don't remember asking me to stay or encouraging me to dance—or saying I was beautiful? You don't remember sleeping with me snugly fitted to your chest, your arm hugging my waist, the same position I woke up in before I snuck out early the next morning?

"It's all hazy," Colton said. "But what'd you expect? I was out of it from the medicine, delirious with fever."

My chest deflated. Oh well, I thought, I guess it was good that he didn't remember. Maybe it would make dancing together less awkward. For him anyway. I still remembered everything with perfect clarity.

Colton crossed his arms. "What other one did you do?"

My entire body heated this time, part embarrassment, part something else entirely. I so didn't want to talk about this with Colton, but he was my coach so… "I ordered some lingerie the other day online," I said. "It's a corset. I was thinking I could use it as part of my costume."

"What color?" he asked.

"Red."

"I'll need to see that."

"What?" I asked, my gaze returning to his. "Is that really necessary?"

Colton's face was impassive. "You heard me. As your coach, I'll need to see this so-called lingerie. It's important that I be included in all aspects of your naughty list."

"Okaaay," I said slowly. "But for the hundredth time, it's not a naughty list. And I definitely picked out something nice."

"I'm sure you did."

There was something in his voice, in the way he was staring that made my throat go dry.

"So that just leaves *Dancer's Edge* and the tattoo, right?" he said. "You decide what to do about that?"

I shook my head. I'd actually thought about this one a lot. "I did some research, and it takes a while for tattoos to heal. Almost two weeks, right? For the dance, we'll have to touch each other a lot, and I wanted it on my wrist—plus, to be honest, I'm not even sure I want a tattoo anymore." A shiver went down my spine. "I've read so many horror stories about pain and infection. Not proud of it, but Google may have officially scared me off."

"Never fear," Colton said, pulling something out of his pocket. "I've got you covered."

Looking at the small paper squares in his hand, I noticed a dragon, daisy, and what looked like some words in cursive. My heart warmed. It was number seven on my list.

7) Get a tattoo (daisy, dragon, lyrics/book quote?)

"See," Colton said, holding them up, "even though I was sick I was still being an awesome coach."

"I see," I swallowed, hoping I could control myself and not

just tackle him right then and there.

"Which one do you want?"

Clearing my throat, I said, "What's the last one say?"

Colton grinned. "It says: I love Mr. Darcy. You know, from that dumb show you made me watch?"

"*Pride and Prejudice*?"

"Yeah, that one," he said. "I finished it and a ton of other movies while Mom kept me hostage in the house—which included *A Walk to Remember*, have to give them props for the tattoo idea, but seriously? That movie is sad as hell. By the way, back to *Pride and Prejudice*, I knew I didn't trust Wickham. Darcy turned out to be pretty decent though."

I nodded unable to speak.

"So?" he said again. "Which do you want?"

"The daisy," I said. Because although I did love Mr. Darcy, he was a fictional character. The guy in front of me, on the other hand, the one who was gently applying the daisy tattoo to the inside of my wrist, brows furrowed in concentration? He was all real. Colton was more real than anyone I'd ever met, and I knew that although I'd never have him, although he didn't feel the same, my love for him was real, too.

Colton straightened after applying the tattoo and caught me staring.

"What?" he said.

"Hmm?"

"Why are you looking at me like that, Sadie?"

I blinked. "Practicing for the dance," I lied. "Remember when I told you how you guys have to look at me? Well, I have to look at you…like I want you. More than anything."

Colton nodded slowly. "You're doing a damn good job. With the hearts in your eyes, even I'd believe you."

"Thanks," I said, shaking myself out of it, and then I took a deep breath. "Ready to get started?"

"Yeah," Colton said. "Let's do this."

With that, we got down to business. Even though I was lovestruck and trying my best to hide it, Colton picked up the choreography so fast, faster even than Kyle, and he had "the look" down pat. Every time his eyes caught mine, I felt something spark inside me. Colton definitely didn't need to work on his smolder. The way he looked at me…the way it made me feel…I had to keep reminding myself this was pretend. I wasn't his type. It was all for the bet. Still… His hands molded to my curves, and Colton wasn't afraid to pull me in close, move with me. The chemistry was undeniable. It was just like when we'd danced at the club multiplied by a thousand, and my heart was trying to beat a hole in my chest.

By the time Kyle came back, we'd gone over Colton's part several times and had everything but the last bit of choreo perfected. The only thing left to do was put it all together and hope like heck it worked.

And miracle of miracles, after two more hours, it did. Kyle really had been practicing; I could tell. When we added him to the mix, everything was amplified, and the heat level couldn't have been higher. The movements really brought out the tug of war between the two guys, and I was able to play off of them, telling the story of passion, desire and power I'd wanted to tell all along.

We agreed to meet again tomorrow night to practice, but before I said goodbye to the Bishop brothers, I laid out my plan.

"So, I'm going to try for the million views," I said.

Colton and Kyle both stared at me.

"I thought it was your dream to be on the *Dancer's Edge* site," Kyle said, looking confused.

"It was," I said—then amended, "I mean, it is. But if

Dancer's Edge doesn't want to give the dance their stamp of approval, I don't want to wait for it. I'm putting work out there that I'm proud of. I love it, and that's all that matters."

Colton was smiling a bit, and Kyle looked stunned.

"Good for you," my best friend said. "What made you decide to go for it?"

Glancing to Colton then away, I shrugged. "Took some good advice."

"Sounds like a smart guy," Colton said. "And how do you plan on getting a million views?"

"Well, I'm not exactly sure yet," I admitted, "but I'm working on it."

Kyle smiled and pulled me in for a hug. "Gah, I'm so proud of you right now."

"Don't be too proud." Colton shook his head, tongue flicking his lip ring. "If we get that million, you're that much closer to losing the bet."

"Yeah whatever," Kyle said, "maybe it'll happen. Maybe it won't, but man, I love that she's trying. Let us know if there's anything we can do to help."

"Thanks for the vote of confidence, my friend, and I will," I laughed. "I'm sure I'll need all the help I can get. By the way, Betty's coming in to do our makeup—which is awesome because she used to do makeup for the stars—and Tim said he'd drive down to film the dance for us on Saturday."

Colton nodded but said nothing. As he stared at me, and I tried but failed to read his mind, one thought ran through my head like a record on repeat.

After we did this last thing, whether it succeeded or failed, Colton would no longer be my coach. The end of the month was in 12 days, and coincidentally so was the deadline for *Dancer's Edge*. That meant the end of the bet, the end of our time together, the end of my time with Colton. I felt my eyes misting and looked away. Strange, I'd always thought finishing my list would make me happy.

But I was already missing Colton even though he was right here in front of me.

CHAPTER 19

The next few days flew by.

Colton, Kyle and I practiced every night—and I noticed Colton was never late even though he was still working long hours at the garage. He and Kyle seemed determined to make the dance the best it could be, making every correction, running the piece as many times as necessary, and I couldn't have been more thankful.

I soaked up those practices, memorizing the feel of Colton's broad shoulders, his closeness.

Every time Colton noticed something like a fluttering pulse (how could my pulse not flutter when he trailed his hand slowly down my neck?) or a gasp (because his hand on my lower back felt freaking amazing), I deflected like a pro.

"Oh that," I'd said. "It's just part of the dance."

"It sure felt real," Colton had grumbled.

"That's the whole point. We want people to believe this"—I'd gestured between the three of us—"is all genuine, right?"

"Yeah, I guess," Colton had said. "If this whole dancing thing doesn't pan out, maybe you should try acting. You're really good at it."

"Thanks, you are, too."

And he was. Although Colton had definitely caught me staring at his lip ring on more than one occasion, I'd noticed him staring at me as well. There were times when we'd hit a pose or come out of a lift, dip or spin, and I totally thought he was going to make a move, was sure he was going to kiss me. But then Colton would blink and back off, once again becoming his normal cool, unaffected self. It was wishful thinking, but if I hadn't known better, I definitely would've thought he felt something for me, too.

If I was a good actor, his performance was Oscar-worthy.

Saturday came, and before I knew it, Betty was doing my makeup, getting me ready to do this dance that I loved with the two guys that I loved.

"This is so exciting," Betty said, adding something called contouring to my face. "You look fabulous, dear, just fabulous. After I finish, you'll be ready to make your grand debut."

"I can't thank you enough for doing this, Betty," I said, but she shushed me.

"Oh, hush now," she said. "I already told you. It's my pleasure. Eyes closed, please."

I did as she asked and felt my eyelids getting the same treatment as the rest of my face.

"Those twins sure are gorgeous," she commented. "Kyle's a peach, and Colton sure seems to be smitten if you don't mind me saying so."

"He's not," I said, lips turning down. "He's doing this to win a bet."

I couldn't see it, but I heard Betty sigh and knew she was shaking her head. "Oh Sadie, you really are blind if you can't see his feelings for you."

"It's fine," I said, lying through my teeth. "It's not like I'm smitten with him either."

"Now, you know I'm far too smart to believe that big of a fib," Betty said which made me blush. "But think about it, Sadie. Why would Colton agree to do the life makeover? Why would he do this dance when, as you've mentioned, he hates dancing? Why would he ask me…"

"Ask you what?" I said when she'd been silent too long. Silence was not one of Betty's strong suits. I was immediately suspicious.

"Never mind," she said. "It's not important. Now, open those beautiful eyes, so I can do your mascara. Has he seen you yet? In costume, I mean?"

I was still suspicious but decided to let it go. If Betty didn't want to talk about something, it was like pulling teeth trying to get it out of her. "Not yet," I said, though I had texted Colton a picture of my corset the other day. I'd laid it out on my bed all nice and proper, snapped the pic and sent it his way.

His reaction had been underwhelmed.

I could see that he'd read the text. The little dots that let me know he was typing appeared then disappeared. This went on for a few minutes before I finally got his response.

Colton Freakin' Bishop: Looks good. I'll see you tomorrow.

Maybe he wasn't a big fan of red satin and lace? had been my first thought, but then a worse possibility. Maybe he just wasn't a big fan of me.

"I can't wait to see his reaction," Betty laughed, "and Kyle's, too. They're going to faint dead away at the first glance."

"Nah," I said, "I don't think so."

Betty just sighed again, putting the finishing touches on my lips. At length, she stood back, tilted her head this way and that, then nodded.

"Sadie Day, you're an absolute knockout," she pronounced, stepping away so I could look in the mirror.

It was my first time getting to see myself since she'd started, and I was truly impressed. My skin looked like porcelain, smooth and flawless. My eyes were smoky, my cheeks high and defined with a rose blush, and she'd accentuated my lips with ruby red. She'd even managed to set my wild hair in smooth waves, falling around my face. I looked like a starlet, a powerful femme fatale with a dash of innocence. It was the perfect look.

"Betty," I breathed, "you're a genius."

"I had a great subject," she shrugged then rested her hands on my shoulders. "Now, you go out there and believe in your beauty and yourself. Once the video's up, I can't wait to watch your dance over and over."

I nodded then went out in search of the boys—but before I could find them, I ran into Big Tim and Little Tim. They'd both come down to help with the video. With the flood lights and spotlights they'd brought, the studio looked like an actual film set.

"It's awesome to see you guys," I said, hugging each of them in turn. "Thank you so much for doing this."

"How could we not?" Little Tim said with a smile. "You've helped us tons of times, Sadie. It's only right to pay it forward."

"First," Big Tim said, "Sadie, you look awesome. Second, that pencil skirt is giving me life. Third, this whole sexy librarian look really works for you. Kudos."

Little Tim nodded. "The lighting's all set up. It's going to frame you and your partners like a dream."

"Speaking of which, do you know where Colton and Kyle are?" I asked.

Big Tim nodded to the corner of the room. "I think Kyle's in the bathroom, and Colton's over there talking to your parents. P.S. They are looking so fine."

"My parents?" I repeated, following his eyes, spotting Colton on the other side of the studio. Mom and Dad were nodding at whatever he said, but I couldn't imagine what they were talking about. As I watched, Colton smiled at my mom who smiled back, and then he shook hands with my dad. A moment later, he disappeared into the bathroom, but I definitely wanted in on that conversation.

Making my way across the floor, I stood in front of my parents.

"Hey," I said, crossing my arms. "So, what was that all about?"

Mom and Dad stared at me, pride shining in their eyes.

"Nothing much, we were just talking with Colton," Mom said, her smile dreamy. "He really is a nice boy."

"I wouldn't go that far," Dad said and ran a hand along his neck, "but yeah, I guess the kid's not all bad."

I nearly swallowed my tongue—Dad wasn't the biggest fan of teenage boys. He'd taken forever to warm to Kyle, and he'd been my best friend forever. Plus, I knew for a fact Dad had never liked Colton.

"What brought on this change of heart?" I asked him.

"Well, if he's helping my baby girl, I have to like the kid a little. Right?" Dad said.

"Right," I said slowly, though I got the distinct feeling I was missing something.

Before I knew it, Mom had grabbed me in a tight hug. "You look stunning, baby."

"You do look beautiful," Dad agreed. "It's kind of scary."

"Thank you," I said, smiling at them, "for saying that and for supporting me, even if my dreams are way out there."

"Always," Mom said, giving me another squeeze.

Colton and Kyle came out of the bathroom, and my parents left just as the guys stepped up to me. Big Tim had been right. They were looking fine in their t-shirts and jeans. Seriously, how was it that guys could rock such a simple look and make it a girl's fantasy come to life? One glance at Colton in his fitted black tee, and I was done for. As his eyes skimmed my outfit, I had to fight the urge to fan myself.

"Library chic," Kyle said with a grin, rocking his plain white tee, while Colton looked me up and down. "I dig it, Sadie. You look phenomenal."

"Same to you guys," I said as Colton's eyes finally came to rest on mine. Betty must've gotten to them, too, I realized, because his ocean eyes were even more pronounced. The guyliner was totally unfair and unnecessary. Colton was already too attractive for his own good. He'd taken in everything from my hair to my white button up, the red corset peeking out, black skirt and stockings to the black high heels, and I couldn't tell what he was thinking. "Thank you so much again for being a part of this. I couldn't have done it without you."

"Yeah, you could've," Kyle said, "but it's cool that you included us."

Colton remained silent until Kyle nudged him.

"Yeah," Colton said and cleared his throat. "You look nice."

My smile fell.

"Better than nice," he said quickly. "Sadie, you look...*damn*."

Damn was a lot better than nice especially when he said it like that, like he couldn't quite find the words, and my spirits lifted. Heck, I almost floated out of my heels and to the ceiling. One compliment from Colton, and I was ready to take flight.

"I'll admit it," Kyle said. "I'm starting to feel more worried about losing the bet."

"You should be," Colton said. "Sadie's been doing a great job on her list."

"That's not what I mean, Colt." Kyle shook his head. "The way you look at Sadie, and the way she looks at you, even I would think there's something going on. I'm sure an audience is going to eat that up."

"That's the point. Right, Sadie?"

"Yeah," I swallowed. "We're acting, and we're just really good at doing it together."

"Really?" Kyle said. "'Cause I would've sworn it was more."

"Well, it's not," Colton said.

"Will you excuse me?" I said suddenly needing to escape, desperate to get away before I did or said something stupid. "I need to check my makeup before we start."

"Sure," Kyle said. "Take your time."

I made it to the bathroom on fairly steady feet, my mind rushing all around. I couldn't do this anymore. I was lying to everyone, Betty, my best friend, the guy I'd fallen in love with. Worse, I was lying to myself if I thought it would all blow over, or I could just keep it in for the rest of my life. Something had to give. Even if I only confessed everything to Kyle, I thought, maybe it would make things a little better. Colton could go on and hook up with as many girls as he wanted. I shuddered, heart shriveling at the thought. He would forget me easily, but I would still pine for him long after this bet and my list were complete. I had to tell someone. I had to, or I'd never be able to face either one of the Bishop brothers again.

Colton had been right. I was brave.

Just not brave enough to tell him.

But who knows? I thought, trying to pump myself up. Maybe if I told Kyle, one day down the road—a long, looong way down—I would finally be able to confess my feelings to Colton and be done with this charade.

Pulling up all of my courage, I marched out of the bathroom and spotted the twins. They were taking a selfie in their contrasting tees. Their backs were to me, but I tugged on Kyle's white shirt and said, "Come with me. I need to tell you something."

Without looking, I dragged him along behind me until we were in the dressing room away from everyone. Dropping Kyle's sleeve, I put my hands on my hips, still facing away, thinking it would be easier to get it all out if I didn't have to look him in the eye. As he started to say something, I held up a hand to cut him off. I needed to get this off my chest and fast.

"I think I'm falling for your brother," I said in a rush.

He said nothing, so I went on.

"Actually, I know I am." I started pacing. "Kyle, it was a total accident. I know you warned me not to fall for him, but I couldn't help it. It all started when Colton stepped up to help with my list, and as we spent more time together and I really got to know him, it was impossible not to like him. Colton's sarcastic and way too honest—but he's also smart, funny, loyal and thoughtful. He's like…one of the best guys I've ever known. Besides you, of course."

Kyle still hadn't said anything. I couldn't read his silence, but I couldn't seem to stop talking.

"And I know what you're thinking," I said. "Colton already told me I'm not his type. He thinks I'm uptight and prissy, all the things he'd never go for in a girl. But like I said, I couldn't help it. It isn't even how attractive he is or his confidence, although those are definite turn-ons."

I waited to see if Kyle would gag or say something then, but he didn't.

"I love Colton because he makes me feel like I could be anything. Do anything." I paused, finally taking a moment to exhale. "He makes me feel beautiful and brave, exactly like the person I want to be. And when he kisses me, sometimes even when he looks at me, I feel it." My hand drifted up to my chest. "Right here, in my heart."

A beat passed.

"Please say something," I begged. "You're my best friend, Kyle. I know this will make it strange between us, but I just couldn't keep it from you anymore. There's nothing to worry about because I'll probably never tell Colton anyway."

"I think you just did."

The voice that spoke definitely didn't belong to my best friend, and as I spun around, my eyes widened. Colton stood there, piercings and all, hands in his pockets—and he was wearing Kyle's white shirt.

"But I thought…" I stopped, voice disappearing as I took in the fact that Colton was here, not a figment of my imagination.

"That I was Kyle?" Colton shrugged. "We switched shirts. Kyle said he wanted a picture to see who looked better in each color, so we changed shirts while you were in the bathroom."

My mind was reeling, still taking in the full ramifications of his being here. I'd never mistaken one twin for the other. *Ever.* Then the one time I did, it was the biggest, most colossal mistake of my life. If I'd looked at him or heard his voice, I definitely would've known, but like an idiot, I'd pulled him in here without checking.

"So…you heard everything?" I asked, voice little more than a whisper.

"Yeah," Colton said. "It was kind of hard not to. You were rambling for a while."

I wanted to die.

"Listen Colton," I said, "I didn't mean—"

"You sounded like you meant it," he said and took a step closer.

Shaking my head, tears of shame pooling in my eyes, I said, "Why couldn't you just be gay?"

"What was that?" Colton stopped short, looking confused by the question, but it made perfect sense to me.

"If you were," I said, "at least then I'd know there was a reason you couldn't feel the same."

Colton exhaled then took another step and another until he was right in front of me.

"If you were, then maybe it would hurt less, knowing you can never love me back," I said, my breath coming short because of his nearness. "God, I wish you were gay."

"Sorry," he said, hands coming up to cup my cheeks. "Definitely not gay."

Colton leaned down until I could feel his breath fanning against my lips.

"But who said I could never love you back?" he said before taking my mouth in a kiss. This one was soul-deep, his mouth moving with a purpose against mine, trying to tell me something I couldn't even begin to fathom, his hands slipping into my hair.

"Wait," I said, breaking away and breathing fast. "I thought you said I wasn't your type."

Colton shook his head and kissed me again. "That was bullshit, Sadie. I've wanted you ever since we met, ever since my brother claimed you as his best friend and got all your attention before I could even say a word. God, I was so jealous of him back then."

"You were?" I asked in surprise.

"Yeah," he said, pressing his forehead against mine. "You're so smart, beautiful, freaking fearless. You know, twin or not, I could kill Kyle for telling you to stay away from me."

"But you did too, remember?" I said. "In the contract before you agreed to be my coach?"

Colton laughed. "That was more for my protection than yours. I knew if you showed the slightest interest, I'd be done for. I've always been gone over you, Sadie. I'm surprised you never knew."

"I didn't," I said, smiling so much my face hurt. "It was too hard to believe. You're Colton Bishop, for goodness sake. Every girl's dream and my best friend's brother."

"Yeah," he said, pulling back enough so he could look me in the eye. "And you're Sadie Day, the one girl I always wanted but never thought I could have."

"Until now," I said.

"Until now," he repeated.

Before he could kiss me again, there was a knock at the door. It was Tim telling us we had five minutes to get to the set. Everyone was ready; they were just waiting on us.

"You ready to do this thing and complete your list?" Colton asked, taking my hand, laying a kiss on the daisy inside my wrist as we walked to the door. It made my breath catch—but who was I kidding? Everything Colton did affected me.

"Yeah," I said, "I'm ready. But what if we don't get accepted to *Dancer's Edge* or get a million views? Will you be disappointed if you lose the bet?"

"Screw the bet," Colton said. "I've already won."

And I could tell by the look he gave me that he meant it.

Betty didn't react when she saw the state of my lipstick, just touched me up without comment. But I could tell she wanted to say something by the knowing smile she wore. We shot the dance in a few takes. Colton, Kyle and I moved like we'd been dancing together for years—at least that's what my parents said. Big Tim asked for my account info so he could upload the video when it was ready. He said he and Little Tim wanted to make some edits to make sure the video was the best it could be, so I gave it to them with my thanks. They also promised to submit it to *Dancer's Edge*.

I didn't know if anything would come of it.

Definitely didn't know if we'd hit a million views.

But Colton was right, I thought as I gazed at him across the dance floor. He'd been talking to Big Tim, but as if he could feel my eyes on him, Colton looked up, caught my gaze and gave me a slow smile.

I'd already won.

CHAPTER 20

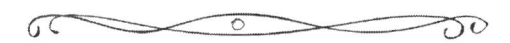

"What's it at now?" Kyle called from the living room.

"999,824 views," my mom said back, "and I'm not answering that question again until at least five minutes have passed."

"That's cool, Mrs. Day. Just checking."

It had been three days since the video posted, and we were already at almost a million views. And it was all because of Colton.

Thinking back, I remembered him talking to people at the video shoot, but I hadn't realized why until later. Betty was the first to break. When I started getting a ton of new followers, many over the age of 50, I'd asked if she knew anything about it, and she sang like a canary.

"It was Colton," she said. "He asked me to use my connections, and I was more than happy to follow through. I got the word out to all my friends and told them how talented you are. Plus, he came to Shady Grove and gave everyone a crash course in social media."

"He did?" I asked.

Betty nodded. "I knew you'd never ask me yourself, dear, but what good is having connections if you can't use them now and again?"

She told me she'd shared my video with everyone she knew in Hollywood. Once they realized she'd done the makeup, it made the views soar.

But Colton had also gotten to my parents.

"When he told us about your goal," Mom said, "your father and I were more than happy to spread the word."

Though my parents owned a studio now, back in the day, they'd been close to ballroom royalty. I knew they'd held world titles for several years in the Latin division, but I didn't want to use that, had never wanted to bring them down if I failed. Ballroom was notoriously attached to the status quo. Sometimes being different or outside the box could get you ostracized.

Mom had scoffed at this.

"Sadie," she said, "your dances are amazing, creative and everything ballroom needs right now. I've always wanted to share your pieces but wasn't sure you'd let me. I was glad Colton asked for my help. I couldn't wait to show everyone and tell them that's my daughter."

It was everything I should've already known but needed to hear.

From what she told me, all she and my dad had done was share the video to their contacts, letting them know I was their kid. That had led to more sharing and more sharing until the video made the rounds of the ballroom world.

And Colton had gone one step further, asking for Big Tim and Little Tim's help in tagging the video, making it searchable and SEO-optimized (whatever that meant). All I knew was the dance showed up on the first few pages of every search with a term or phrase possibly related to the video—which, thanks to Big Tim had one of the best titles ever.

"Taylor Swift Look-Alike dances Tango with Hot Twins?" I'd asked him over the phone. "Really, Tim?"

"Yeah," Big Tim said. "You like? I thought it had a certain flair."

"Oh, it's definitely inspired," I laughed. "Not sure how accurate it is, but I'd totally click on that video."

"Exactly, Sadie. Colton told me to pull out all the stops, so I did. Plus, I want those *Dancer's Edge* people to regret ever turning you down," he said. "They'll be begging you to be on their site in no time."

Thanks to Tim's mad computer skills and his wide-reaching network in gaming circles, the video ended up not only being searchable but somehow landed on the front page of a popular gaming site. He'd gotten it there by telling them I was the creative mind behind "Her Majesty's Revenge," the game we'd created together over a year ago that was currently at the top of the charts.

We were firing on all cylinders, and with all of those shares, my family and friends had helped our dance video go viral. It seemed impossible, but the view counter didn't lie.

"What's it at now, Mrs. Day?" Kyle asked again.

As my mother sighed and said, "999,902 views," I couldn't hold back a smile.

My list was this close to being complete. And none of it would've been possible without Colton. Pulling out the much-used paper, I unfolded my list, holding a pen in my other hand. All of the items were crossed off except the first three.

CARPE DIEM LIST

1) Fall in love with someone who will love me back.

2) Roll down a hill in Ireland.

3) Be featured on Dancer's Edge—or get a million views LOL whichever comes first!.

Strong arms wrapped around my waist from behind as Colton placed his chin on my shoulder. Taking the pen, he drew a line through number 1, and I melted back into him. I couldn't believe I'd gotten so darn lucky.

"How does it feel?" he asked.

"What, finishing my list?" I sighed. "Absolutely incredible."

"Not the list," he scoffed. "How does it feel having the best boyfriend ever?"

Heart skipping, I said, "Are you saying you're my boyfriend?"

"Yeah." He waited until I met his eyes. "Sadie Day, you have bewitched me, body and soul."

My jaw dropped. "Did you just quote *Pride & Prejudice* to me?"

Colton cleared his throat. "I may have."

"I think I'm in love."

"That's good," he said. "Because I love you, too."

Cheeks burning, I shook my head, hesitant to believe—but Colton was the most honest person I'd ever known. Besides, there was no missing the truth in his eyes.

"I love you, Colton," I said quietly and felt him release a breath. I thought maybe he had been nervous, too—but then he shot me a grin, like he'd known it all along, and I rolled my eyes. "How about you? How does it feel winning the bet?"

Colton shrugged. "Normal," he said. "I told you before. I never lose a bet."

"Oh really?" I said, turning in his arms.

Looking down at his phone, Colton held up the screen so I could see. He had our video pulled up, and as he refreshed the page, I saw the view counter now read 1,000,001 views.

With a squeak, I did a little happy dance, not even embarrassed as Colton laughed. "I still can't believe it," I said. "We did everything on my list."

"Why not?" he said, marking off number 3 then pulling me back to him. "You're talented"—he kissed my cheek—"and amazing"—a kiss to my nose—"and all mine."

I placed a hand against his lips, stopping him from any

more kisses to which he cocked his pierced eyebrow. He knew I couldn't resist that look.

"Uh uh," I said, "there aren't any more kisses on the list, Coach."

"But there is Ireland," he said, placing a kiss against my palm. "What are we going to do about that?"

"I guess you'll just have to take me there on our honeymoon."

I laughed at his stunned look.

"Relax Colton, I was just joking."

"Ah, be honest Sadie, you were only kind of joking." I flushed, but Colton shook his head. "You're such a romantic. I'd be offended if you hadn't at least thought about it."

I scoffed, trying to ignore the truth of his statement and his smug expression. "Like you haven't? I've seen all your romance novels, Colton. I know you're just as big of a romantic as me— even if you try to hide it behind piercings and a bad boy attitude."

"I admit nothing," he said. "And you're wrong about the kisses."

"Oh?" I said.

"We've done all the ones on your list," he said, a glint in his eye. "But not the ones on mine."

I smiled up at him. "You don't have a list."

"It's a mental one," he shrugged.

"Oh, I see, and are there a lot of kisses on your list?"

"A few," Colton said, one hand slipping into my hair as he leaned forward. "But once we've completed those, I'm sure I could think of some more. I have a good imagination."

My breath caught as I felt the touch of his lip ring, his next words spoken only inches from my mouth.

"Maybe we should start now."

"Whatever you say, Coach."

Our lips met, and no list or check marks were necessary. No contract, no bet. Just me and Colton and this kiss that was unchoreographed, unscripted and amazingly real. Colton Bishop was my first kiss, and I wanted him to be my last. End scene. Roll the credits. It was simple: He was my person, and I was his.

Absolutely, completely, forever.

Thank you so much for reading!!!

If you enjoyed this book, I'd be so thankful if you'd leave a review. Your thoughts matter, and just a few words can really make a difference. Reviews are a wonderful way to support me and my books, and they help me find new readers! Thank you in advance, and I hope you loved *The Good Girl's Guide to Being Bad*! <3

ACKNOWLEDGEMENTS

Sadie's book has been in the works for a while, and I can't believe it's finally out in the world. Honestly, I wasn't sure I'd ever finish writing another book. Aunt Pat, my best friend, first reader/editor, movie buddy, best-person-I've-ever-known wasn't here to read, encourage and give me feedback. She did read the first chapters years ago before she passed away, and I remember she loved the book—and Colton—so much. I'll always remember that, and I think her faith in the story really helped me push forward. I hope it keeps pushing me because there are other books I haven't finished that she loved, and I still want to make her proud. Pat, I miss you every day. I love you and hope you love how Sadie's book turned out (and that Colton lived up to your expectations <3).

To Aunt Colleen and Mom: Thank you for telling me you don't "bake" pancakes/Rice Krispies and for finding all those titled/tilted mistakes. I love you both more than words can say.

To Stephanie Mooney, thank you for the swoony/awesome/perfect cover! You're amazing.

To Kristen, thank you for being a true friend and always texting at just the right time.

To the dancers and dreamers, thank you for putting your hearts out there for everyone to see. Keep dreaming and know that you are enough.

To my readers, thank you for all of your support! Every review, rating, blog post, share, comment is so appreciated! You bookworms rock, and I hope this one was worth the wait!

And to you, thank you, thank you, thank you for reading this book! I hope you swooned over Colton like I did *sigh*, and I hope you could see glimpses of yourself in Sadie. Oh, and I hope it brought you so many laughs! I feel so honored and glad that you chose to read *The Good Girl's Guide to Being Bad* <3. If you're still searching for what you want to do with your life or have a list you've yet to complete, don't worry. It will come. And in the meantime: Carpe freaking Diem!

SADIE'S CARPE DIEM LIST

Below you'll find Sadie's *Carpe Diem List* (or in Colton's words her *Naughty List* lol!). Do you have a list? Are any of your items the same as Sadie's?

CARPE DIEM LIST

1) Fall in love with someone who will love me back ☺

2) Roll down a hill in Ireland ☺

3) Be featured on Dancer's Edge—or get a million views LOL whichever comes first! ☺

4) Talk dirty (work on better insults). ☺

5) Stay up and watch the sun rise ☺

6) See the inside of a police car ☺

7) Get a tattoo (daisy, dragon, lyrics/book quote?) ☺

8) Get something pierced (ears, nose, belly button?) ☺

9) Sneak out of the house ☺

10) Learn to drive a stick shift ☺

11) Go dancing at a club 😊

12) Crash a party 😊

13) Buy lingerie 😊

14) Have an explosive first kiss (preferably in the library 😊

15) Kiss in the rain 😊

16) Kiss in the car 😊

17) Kiss in public 😊

18) Kiss in my bedroom 😊

19) Skip school 😊

20) Pull a prank 😊

21) Learn how to make pancakes 😊

22) Sleep with a guy (Just. Sleep!) 😊

ABOUT THE AUTHOR

Cookie O'Gorman writes stories filled with humor and heart for the nerd in all of us. Fiery first kisses, snappy dialogue, smart girls, swoonworthy boys, and unbreakable friendships are featured in each of her books.

Cookie is a hopeless romantic, a Harry Potter aficionado, and a supporter of all things dork. Chocolate, Chinese food, and Asian dramas are her kryptonite. Above all, she believes that real life has enough sorrow and despair—which is why she always tries to give her characters a happy ending. She is the author of *Adorkable, Ninja Girl, The Unbelievable, Inconceivable, Unforeseeable Truth About Ethan Wilder* and *The Good Girl's Guide to Being Bad*.

Whether it's about her books or just to fan-girl, Cookie would love to hear from you!

Website: cookieogorman.com

Twitter: www.twitter.com/CookieOwrites

Facebook: www.facebook.com/cookieogorman

Printed in Great Britain
by Amazon